SANDPIPER COURT JOURNAL

A Saga of the Second Civil War and its Impact
on the Lives of the Residents of a Wheaton,
Illinois, Subdivision

DAVID A. BRAGEN

IUNIVERSE, INC.
NEW YORK   BLOOMINGTON

Sandpiper Court Journal
A Saga of the Second Civil War and its Impact on the Lives
of the Residents of a Wheaton, Illinois, Subdivision

iUniverse books may be ordered through booksellers or by contacting:

iUniverse
1663 Liberty Drive
Bloomington, IN 47403
www.iuniverse.com
1-800-Authors (1-800-288-4677)

Because of the dynamic nature of the Internet, any Web addresses or links contained in this book may have changed since publication and may no longer be valid. The views expressed in this work are solely those of the author and do not necessarily reflect the views of the publisher, and the publisher hereby disclaims any responsibility for them.

ISBN: 978-1-4401-8475-8 (sc)
ISBN: 978-1-4401-8474-1 (dj)
ISBN: 978-1-4401-8552-6 (ebk)

Printed in the United States of America

iUniverse rev. date: 5/18/2010

A BEGINNER'S GUIDE TO A SUCCESSFUL CAREER

ForeWord Magazine awarded a Gold Medal in the Career category to **A BEGINNER'S GUIDE TO A SUCCESSFUL CAREER** in its Sixth Annual Book of the Year Awards program. **A Beginner's Guide to a Successful Career** is available online at **Amazon.com** and **Booksamillion.com**.

Excerpt from letter to David A. Bragen as authored by Ms. Susan Driscoll, President and CEO of **iUniverse**…..

"This year's competition yielded a record-breaking number of 1,500 entries. Beginner's Guide to a Successful Career looks like a wonderfully practical guide for those entering the work force (in fact, I'm ordering one for my son!) and I'm delighted that it has now been recognized as one of the finest independently published books ……"

CORPORATE CHARACTERS
Understanding the Personalities of Your Co-Workers

IUniverse has awarded both an Editor's Choice (October 2006) and Publisher's Choice designation to **CORPORATE CHARACTERS** (November 2006). **CORPORATE CHARACTERS – Understanding the Personalities of Your Co-Workers** is available online at **Amazon. com** and **Booksamillion.com**.

Excerpt from letter to David A. Bragen as authored by Ms. Susan Driscoll, President and CEO of **iUniverse**.....

*"Congratulations! iUniverse has awarded your book **CORPORATE CHARACTERS** with the **Publisher's Choice** designation......
designates your book as a high-quality work both inside and out....."*

THE FIVE BUILDING BLOCKS OF SUCCESS
Getting Your Career on Track and Keeping It There

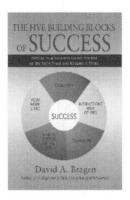

THE FIVE BUILDING BLOCKS OF SUCCESS - Getting Your Career on Track and Keeping It There is available online at **Amazon. com** and **Booksamillion.com**.

The **Five Building Blocks of Success** completes the DAVEN Management trilogy targeted at assisting individuals in developing successful careers.

DEDICATION

To Joe and Tony. Sure do miss you guys.
I know you'll understand me when I say
I hope I don't see you too soon;
but I can't wait to see you!

ANOTHER 'SHOT' HEARD ROUND THE WORLD'

Washington, D.C.
1312 hours
January 22

As Darnell J. Jenkins climbed up the steep, seven step staircase located at the back of the raised red, white and blue draped 1,357 square foot platform, he marveled at the pomp and circumstance that heralded the dawn of a new era in American politics and more importantly, in American history. He marveled at how quickly and professionally the platform had been constructed in the course of the hectic, activity filled week prior to this moment, the beginning of the inauguration ceremony that when completed, would conclude with him being sworn in as the forty-forth president of the United States, and even more importantly, with him becoming be first man of color to fulfill the highest elected office in the world.

Realizing early in his political career that he could not achieve victory in either the primaries or the presidential race itself by revealing his radical agenda, Jenkins had successfully hidden behind the persona of a moderate. His ultimate goal, elevating the position of 'his people', could not be a route directly traveled, so now that he had been elected, he planned to introduce massive, sweeping changes to the social order of things, which became his seemingly innocent political mantra of change, change, change. The change he was looking for was ultimately to improve the lot of 'his people' by taking everyone else down

1

several pegs through increased governmental meddling in all aspects of everyday life. And the money to fund this radical agenda would be obtained through massive tax increases and previously unheard of levels of deficit spending. Jenkins was going to be taking the old 'tax and spend' philosophy of the left to a whole new level.

Man of color indeed! soon to be President Jenkins thought. *They never could figure out how to refer to me with my mixed blood....some black, some white and a touch Puerto Rican. If only grandma could see me now. She lived to see the election, but not the final moment. What a waste.*

Reaching the top of the staircase, Jenkins stopped, straightened his suit jacket, and with a practiced prance, marched up to the podium and stood next to Chief Justice Myron Laubstein, who with bible in hand and a wink in his eye, greeted his old friend, ready, willing and quite able to administer the oath of office in spite of his advanced age of eighty-eight, making him the oldest Chief Justice in history.

Smiles spreading even more broadly across their faces, the two men simultaneously extended their right hands for the customary welcoming handshake and Jenkins thought quickly about the man of color description that the worldwide news media had picked up and started using early in his run for office, the innocuous description he had hid behind during that race.

As soon as this ceremony is over, I'm going to make it clear that as the first African-American to hold this high office, I am going to take great pride in my black heritage and embrace it in every action that I take as President. My people have finally become a force to be reckoned with and we now have, for the first time ever in this country, the power we need to right the multitude of wrongs since they first began shipping us here in the holds of so many slave ships.

And you, too, Myron. My little Jewish lap dog, my lifeline to the American Jewish community, and their deep pockets. You, too, will understand what happens when you elect a nigger to the office of President of these here United States!

A fraction of a second before their hands met, a large caliber bullet entered the head of the soon to be dead Darnell J. Jenkins, one and a quarter inches above his left ear. Within twenty minutes of the shooting, his exploding head, surrounded by an expanding mist of red blood, black scalp and whitish brain matter could be seen worldwide on numerous YouTube postings and mainstream news programs on the Internet. And, as mentioned repeatedly by the news media during the thousands of news reports issued during the course of the next several days, was the observation that since the inauguration ceremony was never consummated, the history of the United States would continue to show that only white men have held the highest office in the land. These reports only added fuel to the fire that was already starting to burn from border to border and coast to coast.

The on-scene crowd attending the inauguration ceremonies had been conservatively estimated to be in excess of eight hundred thousand souls, with the majority clearly being 'people of color', wanting to see one of their own finally take his rightful place in the pecking order. Within seconds of the gunshot, a man with a rifle emerged from a closed down corner newsstand yelling, with great pride in his voice, "I shot the nigger! I shot the nigger!"

Within seconds of emerging from that corner newsstand, Frank Miller, an unemployed carpenter and card-carrying member of the white supremacist, neo-Nazi organization known as the Sons of Hitler, South Carolina Chapter, was beaten to death by a revenge filled, angry mob, all of whom were 'people of color'. And once again, like a flock of vultures, the news media captured each and every blow on camera, beaming the images around the world in real time. The cameras also captured the transformation of a crowd, which moments ago had been blended together under the banner of change, begin to divide into islands of white faces, surrounded by a seemingly endless sea of non-whites faces. The cameras then captured numerous instances of non-white on white violence. The butcher's bill at the end of the day listed eighty-four killed and thousands injured.

Several months later, the country remained in a state of heightened tension. In an effort to quell the mounting pressures, the Congressional Committee rushed its investigation and issued a final report proclaiming that the assassination was the act of a single, deranged mind. However, the truth, which was missed in the rush to judgment, was that the assassination was a well thought-out plot orchestrated by a New York City based sect of a fundamentalist Islamic group whose goal was to bring down the Great Satan by initiating an internal struggle of epic proportions. Fortunately for the Islamic extremists, their participation was not uncovered during the rather hasty investigation since its exposure would have explained the one key fact that could not have been overlooked.

The Islamic sect had been comprised of a fringe group of African-Americans intent on bringing down America. Had their involvement and responsibility been uncovered, it may have helped mitigate the fact that the gunman, though hired by blacks, had been white. Unfortunately, the truth never came out. As far as the nation was concerned, there was only one key fact, the color of the gunman's skin, which became the rallying point that helped the racial radicals drive the final nail into the coffin. And that great melting pot, known world-wide as the United States of America, went from a roiling simmer to a full-blown, raging boil. Both sides in the national conflict immediately started referring to the three month, all-out fight as the United States of America's Second Civil War.

SANDPIPER COURT
JOURNAL

I

Wheaton, IL
0935 hours
November 6

Rolling over the bloody corpse, the soldier leaned forward and opened the backpack strapped to the body. Moments before, the boy, he guessed him to be around seventeen or eighteen, had been snooping around the ruins, looking like he was looking for something; probably a place to setup another ambush. The soldier, seeing this from across the cul-de-sac, put a 7.62mm slug through the boys' head, watching it explode like an overripe melon, spraying blood and brains into an expanding cone of flying gorge.

The soldier reached into the Elmhurst College backpack and pulled out some ammunition, a pair of binoculars, and a notebook. The soldier then stood up and pursing his lips together, tried to whistle to get Pierce's attention. All he accomplished was to make a strange blowing and hissing sound. Without those two front teeth, lost during a misunderstanding with his sergeant a few weeks back, whistling was no longer part of his oral repertoire. In the end, he just yelled to his sergeant.

"Hey, Sarg! Take a look at this."

A couple of houses further to the west, a tall, well built soldier rose from his half crouching, half kneeling defensive posture. Even up close, his six feet, four inch frame appeared smaller due to the seemingly near perfect symmetry of his rugged, battle-honed muscles.

Thirty-five year old Master Sergeant Franklin B. Pierce, wearing dirty white, gray and black zigzag block, urban camouflage combat fatigues, looked up from the rubble of what used to be a $350,000 - $400,000 residence to see what Jones was hollering about. In stark contrast, eighteen year old, scarecrow built Lance Corporal Tyrone Jones, also dressed in urban camouflage, looked like some militaristic marionette from the early days of black and white television.

He's going to be the death of me yet; literally, Pierce thought. *Here we are, walking around in an unsecured combat zone and this joker's standing in the middle of another used-to-be-house yelling and waving his arms around like some kid during schoolyard recess.*

"Goddamn it, TY! Get under some cover before you get your ass blown away! How many times do I got'a tell ya we're still taking fire in this subdivision?"

Jones started to crouch down next to what was left of a three story high stone fireplace that towered from the center of the destroyed house as his sergeant dodged across the litter filled cul-de-sac.

Pierce took his time getting over to Jones. Snipers were all around and he'd just lost Private Riggins a couple of blocks over. These kids are too damn young to be fighting a war; yet he knew that given the circumstances, he desperately needed all the help he could get. He also knew he'd give his left nut for a trained company of combat hardened soldiers; hell, make it a platoon or even a squad and he'd be happy!

As Pierce scurried nearer to Jones, he saw that Ty was holding something in his hands, apparently fascinated by it. A book, or notebook, or something. When Pierce squatted down next to him, Jones handed him a leatherette bound notebook; the kind sold in hundreds of stores across American; the kind that used to be used by thousands of people to record their thoughts and dreams.

"Whad'ya find, Ty?" Pierce asked.

"Not sure, Sarge. It's pretty bad beat up. Looks like a diary or something. The damn things full of blood and it's burned up on the one side," replied Jones.

"Looks like you're right on the money, TY. The first page has a title on it," said Pierce as he held the notebook open for Jones to see.

Jones reached out and took the notebook from his sergeant. He looked at the first page, getting a chill down his spine when he saw the date the diary was started.

Journal

Anthony Joseph Bender
3437 Sandpiper Court

September 22
Wheaton, IL 60188

As Pierce moved over next to Jones, Ty turned the page and they both started to read.

II

September 22 - Day One

My name is Anthony Joseph Bender; my friends call me Tony Joe or TJ. I'm starting this journal to record my thoughts so I don't go out of my fucking mind. I still can't believe this is happening and I want to get this stuff down in the hopes it will start to make sense, or until I wake up from this nightmare.

I live in a pretty new house in one of the newer subdivisions in Wheaton, a western suburb of Chicago, IL. Joyce and me got two sons (Joe - 18, and Rich - 16), a daughter (Jenny - 13), a dog, cat and guinea pig. An all-American family with two cars, actually a couple of Jeeps, and a big fat mortgage. But now, none of that seems to matter much anymore.

I guess we should have known something was up. You know the old story: hindsight is 20/20. I'm so fucking pissed that no one, not one fucking politician, not one fucking soldier, not one fucking media type, not one fucking nobody ever put it all together until it all came apart!

Even though Jenkins' assassination was the last straw, it really started small. Things that wouldn't be noticed. No way to tell how long it was going on; probably years. And so damn well organized.

A newspaper article that enlistments were up in the Army and Air Force, but not the Navy. Increased turnouts at the polls on election days. And not just the national election, all elections.

Some statistics that Blacks and Hispanics were entering colleges and universities in increasing numbers. That the racial mix of the Armed Services were changing. More Blacks and Hispanics on City Councils, School Boards, more of them Mayors and Governors.

But no one really noticed. In fact, everyone felt pretty good that the old days of separatism and all that old racial prejudice bullshit seemed to be a thing of the past; at least statistically.

Yeah, there were still problems here and there. Mostly isolated gang stuff. But no more Rodney King and Reginald Denny crap.

In late '95, the NAACP and SCLC merged and formed the National Coalition for Non-White Citizens. This caught middle class, White America by surprise. Not a fearful surprise but a grateful 'thank you God' euphoria for the first few actions of the newly formed NCNWC were aimed at what Whites and Blacks together called "niggers and red-necks".

The NCNWC did not condone or promote violence, or gangs, or ganging up on Whitey. They did preach a brand of separatism, but were very hard on their own problem children.

'96 ushered in the year of the Hispanics: they also formed a Coalition and went after the trouble making spics and wetbacks, and eventually merged with the NCNWC in April. I clearly remember the press interviews with soon-to-be ex-President Clinton trying to capture some positive results from the NAFTA fiasco saying that "even though the economic downturn fueled by NAFTA was disastrous on the American economy, the positive, more significant achievement was the equalization of people of all races and religions in these United States".

Once again middle class, White America felt that Nirvana was in sight. This peaceful separatism was viewed very positively. Integration was a thing of the past. Separate but equal really meant separate and equal. Blacks and Hispanics fled the cities in droves to establish non-White suburbs and rural communities. There was a big back-to-nature movement as many of the NCNWC proponents started farms and stuff. The White establishment was so happy about these changes that they extended credit like it was going out of style. With crime and drug wars and stuff like that decreasing, American business enjoyed the largest increase in productivity since the Viet Nam war. Factories were producing seven days a week as the NCNWC used its new found credit to the max buying everything from canned food goods, to medical supplies, hunting equipment, farm machinery; the list was endless.

The biggest clue that was missed by everyone, dealt with a series of news reports in mid-'97 about some sort of radical group of Army and Air Force personnel who were arrested and charged with conspiracy to defraud the government. The group included thirty-three members of these two branches of the service: three generals and six colonels among those arrested. Apparently, or so the story went, this group was engaged is some sort of black market activity regarding missing government property and falsified records. They had been caught 'appropriating war materiel' and were accused of sending the stuff to help support the cause of Black Separatism in South Africa.

The story died down pretty quickly as the government stepped in to cover-up this major breach of security. The NCNWC publicly declared that South Africa was a problem for South Africans and that the NCNWC did not in any way, shape or form endorse the policies and practices of this obviously radical splinter group.

No one seemed to notice or care that of the thirty-three arrested soldiers, eighteen were Hispanic, the rest Black.

Then September 11, 2001 came. Yeah...that 9/11. Well, for once, Americans seemed to band together, at least for a while. Color meant nothing. It was us united against them. Black, white, yellow, brown, whatever. Americans everywhere, all standing side by side, ready to take it to the world. But, that, too, faded as time went on.

Yet, things seemed to once again come together with the nomination and eventual election of Darnell J. Jenkins, the first term Governor of Indiana. Operating under the banner of change, this virtual political unknown leapt onto the center stage of the American political scene and never looked back. And somehow, against odds that seemed insurmountable at the onset, Jenkins was actually elected President. Everyone thought change had finally become a reality. Obviously, those on the fringes of racial issues felt uneasy, and in some cases extremely vocal.......but most people were filled with hope.

Then, Jenkins gets his head blown apart.

And then things really changed. Then the shit hit the fan.

Once again, it was us against them except that the us were the Whites including Jews, Italians, Eastern Europeans and other, darker skinned 'Whites' and the 'them' was pretty much everyone else. Uneasiness settled over the country after Jenkins stopped that bullet, especially amongst the fringe radical groups on both sides of the issue. I guess it's hard to ignore the differences between people when you can see what side of the issue they support merely by looking at them and seeing the color of their skin.

September 15, 2009 was a very memorable day. A day forever branded into the heart and soul of America, and the world. A day even more memorable that the January 22nd assassination of Jenkins.

A week before, on September 8th, the NCNWC called for a one day, general strike of all non-White Americans as a sign of solidarity. The day selected was September 15th. The NCNWC asked all of its members and all non-member, non-White Americans to stay home from work that day starting at 8:00 a.m. Eastern Standard Time.

By 8:30 a.m. on the 15th, the media was reporting that over 85% of Black and Hispanic workers, at all levels, and in all walks of life either walked off the job, or simply didn't show up for work. Figures suggested that at least 50% of US citizens of Oriental extraction participated as well. Some cities were reported to look like 'ghost towns' in that the only people walking around were White.

At 8:45 a.m., a spokesperson for the NCNWC went on the radio and TV to thank those people for their show of support. He closed his statement by saying 'Our time has come, my people. What has been denied, is now ours'.

At exactly 9:00 a.m. EST, America as we had known it, ended. Over three thousand homemade bombs of various power exploded at once in various locations throughout the United States.

Twenty-six airliners were simply blown out of the sky. It was later determined that baggage handlers had loaded bombs in the cargo bays.

A number of trains were destroyed, either by explosive devices placed on the trains, or when the trains tried to cross bridges that were now lying in ruins, themselves the victim of well placed bombs. The biggest buildings in Chicago, New York, San Francisco and numerous other cities were rocked by major explosions.

Fighter planes and tanks were reported to be attacking major military bases. Para-military troops came out of the woodwork to attack major supply depots, police stations, power plants, telephone switching stations, city halls and state capitals. And atom bombs destroyed Washington DC,, Cheyenne WY , Dallas TX and Seattle WA.

In the course of 20 minutes, over 6,000,000 million Americans died; white, black, brown, whatever.

Civil War had broken out in the United States. The fucking niggers and spics had set us up and we bent over and took it up the ass. I still can't believe it happened. How could we let it come to this?

September 15th was also my 45th birthday.

Well, that was seven days ago. I've got to stop now. I drew midnight to seven guard duty.

September 23 - Day Two

By 11:30 a.m. EST on September 15th, the war was really in full swing. Things were happening so fast that the authorities, those that were left, couldn't function properly. The old American attitude of innocent until proven guilty continued to hamper the actions of the Whites. We just couldn't believe what was happening, field reports were sporadic and confusing, information often delayed or garbled. We just couldn't believe that all non-Whites were the enemy.

And that's exactly what the NCNWC counted on. Our sense of ethics allowed a number of suicide squads to continue to wreak havoc in major proportion. Car bombs driven into hospitals. Schools set on fire. You name it; they did it.

The NCNWC had a significant strategic advantage over the Whites. Their attack, modeled after the Viet Cong's Tet offensive, simply took us by surprise. And there were no limits imposed on NCNWC field commanders.

They were authorized to do whatever it took to succeed. Their objective was singular in purpose. Extermination of Whites. No compromises, no mercy, just complete and final victory.

I'm not a rocket scientist but even I could tell that something had gone so wrong that survival was the only option available to us. We couldn't sit back and wait for Uncle Sam or the police or anyone else to help. We had to do it ourselves.

I had a couple of shotguns in the basement that I used for hunting. The boys and I went to get the guns and prepare some rather basic defensive positions at the front and back doors.

I told Joyce to take the Jenny upstairs and stay away from the windows. I knew we didn't stand a chance by ourselves. Nothing had happened in Wheaton yet, but it was clear that something would.

Then the power failed. Someone must have blown the transfer station or something.

I went over to a couple of the neighbors, Ed Flanders and Bill Komanski, to compare notes and come up with some plans. We decided it was best to get our families together for safety. We only had my two shotguns and each family had some small amount of foodstuffs. And with the electricity gone, the refrigerated stuff wouldn't last too long. We walked out of Ed's house and saw the street and cul-de-sac filled with the rest of our neighbors, walking around dazed and shocked. Battery operated radios were giving some pretty gruesome reports and the NCNWC was broadcasting their intentions to win at all costs.

Ed, Bill and I called everyone together to try and organize some kind of defensive group to help protect us.

People were screaming and shouting and just going crazy. I finally fired the shotgun in the air to get some attention. After about an hour of planning, the result was the formation of four groups or committees: Defense (18 men and older boys, 6 women), Food & Medical (one doctor, 12 women and older girls, 3 men), Children Protection (1 man, 6 women and 23 children under the age of twelve), and Scavengers (9 men and older boys).

The Defense group was charged with barricading the streets and spaces between the houses with cars, trucks and whatever else could be used. Their responsibilities were to secure this perimeter with guard positions and observations posts.

Food & Medical was responsible for gathering all food and medical supplies that they could get their hands on. Doc set up a field hospital of sorts and was told to train a couple of the women to be assistants.

Children Protection was self-explanatory. Keep the kids safe and out of the way.

I was one of the Scavengers. Since I had the one of the few guns, the group elected me leader. We debated for about thirty minutes what we should do first. We discussed getting food, getting in touch with the authorities, banding together with other groups and getting more defensive firepower. Guns won over butter!

We formed a six-car caravan and headed north on Pleasant Hill, the road that formed the western boundary of our subdivision. We turned right on North Avenue and headed east. Chicago lay in front of us, about thirty miles to the city's western edge. We saw huge plumes of smoke on the horizon, which only served to make us more nervous than we already were. Surprisingly, we saw very little traffic of any kind. A couple of police cars went roaring by with their lights and sirens on, but no commercial traffic of any kind.

A couple miles down the road we found a sporting goods store, one of the big places that used to advertise on Midwest Outdoors, on a local cable station.

We pulled up into the parking lot, gathered our small force and walked up to the front door. As we walked in, we were immediately pounced upon by two big, burly guys, each holding a rifle. They also had 45s in their belts. It looked pretty scary for a few moments until the blond guy, looking to be about twenty years old, asked us who we were and what we wanted. We told him we represented a group of homeowners who were looking to increase our defensive firepower. We offered to buy guns and ammunition but felt pretty stupid in making this offer in that the economy probably went to hell in a hand basket so who needed money?

Well, the blond guy started laughing. His partner, about the same age with dark hair, laughed so hard he started crying. We all joined in and friendships borne of adversity quickly developed. We found out that these two guys lived in Chicago, attending Northwestern University, senior year. The blond, Jason, was from Pittsburgh and Danny, dark hair, was from Dallas. With all the shit going down, they left their apartment just after the news reports started telling about all the problems. They headed west in hopes of finding a place to hide, maybe join up with some people. They found the sporting goods store and had planned to spend the night.

They told us some pretty scary stories about what they saw in Chicago. Their apartment was on the outskirts of downtown and just after 9:00 a.m. on the 15th, explosions and fires were happening all over. They talked about roving bands of Black and Hispanic men, not gang members or anything like that, but organized para-military groups who simply attacked all Whites they saw. People getting shot down in cold blood. The cops tried to stop these guys, who were carrying NCNWC banners, but didn't stand a chance. The cops were out there with pistols and riot guns while the NCNWC had automatic rifles, grenades, armored cars, etc. It was a massacre.

Jason said they got out just in time. Danny asked if they could join our group and we had our first two new recruits.

I told everyone to go through the store and take anything that looked useful. We ended up spending just over an hour in the store and after our little shopping spree, had a bunch of rifles, shotguns, handguns, ammunition, knives, lanterns, canned kerosene, fishing gear, medical kits, tents, and sleeping bags. Just about anything we could think of, we took.

When we came out of the store after our last walk through the aisles, we noticed that a small group of people had gathered across the street, near the Mobile station. They we looking at us and we could see that they had a couple of guns with them. Here we were, robbing this store blind and this other group, who apparently had the same idea, were standing there like hyenas, waiting for whatever the lions left over. We also realized that we hadn't left a guard or anything outside during our shopping trip. Had these guys been NCNWC, they could have walked right up to us and killed us when we left the building. We also realized that they were people we didn't know and we were concerned about whether or not we could trust them to help us or if we should leave right away. As we were talking about this, the people across the street broke up into three groups, about seven in each group. Two groups stared to move around on our flanks. We fired a couple of shots in the air, jumped in our cars and got the hell out of there.

As soon as we got back, we appointed Danny and Jason to take charge of the weapons and set up an armory in the basement of one of the houses. Komanski, also a Scavenger, said it would be a good idea to split up the arms cache into two locations as a preventative measure. We agreed and did this.

I also told Flanders to take a couple of guys and set up a Security detail. Security would provide protection for the Scavengers during our little trips out and about the countryside.

The electricity came on about 3:00 p.m.

The water never stopped, though the suggestion was made that we boil all water just in case the NCNWC tried to poison us.

Food became the next issue for the Scavengers. Our caravan left Sandpiper Court at 3:30 p.m. to go see what we could find. We traveled east on Geneva and once again saw the smoky horizon. The fires in and around Chicago must have been burning pretty badly for all that smoke to be there.

We got to the Jewel Food Store at Geneva and Schmale. The parking lot was jammed with cars, trucks and people by the hundreds. Everyone was keeping in some kind of order, which finally made sense when we saw that the Wheaton Police had set up some barriers around the doors. We parked across the street and sent Flanders and Danny to see what was going on. They reported back that the 'store was open for business and people were paying for food'. Do wonders never cease?!

When we checked, we found we had about $300 between the seven of us. I told everyone except Flanders to go buy some canned goods, no perishables. Flanders and I drove to the bank to see if it was open. It wasn't. We all left the Jewel around 6:30 p.m. without much to show for our efforts.

We all sat around a campfire we had built in the middle of the cul-de-sac to compare notes on what happened during the day and to listen to the latest news reports.

It struck me as ironic that here we were, our little community, people who had lived near each other for a couple of years and yet few of us knew each other's names. We had gotten used to just waving 'hi' to each other and never really got to know one another. We spent over two hours that night simply getting acquainted. We all recognized that we were being thrust into a situation that was beyond any one of us as individuals. We found hope and solace in knowing that we were in this together, and that by trying to work through these trying times as a group gave each of us the best chance for survival.

Each of the groups elected one of the members to act as its head:

```
Scavengers. . . . . . . . . . . . . . . .Me
Child Protection . . . . . . . . . . . .Frank Smyth
Food & Medical. . . . . . . . . . . .Doctor Hank Furgeson
Defense. . . . . . . . . . . . . . . . .Bruce Jamison
```

I don't remember all of the particulars but the news reports we heard that night included the following:

National Guard troops were all being called to assemble at their training stations.

The atomic explosion in Washington DC had utterly destroyed the seat of national government. The EMP (electro-magnetic pulse) wave had left the DC area in a shroud of silence. No radios would work and the full extend of the devastation was unknown. Ditto Dallas, Cheyenne and Seattle. All totaled, over 6,000,000 dead of all colors, races, creeds, etc. A huge waste of life

White soldiers of the Army, Marine and Air Force units were in control of the areas surrounding some military bases while NCNWC forces controlled others. The Navy was experiencing a number of incidences of sabotage and had already lost a couple of ships to suicide squads. Each state's National Guard was to protect its own citizens and we were told not to rely on Federal troops for the foreseeable future. And obviously these forces were also divided along color lines.

We posted the night guard watch at 9:30 p.m.

September 24 - Day Three

Our first real problem occurred early in the morning. It seems that during the night, a couple carloads of people showed up at one of our guard posts. They told the guys on guard duty that they were from Chicago, had barely escaped with their lives and wanted to spend the night, get some food and protection. The guys on guard said 'Okay'.

It seems that these cars held nine people, no food of their own and they had no intention of leaving now that it was morning. The four committee heads, Bruce, Doc, Frank and me felt pretty strongly that our group needed to be self-sufficient and that there wasn't enough to go around for every Tom, Dick or Harry that showed up asking for help.

That's when the problem got bigger. A number of the folks inside our little enclave felt that we should take in these strangers. We're all Christians, Whites, etc. We saw our first major problem coming in spades.

The four committee leaders decided to establish the law pretty quickly. At gunpoint, we forced the overnight visitors to depart. We held a group meeting to lay down the law. We told the folks that our supplies were limited, that no help was in sight and that we intended to protect our own and only our own. We gave everyone a choice: abide by the rules or they were free to leave. Not everyone saw the wisdom. Some didn't like it, but there wasn't any alternative that they could offer. We finally agreed to modify the rule. If anyone seeking to join the group could prove to be self-sufficient like having a special skill, or bringing food, fuel, firearms or medical supplies, they could join us, however, they would be required to pledge loyalty to our group and obey our laws.

This problem, once dealt with, also pointed out that we'd have a tough time living a democratic existence in our little community. We decided that the four committee leaders, along with an additional representative from each of the four groups would form a governing committee. The committee would elect a committee chairman. Whichever group the chairman came from would get to replace him on the committee with another member of the group. This resulted in a nine-person management committee with one chairperson.

We spent a couple of hours selecting the people. The result of the initial effort was:

Scavengers	Me & Ed Flanders
Child Protection	Frank Smyth & Janice Pedopoulos
Food & Medical	Dr. H. Furgenson & Susan Hollis
Defense	Bruce Jamison & Larry Findler

The eight of us discussed the chairperson's position and no one really wanted the responsibility except me, so I took it. Bill Komanski replaced me on the Scavengers.

The committee was formed and we spent the balance of the time deciding upon our course of action.

That election was held on September 16th. I'm not going to detail what happened between then and today, September 24th. Nothing significant happened. We simply took the steps necessary to stay alive.

Tomorrow, I'll pick this up on a current basis.

III

Wheaton, IL
1008 hours
November 6

They say you never hear the shot that kills you. Sergeant Pierce learned the hard way that what they said was true.

The sledgehammer blow to the head knocked his helmet off and him down, hard. A sea of blackness outlined his vision for a few moments as he struggled to understand what had happened.

Jones, in the meanwhile, buried himself even deeper in the ruins. *Sniper!* he thought as he fought to remain in control of wind and water. Unlike Pierce, he had heard the sharp report of the small caliber rifle and saw Sarg hit the dirt. Hit it hard and not move. Scared the shit out of him.

Jones crawled closer to Pierce, quickly got to his knees and fired off a burst into the tree line, where he thought the shot had come from. Five quick shots and on the ground, crawl a little more and repeat the procedure until he was safety behind a section of the foundation that was still intact.

Jones peered at Pierce and was surprised to see him breathing. *Man, that's just great. A fuckin' head wound and I'm stuck out here all alone. I sure ain't no doctor. Now what am I going to do?*

As Jones looked back towards the tree line, another sharp report made him flinch reactively; only this time it was a stream of words, not lead. "Goddamn that sonofabitch!" Pierce yelled.

Jones was shocked that the Sarg could talk with the head wound and all. He turned around and looked at Pierce, seeing him holding his head and hearing him swearing so loudly that he finally said "Hey, Sarg. Take it easy, or you'll bleed to death for sure."

"Jones, just shut your mouth and look for that fuckin' sniper. Man, does my head hurt. Good thing the guy only had something small. Bullet didn't even go through the helmet liner though my head feels like it went in one side and out the other."

"You mean you ain't even hit. Jesus Christ, Sarg! You scared the shit out' a me. What the hell am I gon'na do out here all by myself if you get yourself killed?" asked Jones, now just as mad as his sergeant.

Pierce's response was to pick up his M-16, seemingly aiming it right at Jones' head and before Jones could let out a shout or hit the dirt, pull the trigger. Jones later told the sergeant that he could hear the bullet, which had only passed an inch or so away from his left ear as it sped past into the chest of the sniper who was naive enough to give Pierce a target.

Chuckling, Pierce said, "If you can hear it, it won't kill ya!"

After the excitement died down, Pierce crawled back over to where he had dropped the Journal. Putting in under his shirt, he motioned for Jones to follow him as they made there way back to the encampment. It was starting to get dark and being out here in the ruins without any more firepower was a sure invitation to disaster.

IV

After reporting in to the Lieutenant and telling him about how Riggins stopped a sniper's bullet on MacArthur Lane , Pierce and Jones walked over to the mess tent for a late meal. The war was a hardship on everyone and Pierce could tell by the smell, or was it more of an odor, that tonight's feast was not too tasty. One look in the big pot told him his guess was right on the money.

"Hey, Cookie. I thought you threw away that shit-on-a-shingle recipe years ago," Pierce said, half jokingly.

"Now, Master Sergeant Pierce, you know I do my best with what I'm given. Ain't nobody in this here man's army doing better than me. Why my shit-on-a-shingle's the talk of the town, " replied Cookie.

Pierce had a hard time being mad at Cookie. They'd enlisted together almost seventeen years ago and spent most of their careers serving in the same company. They'd even done the Gulf War together.

Yeah, nothing like shit-on-a-shingle under the hot, desert sun.

Cookie filled Pierce's plate, gave some to Jones and handed out some day-old bread to both of them. Pierce motioned to Jones to follow him and together they walked over to the burned-out warehouse the unit had commandeered as temporary barracks during this engagement until their equipment could catch up with them.

Getting comfortable, Pierce reached over into his haversack and pulled out a couple of beers; warm, but still beer. Handing one to Jones, he popped the top of the second one and took a long pull.

"Thanks, Sarg. Hey, why don't we get out that notebook and read some more?"

"Lance Corporal Tyrone Jones, that's an excellent idea."

Reaching back into his battle worn haversack, Pierce reached in a second time and removed the journal. He thumbed through the first few pages until he came across the last entry that they had read together. He turned to the next page and together with Jones, they began to delve further into the written record of one Anthony Joseph Bender.

September 25 - Day Four

Ten days after it started, the Civil War seems to have stabilized. Neither side making much progress against the other; neither side really wanting to!

The NCNWC shot their big wad during the first week. They needed to conserve their weapons and supplies since the major industrial capacity was still in the hands of the Whites. The Whites on the other hand, couldn't disengage from protecting the cities and military bases to ferret out the NCNWC from their rural enclaves. Additionally, many industries suffered from lack of people to run their plants effectively. People still feared that random attacks and guerrilla raids would continue and many simply didn't show up for work. Factories sat idle or operated at levels way below their intended throughput. Everything stagnated.

Many non-Whites didn't join the NCNWC or even support their ideals, yet Whites felt that all non-Whites were potential enemies. A great deal of effort and resources were consumed trying to corral these people and keep them from either linking up with the NCNWC forces, or being allowed to be in positions to attack Whites. Detention Centers, ala our treatment of Japanese Americans in California during World War Two, and the right side/wrong side of town boundaries started to be established.

This became a self-fulfilling prophecy. The non-aligned non-Whites felt slighted by the Whites for treating them like the enemy. The NCNWC encouraged this disruption by infiltrating agents to fuel this building frenzy. Words became blows, blows became gunshots and firebombs, and the Civil War re-ignited.

The world community didn't know how to respond. Previously, when the US had maintained its position of global policeman, most conflicts tended to have a right and a wrong side. People were able to judge a conflict on the merits and most people tended to easily recognize which side represented good.

In the current US Civil War, rightness or wrongness didn't seem to be an issue. This wasn't a small country were thousands of people were joined in an internal dispute. This was one of the largest, most powerful nations on earth being brought to its knees by a nationwide, ethnic/racial maelstrom.

Most countries don't have all White, or all non-White populations therefore almost the entire world community passively watched from the sidelines.

Europe figured they had suffered enough with their own two World Wars and the collapse of the Common Market, which they attributed to the NAFTA deal. Besides, they still held grudges over our bungling of the Bosnia crisis.

Canada, also bitter at having to suffer under NAFTA plus having suffered the added humiliating experience when the US said they wouldn't consider the Canadian Provinces for statehood, closed their borders and offered no assistance whatsoever.

The Africa nations didn't have a whole lot of anything to send and their internal problems continued to be significant.

The South American Hispanics tended to watch since they feared the retaliatory power of the US Armed Forces.

The Asian nations found the war amusing. Though a major market for their goods was being crushed, a major competitor was also being eliminated. Red China also heralded the Civil War as a classic case of class struggle, a situation that Communism wouldn't allow to occur in the first place since all Communists are equal. Simply put, no one wanted our fight.

The economy pretty much ground to a halt. There were marginal efforts to keep the plants and factories open, however, raw material supplies were quickly depleted. Though the US Navy still controlled the seas and major ports, foreign companies were reluctant to send their ships and people into a combat zone. The result, raw material flow slowed to a trickle.

Schools were shut down as parents refused to be separated from their children.

Hospitals remained open, but they were operated as forts with sandbag barriers erected around their perimeters and police and National Guard troops assigned for protection.

Every day on the national scene still had some amount of attacks; sniper fire, suicide squads, car bombs, etc. Each side was losing a couple thousand people per day. The radio reports indicated that the ebb and flow of the battles were resulting in fluid front lines. Areas that were safe yesterday were coming under fire today. The only certain thing about the situation was the uncertainty.

The Sandpiper Court Group was doing pretty good considering the circumstances. I told the governing committee that I was keeping this Journal and they suggested that I include a list of names showing the members of our little encampment, just for posterity sake.

It is my privilege and honor to introduce you to the Sandpiper Court Group (Committee, Name, Age):

Sandpiper Court Committee Chairman:

TJ Bender - 45

Defense

Bruce Jamison - 36	Larry Findler - 29
Steve Granger - 40	Jim Sawyer - 33
Bill Jenkins - 47	Brian Jenkins - 17
Phil Savatini - 33	Roger Dalton - 50
Jeff Dalton - 16	Bob Pedopoulos - 44
Joe Oliver - 55	Joe Olive Jr. - 18
Jim Stantree* - 36	Bob Stantree* - 33
Jason Furgeson - 22	Jack Furgeson - 19
Bill Flanders - 16	Rich Bender - 16
* = brothers	

Linda Savatini - 31	Mary Dalton - 47
Sheri Findler - 28	Sue Oliver - 53
Mary Kornat - 26	Jane Flanders - 17

Food & Medical

Dr. Hank Furgenson - 62	Bill Donovan - 55
Frank Farmer - 70	Juan Hernendez - 55
Rosa Hernendez - 52	Susan Hollis - 40
Julia Farmer - 69	Ann Donovan - 16
Rita Hernendez - 17	Anita Furgenson - 17
Mary Pedopoulos - 15	Sara Hollis - 14
Kathie Oliver - 17	Mary Oliver - 16
Jennifer Bender - 13	Suzie Smyth - 16

Child Protection

Frank Smyth - 48	Janice Pedopoulos - 42
Joyce Bender - 47	Mary Komanski - 50
Mary Donovan -55	Kathleen Granger - 30
Nancy Sawyer - 31	Staci Sawyer - 2
Billy Sawyer - 5	Steve Jamison - 7
John Jamison - 3	Kyle Granger - 12
Lisa Granger - 10	Linda Granger - 8
Katie Findler - 18 mos.	Karen Stanley - 4
Sean Jenkins - 9	Helen Pedopoulos - 6
Brian Chang - 6	Beth Chang - 3
Patti Savatini - 2	Paul Savatini - 6
Suzie Kornat - 7	David Kornat - 6 mos.
Jason Komanski - 11	Donna Donevan - 8
Jimmie Farmer# - 3	Staci Farmer# - 6
Alice Furgeson - 12	Josh Oliver - 11
#= visiting grandchildren	

Scavengers

Ed Flanders - 50	Bill Komanski - 46
John Dalton - 20	Joe Bender - 18
Jason Waholik - 21	Danny Davidson - 20
George Davis - 48	Steve Kornat - 31

<u>Sandpiper Court Subdivision Residence Out of Town at Outbreak of CW II</u>

Janice Jamison - 33	Betty Furgeson - 57
Frank Hollis - 42	Lee Chang - 36
Kathy Flanders - 46	Jean Chang- 35

September 26th - Day Five

The War came to Wheaton today.

A group of NCNWC irregulars shot up some store fronts on Hale Street just across from the train station. The station has been closed since September 15th and no one bothered to set up any guards or anything. Apparently, the irregulars drove into town in two panel trucks. They arrived without anyone sensing that they were NCNWC.

The two ordinary, everyday vans drove up Hale and the NCNWC open fired on the storefronts with automatic weapons fire. Eleven people were killed outright and thirty-six people wounded. The bitch of it was that the two vans escaped without so much as a return shot being fired. Since no street blockades had been established anywhere, neither the Police nor the few National Guard Troops that were on duty had an opportunity to prevent the attack and protect the citizens.

Immediately after, Police and National Guard representatives held a meeting and requested the attendance of a variety of community leaders, including me and several other Committee members from Sandpiper court. The meeting was held at City Hall.

The gist of the meeting was town security. Street maps were produced and there was much discussion as to how much of the town could be protected. There were simply not enough troops and police available to protect all citizens and property. It was agreed that the Police, comprised of twenty-six full time and eighteen part-time officers, would provide defensive forces for downtown

Wheaton in the form of traffic barriers to avoid a repeat of the day's ambush by NCNWC irregulars. Additionally, their squad cars would provide a mobile force to patrol the major streets in Wheaton. The National Guard unit, a total of eighty-seven officers and soldiers, would establish traffic barriers at the major intersections at the town's perimeter, reserving about thirty men to provide a mobile defense deterrent.

Individuals with firearms were requested to band together to form neighborhood watch group while outlying, unincorporated subdivision like ours were encouraged to form our own defensive organizations. The National Guard committed to send us some people to help organize our effort as well as to give us some weapons and ammunition if extras became available. We didn't mind this to much since we were already organized, however, some of the other groups, especially those subdivisions on the south side of town were really upset as they felt that the police and National Guard had the responsibility to defend them. The meeting started to deteriorate into a running argument and since we knew what we had to do, we left.

When we returned to the subdivision, we told everyone about the results of the meeting and continued with our own effort to reinforce the barriers we had established and make sure we had a guard rotation set up. Everyone over the age of fourteen was expected to pull guard duty at some point during the day. Most of the teens and all of the women were assigned daytime watches.

Food and water are still not a problem. Everyone is rationing what they have and we continue to boil the water.

We've had no problem with the few non-White families that reside in Wheaton, two families of which live in our subdivision. The Hernendez and Chang families have been accepted as colleagues by most everyone and hopefully nothing will happen to change anyone's mind.

Electric service is intermittent. We have it about twelve-fourteen hours per day.

Mail service is a thing of the past, at least temporarily. So is TV other than news programs, all of it bad news and sporadic in nature. With the majority of organized government wiped out on day one, the lower forty-eight are quickly becoming state and

David A. Bragen

region sufficient. There is little national anything any more. Even the military has been instructed to operate its various bases as somewhat autonomous, regionally oriented units.

Fuel, both heating/cooking and gasoline, have been relatively constant in supply. Long lines at the pumps, but so far, so good.

September 27 - Day Six

Lieutenant Colonel Ralph Emerson, Illinois National Guard, arrived at our Geneva Road barricade at about 9:00 a.m. this morning. He came in one of those olive drab military HUMMERs and looked pretty impressive in his battle fatigues.

He met with me, the Defense representatives, Bruce Jamison and Larry Findler, and the Scavenger's Bill Komanski and Ed Flanders. His basic message was that he admired what we had accomplished, that he wished other groups were so well organized, that it was clear we didn't need much help and that he would stop by in a couple of days to see how things were going.

What we heard was that we were on our own.

We did follow a few of his suggestions though. We emptied the gasoline out of the cars and trucks we were using as barricades to avoid fires and explosions should a fight happen. We also moved the Child Protection group into the basement of one of the smaller houses to make a smaller target. And we issued orders that people would not walk around in groups smaller than five after it got dark outside.

September 28 - Day Seven

The day started out with some rather startlingly news reports coming over the radio. Apparently the United Nations, which both sides had respected thus far during the Civil War, had announced that they were relocating the UN to Paris effective immediately. Estimates ranged from seven to ten days to complete the transfer of staffs and paperwork to the new UN headquarters just outside of city central Paris. United Nations Secretary General Mary McDonald of Scotland cited the instability of the political situation in the United States, coupled with the world-wide condemnation of the Civil War, had made it unsafe and untenable to remain in the city of New York.

It looks like the world community is abandoning us to forge our own destiny.

Interstate Highway #55
1942 hours
November 6

As Pierce and Jones poured over the journal, the Mid-Night Express was barreling down Interstate 55 between St. Louis and Chicago somewhere around Pontiac, IL. A GMC pickup, followed closely by a beat-up old yellow school bus, pursued by two more pickups, a Dodge and a Ford. This eclectic caravan moved quickly through the night, following the dashed white line in the middle of the two lanes, moving fast enough so the white lines almost blurred into a single, hazy snake.

Frank Hollis, husband of Susan Hollis and father of Sara Hollis, was one of several Sandpiper Court subdivision residents who had been stranded out-of-town at the outbreak of hostilities. Frank, a salesman for a plastics company in Itasca, had awakened mid-morning on September 15th with a hangover induced, splitting headache; drinks courtesy of a late night celebration closing the biggest deal of his short four-year sales career at Acme Plastic Extruders. McDonnell Douglas needed to replace a small, circular wire harness that was used to bundle the huge mass of wiring running throughout the hydraulic systems in their airplanes.

The crash of the MD-80 airliner, operated by Southwestern Airlines in June '97 had been traced to a simple, single piece of non-operating equipment; a small, circular wire harness. Apparently, the harness, which held a series of electric cables in a fixed position, wasn't secure enough to hold the wires together during extreme turbulence. Murphy's law one again proved true on Southwestern's flight #343 from Dallas to Houston. Severe weather had hit the flight unexpectedly during final approach. The thunderstorm looked manageable until a wind shear condition arose. The warning systems worked great. The pilots had over twenty seconds to react to the bleating 'wind shear wind shear' screech of the computer simulated female voice only to find that the hydraulics operating the flaps failed to respond. The cockpit recorder's last recorded sound, in addition to the screams of the co-pilot, were the words of the pilot, "Comin' to see you, dad!", followed by a momentary sound of an explosion.

The National Transportation Safety Board determined that three minutes of rough turbulence has caused the harness's failure and allowed the electronic cables to rub against one another, exposing their metal cores. When two exposed wires touched each other, they grounded and sparked, thus failing to conduct the proper signal. Despite the frantic actions of the cockpit crew, the plane plunged into an open field sixteen and a half miles from the runway at the Houston International Airport twenty seconds after the wires grounded. McDonnell Douglas immediately ordered the replacement of all such harnesses in all of their planes, as well as issued orders to destroy all existing harnesses in inventory and replace them with new ones.

McDonnell Douglas' smallest plane used one hundred eighty eight harnesses; their largest plane, two hundred sixty-seven. There we over twelve hundred planes manufactured by McDonnell Douglas in operation worldwide and over twenty seven thousand harnesses in various replacement or work-in-process inventories. At $5.87 per unit, Franks' sale grossed over $1,700,000. A 20% commission rate explained his giddiness over consummating the deal.

Realizing he missed his 8:15 a.m. flight, Frank turned on CNN to listen to the news during the wakeup, shave, shower, get dressed routine. Missing the flight turned out to be a great stoke of luck since that plane exploded during its final approach into Chicago's O'Hare field, the result of thirty-five pounds of C-4 explosives hidden in a soft-sided piece of ugly, puke-green Samsonite luggage that had been loaded into the belly of the plane by a baggage handler of Nigerian extraction who just happened to have been a ardent NCNWC supporter.

Frank had been stranded in St. Louis ever since.

The Mid-Night Express started operating three days after the Civil War broke out. Adversity always seems to uncover that breed of human who loves to profit from the misfortune of others. It dawned on Charlie Lewis, an overweight, plug ugly tub of a man, that people had been stranded in St. Louis as a result of the War. People who wanted to get home. People willing to pay anything to get home. Voila! The Mid-Night Express was born.

For $10 per mile, forty people minimum, Charlie and the boys would take you anywhere within a 750 mile radius of the Gateway Arch. Some were stupid enough not to realize that the guarantee deliver you 'safe and sound, or your money back' was hollow. The only reason you wouldn't make it was if the NCNWC caught your ass and killed you. That's why Charlie demanded cash up front. That's also why Charlie stayed in the office!

Frank Hollis, and his seat mate, Lloyd Campbell, from Rosemont, just outside of O'Hare Airport, occupied seats 12A and 12B, twelve rows behind the bus driver. They had struck up a friendly conversation as the bus left St. Louis and by the time they had reached Springfield, IL, they had formed one of those quick relationships travelers develop with the stranger sitting next to them. Their conversation had turned to some rather mundane topics and they really where not paying much attention to anything in particular when there was a brilliant flash of light in front of the bus, followed immediately by the sound of a large explosion. The lead support pickup had been lifted six feet in the air in a tremendous fireball and literally thrown into the culvert that ran next to the highway.

The bus driver, in a reflexive maneuver, stepped on the accelerator, swerving right and left, barreling down the highway, struggling to maintain control of the bus and never looking back.

A thousand yards across the field on the left side of the highway, the crew of the NCNWC M60 tank, hunkered down in a hull down position, awaited the commanders' next order.

The MBT (main battle tank) M60 is a fifty-three ton, tracked tank. Coupled with a 105mm main cannon and supported by a crew of four, the M60 is one hell of a fighting machine. The driver of the tank occupies a position in front. The tank's turret, which houses the 105mm main cannon, is located in the center of the vehicle and provides working space and protection for the balance of the crew; a commander, a gunner and a loader. The normal inventory of ammunition included approximately 60 rounds made up of both armor piercing, for use against other tanks and fixed emplacements, and high explosive, used for troop concentrations and thin skinned vehicles (e.g., trucks and APCs or armored personnel carriers). Additional armaments included a coaxially mounted 7.62mm machine gun, located adjacent to the main cannon and fired by the gunner, as well as an externally mounted 12.7mm machine gun, which was usually fired by the commander. The use of this weapon resulted in the commanders' head and shoulders being exposed to enemy fire as he positioned himself above the tank's cupola to fire the machines gun. A great John Wayne scene in most war movies but rather impractical in real combat.

Having a huge, fuel consuming 800+ horsepower engine limited the M60's range to somewhere between 40 and 80 miles, depending upon terrain and speed. Communications were provided through VHF, HF and intercom systems.

"Load another HE round and go for the bus."

The bus glowed a ghostly greenish-red as the gunner looked through the infrared sights while the loader pushed the buttons instructing the automated loading mechanism to insert another shell into the breech.

"Round up, loaded and locked, sir!"

The gunner, looking through the sights, placed the crosshairs on the very center of the bus.

"Target in the crosshairs, sir!"

Frank just happened to be looking out the window when he saw the small flash on the horizon. As he opened his mouth to ask Lloyd what he thought it was, the HE round crashed through the side of the bus between rows eight and nine, about thirty-six inches below the bottom of the windows. In the microseconds necessary to cover the distance from the outer shell of the bus to the protective shield around the massive, eighty-five gallon gas tank, the shell started to explode. A microsecond later, the protective shield vaporized as did Frank, Lloyd, the rest of the passengers and the bus itself.

Glenn Ellyn, IL (NCNWC bivouac area)
1753 hours
November 6

Pierce turned to the last page of the entry for October 29th.

Not too much else was going on. Susan Hollis once again stopped by to see if we had heard anything about her husband. No word yet. She's hanging in there but I'm starting to get worried.

Well, tomorrow's another day.

Glenn Ellyn, IL (NCNWC bivouac area)
1754 hours
November 6

"Whad'ya think? Read a little more or you want to wait until later?"

"Keep going, Sarge. Gettin' interesting," Jones replied as he watched Pierce turn the page to the next entry. "Besides, chow's kind'a just laying like a lump in my gut, I swear Cookie's trying to kill me, and it's way too early to hit the sack. Might as well keep on going. Maybe I can begin to digest that goremet meal, and I do stress the 'gore' part. If I didn't know any better, I'd swear Cookie got'a be using that soylent green cookbook I heard about in the movies. Why I....."

"Jones, shut your yap cause I'm tired of the rap," Pierce rhymed. "Let's just read the book, okay?"

V

September 29 - Day Eight

The Committee met most of the day on housekeeping issues; most of that time devoted to Food & Medical and Child Protection.

Food supplies remain pretty decent. We stock up on canned goods and other non-perishables as they have become available at the stores. The Police set up a ration program that is fair. It's based upon headcount, not ability to pay (though the concept of money is almost becoming a joke at this stage of the game). They are strictly enforcing a residency requirement. It seems that a number of displaced persons have been wandering into town looking for food, shelter and protection. Supplies are already stretched and while the Police have attempted to be understanding, they have established a minimum relief package that includes three square meals, a place to sleep for one night and then the non-residents are escorted to the town's boundaries. It is made clear that they are not invited to return, nor will they be given any additional aid. As brutal as this sounds, we are all in agreement as to the nature of the decision to enforce such tactics.

The biggest problem with food stuffs is that fresh products such as meat, eggs, milk, juice, produce, are all in short supply.

A black market, no pun intended, has sprung up pretty quickly. Most everyone is out to make a buck if they can. Since most people are not working and the banking system is still screwed up, money is tight. The black marketers must figure that CW 2 will end soon therefore they're trying to take advantage of the situation. Long story short, this makes fresh food tough to get and expensive to buy. Though us folks in Wheaton don't have to individually pay for the food, the Police are controlling our community's investment in the food flow and they have to dole out the money. I better explain how the system works.

It became apparent a couple of days into CW 2 that things were going be tough. By the way, everyone is now calling the Civil War CW 2. Anyways, the Police, National Guard and the City government saw that though the economy was being savaged, money was still important and some stability needed to be introduced into the community to avoid an internal class struggle of our own from erupting. The income swing in Wheaton went from a high of well over $1,000,000 per year income to a low of subsistence level.

It was decided that the community needed to operate as a true community and we basically pooled our financial resources. Disbursements were to be made by a financial board consisting of the mayor, Linda Levinson, the Police Chief, Dan Himmerman, the Principle of St. Michael parochial grammar school, Sister Elizabeth Marie, the National Guard senior officer, Lieutenant Colonel Ralph Emerson and three members of the town council, Lou Vianni, Nancy Parker and our very own Bill Komanski.

The financial board contacted the various sources of food, medical supplies and the like and arranged for mass purchases and delivery. So far so good.

Medical supplies are doing great. No real pressure here. Central DuPage Hospital, in Winfield, is in the community next door and under National Guard control. That unit reports to our Lieutenant Colonel Emerson. Enough said.

The only real major medical situation thus far, beyond the normal heart attacks, broken bones and newborn babies, was the massacre downtown on the 26th. That did result in a short-term problem, however, with the increased vigilance we honestly don't expect any more attacks of the same nature.

Child Protection was a heated debate for quite some time. Frank Smyth and Janice Pedopoulos argued strongly that we should increase security for the kids, essentially build them a fortress, and that we should fight with the community Committee to reopen the schools. Talk about dropping a bomb!

We finally agreed to increase the barricades around the area we designated for the Child Protection base of operations but flatly refused to push the town government to open the schools. The risks are simply too great. The transportation up and back would need serious defensive support plus we found that having all of the children in one spot at one time in an obvious target, the schools, were risks that we were unwilling to accept.

One thing that is very distasteful to have to acknowledge is the depths to which humanity has already sunk to. I guess I'm not in a position to speak authoritatively on the politics behind CW 2. Personally, I think it stinks and I'm pretty pissed off at the NCNWC. But, maybe they felt justified to start this whole mess - or did we really start it years before. I'll leave that one to the historians.

What really upsets me are the worthless sons of bitches, White no less, who are too fucking lazy to settle down and organize their life. They selected the path of renegades, living off their fellow man. And I'm not talking about the displaced persons who are just struggling. I'm talking about the assholes that have formed marauding gangs to live off everyone else's efforts. We haven't actually seen too much of this in Wheaton, though the radio carries nightly newscasts that describe the difficulties being experienced in some of the larger towns and cities. Chicago alone is publicly executing an average of twenty people a day for looting, rape, pillaging, murder and mayhem. A war inside a war; just what we need.

Glen Ellyn, IL (NCNWC bivouac area)
2012 hours
November 6

Pierce looked up and over at Jones.

"You got'a admire these folks. There was an awful lot to think about. Us, we just worry about running out of ammunition and where the next hot meal is. These folks, man, I guess no one had it easy."

"It must really be tough on you, Frank. I mean not seeing your wife and kid," said Jones with an obvious look of concern on his face.

Apparently not noticing, or at least not caring that Jones didn't call him Sergeant, Pierce simply shook his head saying "That's a fact, TY. That's a fact. Well, before I start crying like a baby and all, whad'ya say we get some sleep. Another long patrol tomorrow."

"Sure thing, Frank. uhh, I mean, Sarge. Good night," Jones replied, feeling that the friendship that had been threatened a few weeks earlier when they had had that disagreement was once again back on track. He lay back on his cot as Pierce doused the Coleman lantern.

It might not be a bad idea to get me a wife and family when this here war's over. Yeah, that's exactly what I'm gon'na do. If it's good enough for Sarge, it can't be half bad.

Glen Ellyn, IL (NCNWC bivouac area)
0545 hours
November 7

Dawn seemed to come early; too early.

Jones would have bet a bundle that he had just gone to bed and here he was, pulling on the boots and getting ready for another day. He remembered that Pierce had mentioned another long patrol. He wondered what that was all about. Ever since the big fire-fight just outside O'Hare Airport, the trek south had been relatively uneventful. Yeah, some brothers bought the farm, but you expect that in war.

Their Airborne Battalion had initially landed with over eight hundred officers and men arriving on the jumbo Hercules transports. Even though three weeks had passed since the landing, he still couldn't believe they were able to come in under cover of dark and convince those assholes on the ground that they were National Guard troopers coming in to relieve the ground forces in the northwestern Chicagoland area. By the time people knew what was going on, they had secured the airport and moved in some armored support. That, plus a mixed score of National Guard tanks and APCs they were able to commandeer on the ground, gave them a pretty decent chance at achieving success.

While this midnight raid was happening, the NCNWC's 3rd Brigade, over thirty-five hundred soldiers strong, supported by the 2nd Tank Battalion's sixty-seven tanks and APCs, embarked on their attack, moving north from Frankfort, on the far southwestern edge of the Chicagoland area. The overall plan; link up forces around Wheaton, prepare defensive positions, and cut off Chicago from their western supply routes. A bold plan indeed, but a plan that was working beyond the wildest expectations of the NCNWC senior staff.

As Jones finished lacing up his left boot, Pierce came back into the tent.

"Well, Corporal Jones. So nice of you to join us today. Did you have a nice rest? Could I get you some breakfast, or maybe the paper to read," Pierce's voice raising to just about a yell, "or is there any other fuckin' thing I could do to make your day a little more pleasurable?!"

"No, Sergeant Pierce. I'm just fine Sergeant Pierce," Jones stammered as he quickly jumped to his feet. "I'm all set to go, Sarge."

"Let's be on our way then."

Jones ran after Pierce who was already crawling into the back of the APC. After crawling into the back of the fighting vehicle, Jones closed the door since he was the last of the squad to enter.

"Hey, Sarge. Where we going?"

"Yeah. How come we always the first one's to go. Someone mad at us or what?"

"I'm getting sick and tired of this bullshit," yelled another squad member. "How come First Recon is always first?"

With the gun ports closed and the lights down, it was almost impossible to tell who was saying what. Pierce knew the voices well enough, but the anonymity of the dark was respected.

"I sure am glad I don't know who is saying all this shit because if I did, someone would find it very uncomfortable sitting there with my number twelve combat boots stuck up their ass," Pierce said softly. "Yeah, it's a good thing it's dark in here. Right, Jones?"

"I didn't say nothin'," Jones quickly added amongst the muffled snickers.

"It wasn't an accusation Corporal Jones. I'm just saying it's a good thing it wasn't you saying such shit. You have been here long enough, in fact longer than anyone but me in this squad, to know that the First Recon gets the tough jobs because we're tough. Eat steel and spit out nails kind'a guys. We da the big, fighting machine. Ain't that right, Jones?"

Jones finally caught on that Pierce was just hosing him a little. Breathing a sigh of relieve, he added in a chant "Right on, Sarge. Da big…. black…fightin' machine. We da big… black… fighting machine!"

By the time he finished saying it the second time, the whole squad, Pierce included, were clapping their hands, stomping their feet. Psyching men up to prepare themselves to become cannon fodder was never an easy challenge for the guy in charge. Yet, Pierce was able to do it time and time again. That's why Recon One always got the tough assignments. Pierce's superiors knew that if was humanly possible, Pierce and his boys would find a way to do it.

"Goddamn it back there," yelled the APC driver. "Stop that shit. Not only can't I hear myself think, you guys are rocking this whole damn vehicle." The driver pronounced it "vee-hickle" in standard military intonation.

"Hey, taxi man. If you could think, you wouldn't be no fuckin' cab driver in the first place!"

"Yeah. You do the driving, we'll do the jivin'!"

After the laughter died, it started again.

"We da big, black, fighting machine. We da big, black, fighting machine. We da big… black… fighting machine!"

VI

Wheaton, IL (between Route 56 and Blackwell Forrest Preserve)
0638 hours
November 7

Like a low intensity spotlight, the shaft of light cast a muted glow over the interior of the APC. The ghostly pallor of the nine black faces, caused by the sudden and unexpected intrusion of light, made all pause in reflection. The only sound beyond the grinding gears and the strain of the engine was the sharp, staccato harmonic gasps of the nine scared men. Between the seven men in his squad and the APC's crew of two, Pierce couldn't comprehend the incalculable odds of them still being alive.

"Jesus, Fuckin', Christ!"

"What the hell was that?"

"What happened?!"

"Everybody OK? Anybody down? Anybody hurt? Jesus, this fuckin' thing's still moving! Get us out of here, Taximan!" Pierce shouted. His voice noticeably quivering like some young virgin on her wedding night. Mr. Reaper had just flown through. But this time, this one time, he hadn't been carrying any names on his stone cold lips.

Looking from face to face, Pierce knew he was looking at a group of dead men. Ghosts. There was no fuckin' way they could still be alive; but they were.

Somehow, the sabot round fired by the U.S. Army M1A1 tank had failed to explode. It simply, and quite quickly, pierced the thin metal alloy skin of the APC several inches below the roof line, rifled on through and poked another neat, round hole through the other side. And somehow, miraculously, it hadn't detonated.

The M1A1 General Abrams Main Battle Tank is recognized as, if not the best, one of the top three main battle tanks in the world. Crewed with four professionals, the M1A1 is hell on wheels. The large, almost over sized turret, though still centrally located like its predecessors, now provides space and protection for the entire crew. The low profile tank is equipped with enough electronics and communication systems to make its predecessors look like tinker toy models.

The M1A1 was equipped with three different types of imaging systems allowing the commander and gunner to virtually see through anything and everything encountered on a modern battlefield. Six fixed periscope locations with various fields of magnification tied to a computer aided aiming system provided thermal sights for night vision, laser range finders for accuracy, and computer controlled stabilization mechanics to provide combined fire and movement accuracy, even when running at full speed.

Even Nintendo couldn't beat the real thing!

Sabot rounds are tank killers. Their depleted uranium heads carry enough kinetic energy when fired from the muzzle of the M1A1's 120mm cannon to open up the thickest armor on any tank manufactured anywhere in the world. The destructive principle of the round was for the head of the sabot to punch through the protective armor shield, allowing the explosive force of the round to devastate the interior of the vehicle as opposed to being wasted in a colorful, yet ineffective pyrotechnic display on the tank's exterior armor. Everything worked this time, except that this time, the sabot failed to explode.

The gunner on the M1A1's crew knew he had a hot target dead in the crosshairs when he gently squeezed the trigger, propelling the sabot on its way. He saw the hit and almost felt the jolt that had rocked the APC. But it kept going. In fact, it started going quicker. And he was stunned. The tank commander, watching the action through his own periscope said "Let 'em go, Gunner. Ain't their time to die. Not yet anyways."

Pierce had often heard the phrase, even joked about it himself, that you never hear the shot that kills you. Absolutely nobody in the APC heard the sabot round coming. He knew that by all that was holy in heaven, a strange thought he realized to have in the middle of a battlefield, that everyone in the APC should be toast.

God sure does move in mysterious ways.

"Hey, Taximan! If you wanted some cool air, why didn't you just open the fuckin' window?

The APC driver, turned around to look at Pierce and just smiled. Smiled at the attempted humor. Smiled at seeing his buddies alive. Smiled at the simple thought of being able to smile; at simply being alive.

"Well, Sergeant Major Franklin B. Pierce," he drawled, "I was getting mighty hot mighty quick when I sees this big ol' enemy tank sitting there on the ridge. Now I been around long enough to know that this joker just loaded up a dummy round and I figure, why not? Why not gives this poor ol' White boy a target he can't pass up. Now I knew the fucker couldn't shoot worth a shit and what the hell? By the time I would've of asked your permission to ventilate this here vehicle (once again pronouncing it 'vee-hickle') why we'd have be out of range and behind the trees. Shit, Sarge. You just looked kind' a hot. I was just trying to be of service"

As if responding to some unspoken cue, the chant once again arose quickly to a fervor pitch.

"We da big... black... fighting machine. We da big... black... fighting machine!"

VII

Glen Ellyn, IL (NCNWC bivouac area)
1925 hours
November 7

Thinking back on the day's excitement, Pierce, leaning up against a tree in the area where the squad was to bivouac for the night, called out to Lance Corporal Tyrone Jones, "Hey, Ty. Come here."

Jones looked up from his cubby-hole under the rear half of the APC, stood and walked over to Pierce.

"Yeah, Sarge. What's up?"

"What the hell you hiding under there for like some mangy dog?"

"Sarge, I ain't never come so close to dying before and I got to tell you man to man, I don't like it. Don't like it at all."

Laughing as he stood up, Pierce confessed, "You wan'na know something, TY. I don't like it none myself."

"Frank," Ty said, forgetting military courtesy for a moment, "we could've been killed today. Man, this shit's getting serious. I don't wan'na die, Frank. I just do not wan'na die. Not that way."

Pierce reached over and placed his hand on Jones' shoulder, much like a father comforting his own son who just emerged from some horrible experience. He fixed his gaze deep into Jones' eyes. "Ty, I'm real glad you didn't get killed. I'm real glad I didn't get killed. I'll be forever grateful that the good Lord seen fit to spare all our sorry asses this day. It kind'a makes you wonder why."

"Sarge. I don't want to be scared. But I was, and I still am."

"Ty, you'd be a fool if you weren't scared out of your mind. I doubt that what happened to us today ever happened to any squad in this whole crazy war," Pierce said calmly. "You did good. We all did good and together, we'll all make it out of here somehow."

"You sure about that, Sarge?" Jones queried.

"Would a brother lie to a brother?"

With his arm still on Jones' shoulder, Pierce led him back to the tree where he had been sitting. "Whad'ya say we check back in with TJ and see what he's been up to lately?"

"Great idea, Sarge. Anything to help me forget this day. I swear I saw that fuckin' round go right through that armor like a hot knife through butter. Damn."

Sitting down, Pierce opened his haversack and pulled out the battered journal. Jones sat down next to Pierce, and offered him the use of half the poncho as a ground sheet. It could pretty damn cold and wet just sitting there on the dirt.

Pierce was about to mumble "Okay", when he realized that a bond was forming between the two men. A bond the extended beyond the military relationship between a master sergeant and one of his lance corporals. It's nice to have friends he thought. He immediately pushed that thought from his mind. War was no place to have friends. People get killed in wars and he didn't need any friends getting killed. So Pierce simply said "No thanks".

September 30 - Day Nine

Today we buried Steve Jamison - 7, Linda Granger -8, Paul Savantini - 6, Suzie Kornat - 7 and Brian Chang - 6.

Lisa Granger - 10 and Jimmie Farmer - 3, were still in the Emergency Room at Central DuPage Hospital, condition critical. And I'm personally responsible for their deaths and injuries.

Wheaton, IL (Sandpiper Court subdivision)
1850 hours
September 30

A tear struck the page as TJ stared down at what he had just written. He was responsible. Just as responsible as if he had picked up a gun, put it to the kids' heads and pulled the trigger. How was he going to live with this weighing on him, weight heavy enough to crush the very spirit out of any human being?

The day had started out like most of the recent days in CW II. Chores to do, positions to check, problems to solve. Another ordinary day on the ad hoc, subdivision battlefield.

He was sitting with Defense committee leaders Bruce Jamison and Larry Findler, reviewing their new plan to move the ammunition supply to a central, more easily defended location. He remembered that several times, he had to get up and ask the group of kids playing outside of the room to please be quiet; that they were making too much noise and bothering the grownups and "Go find something, anything, to do".

About twenty minutes into the meeting, Jeff Dalton, one of the guards at the main entrance to the subdivision, escorted Lieutenant Colonel Ralph Emerson, Illinois National Guard into the room.

Emerson excused himself for the intrusion, but had previously promised to supply some weapons and was stopping by to drop off a small shipment of twenty Claymore mines.

He explained that Claymore mines were anti-personnel weapons. The convex shaped canister was placed in the ground using the attached spikes or strapped to a tree or some other stationary object. The mines could be operated independently via a trip wire that had been stretched across a trail or any potential entry point for the enemy. When the enemy reached the killing zone of the mine, a simple depression on the firing button would launch approximately one hundred fifty marble sized steel balls into a cone of death that would kill or maim anyone who was in front of the 9" x 15" mine when it detonated. The shotgun pattern of the projectiles had an effective kill radius of twenty yards wide by thirty yards deep. The mines could also be operated manually by removing a small wire from the firing mechanism, thus activating a small plunger. Hit the plunger and the mine exploded twenty seconds later.

Thinking back, TJ remembered once again that he had to tell the kids to be quite and at one point, had to tell them to get away from the door and leave the grown-ups alone.

After giving them the Claymore mines, Emerson expressed his apologies about having to leave so quickly. He needed to visit several other self-defense groups later today and would he unable to stay longer and demonstrate the operation of the mines. He scheduled a visit for the day after tomorrow to hold this training session.

TJ remembered telling Jeff to help the troopers with Emerson to unload the Claymores and place them in front of the house. A few minutes later, the meeting ended and Bruce and Larry took the mines over to the ammunition storage site. Neither noticed that they only transported nineteen mines, not twenty, which is what Emerson left behind.

Thirty minutes later, they heard a large explosion. Tracing the source to the backyard of the house where TJ, Bruce and Larry had held their earlier meeting, they discovered the kids lying on the ground. The carnage was indescribably gruesome and bloody. It took some time to recognize a couple of the kids, with parents having to perform the awful task.

The tragic toll; six dead, two critically wounded. The killer; an exploding Claymore mine.

Lisa Granger, who had had her left arm blown off, said, before she lapsed into unconsciousness, that they were just trying to get the marbles. They had thought these were presents for the kids and didn't want to wait. They wanted the marbles so they could all play. They wanted to play marbles.

TJ realized that the kids must have heard bits and pieces of the conversation they had had with Emerson about the Claymores. He remembered that Emerson had used the word "marbles" several times when talking about the mines.

TJ also realized he had simply told Jeff to unload the mines right out in front of the house. Right out in front of the kids.

If only he had told Jeff to unload the mines at the storage site. If only he had told Bruce and Larry to count the mines before they moved them. If only he had done something right, anything right, these poor kids would still be making noise and he'd still be telling them to be quiet.

And worst of all, TJ realized he was responsible for this death and destruction.

Another tear hit the page as he continued to write.

By 2:00 p.m. this afternoon, we had made the difficult decision to bury the children quickly, after a small memorial service. The devastation was unbelievable. Doc was unable to do anything to help Lisa and Jimmie. Their wounds were so severe that he wasn't sure they would even survive the trip to Central DuPage Hospital.

The kids that were killed were really chewed up. They must have all been gathered around the mine, trying to open it. We found a screwdriver nearby afterwards. We figure they must have grounded the low voltage firing mechanism somehow.

Wheaton, IL (Sandpiper Court subdivision)
1932 hours
September 30

Another tear formed as he as he turned the page.

Most all of the wounds were to the head and upper body. They must have died instantly. When we found them, not one sign of life. Even Lisa and Brian were lying so still we figured they were all dead.

The memorial service was held in the only empty lot in the subdivision, over on MacArthur Lane. Doc presided and a number of the grieving parents had very touching, poignant comments to share with all of us.

Everyone attended, even those on guard duty. This was our first tragedy. We decided to bury the kids in the empty lot and agreed to fix it up as our own private subdivision cemetery. Just about everyone volunteered to help clean it up and make it look okay.

I want to get it down for the record that I, Anthony Joseph Bender, am solely responsible for this tragedy. No one else did anything wrong. It was all my fault.

Wheaton, IL (Sandpiper Court subdivision)
1946 hours
September 30

TJ threw the pen to the floor, slammed the notebook shut, buried his head in his arms and cried the cry of one possessed.

Up until today, he had thought that this whole CW II was kind of neat. Yeah, people were getting killed and the US was falling apart, but they were other people, strangers. And in spite of the ongoing carnage, here he was, the king of a small kingdom. He wasn't really interested in it for the power. Yet he was glad that he was the guy everyone was relying on for direction, advice and decisions. And he had made the decisions; easy ones and tough ones alike.

Now everything had changed. The excitement turned into responsibility. The fun had turned into responsibility. The heady feeling that comes with command had turned into responsibility.

He thought about quitting, even thinking about ending it all. He wasn't a quitter; however, this was too much for him, too much for any human being.

"Excuse me, TJ" the barely audible female voice wavered. "Could I speak to you for a moment?"

TJ looked up, tears streaking his face, his eyes a crazy quilt work pattern of red and white. There stood Mary Kornat, Suzie's mother. He stumbled to his feet and looked at her, surprised to see her here.

In unison, they walked towards each other and hugged. Both crying; both unable to speak.

After several minutes, TJ found enough of a voice to offer "Mary, I'm so goddamn sorry about Suzie. I'd give anything to undo what I did."

Mary pulled back and slapped him hard. Harder than he'd ever been hit by any women before.

He didn't flinch. He had even expected it. After all, he had just killed her daughter. What he hadn't expected though, was to hear what Mary Kornat screamed at him.

"You miserable son of a bitch! This isn't about Suzie and this certainly isn't about you! You're the one in charge. We all agreed with that. We all agreed that you would lead us. Well, a terrible thing happened today. No one wanted it to, but it did happen. No one is going to forgive you. No one. As much as it hurts to have buried my daughter and to see the other parents put their too young to die children in the ground, what I'm worried about, what we're all worried about are the living. If you're not prepared to lead, get the fuck out of the way. If you are going to lead, then start leading."

Reeling from this unexpected verbal blow, TJ drew a breath, started to open his mouth to once again express an apology, but saw that he was looking at Mary's back. She had already wheeled around on her heels and sped out the door.

TJ had a lot to think about that night.

Glen Ellyn, IL (NCNWC bivouac area)
2018 hours
November 7

Pierce reached over and turned another page of the journal.

October 1 - Day Ten

The events of yesterday were tragic and avoidable.

I called for a full Committee meeting at 10:00 a.m. to review all of our procedures in order to avoid a repeat of yesterday. Each group was requested to review their own operating procedures and develop revised plans if any shortcomings were identified. We agreed to meet early the next day for a more formal review of the actions that needed to be taken.

At noon, we called for a gathering of all subdivision residents. I reviewed the events of yesterday and explained the actions that we were going to take to prevent such a tragedy from occurring a second time. It was a very emotional meeting. The wounds of the previous day were still painfully fresh in everyone's heart and soul. We knew we were involved in a war but these kids weren't war casualties. These innocent kids died because of a bunch of civilians playing soldier didn't know how to handle the dynamic and fast moving situation that was developing around us.

I offered to resign, if that would help get our group back together again but just as Mary Kornat had predicted the night before, no one was looking for someone to blame. They were looking for someone to lead them. In fact, Mary Kornat was one of the more vocal members of the group insisting that I continue in a position of leadership.

I never intended this journal to be a diary of my activities. I feel bad in taking the time to detail the events on the matter of the children's deaths and my personal feelings but I do want to make it clear that at the end of the day, no one can be blamed but me. I have accepted this fact and am pledging, just as I pledged to the group at the Noon meeting, that I am completely committed on behalf of everyone to provide the leadership required to help us through this mess, and that I will do my best to represent the trust they have all placed in me.

News arrived at 4:30 p.m. from Central DuPage Hospital that both Lisa Granger and Jimmie Farmer died from the wounds received from the Claymore. Immediate plans were made to recover the bodies and hold yet another memorial service tomorrow.

Glen Ellyn, IL (NCNWC bivouac area)
1939 hours
November 7

"Say, Ty. How about getting us some coffee?" Pierce asked softly.

Jones, seeing the tears welling up in the sergeant's eyes said, "Yeah, sure Sarge. If you don't mind, I'm also going to hit the head? Might take a few extra minutes."

Pierce nodded, waving Jones away.

Thinking back to his own family, Pierce wondered how they were getting along without him. Cindy, his wife, had been his childhood sweetheart. They had grown up together in Manchester, a western suburb of St. Louis, MO. It was a real classic childhood sweetheart story. They had been born in the same month and year, October, 1962, though he constantly reminder her that she was after all an older women, three days older to be exact. He could never understand why a woman with her looks had felt it necessary to rob the cradle just to get a husband. And every time he said this to someone new they had just met, he would get a programmed sigh from Cindy as well as a playfully painful shot to the arm. You would think he'd be smart enough after all these years to consider that the humor had gone out of the little, minuscule joke.

They had lived on the same block, three houses apart. Their parents were truly good friends unlike most neighborhood relationships where people simply nod, occasionally saying "hi" to each other. Thus the friendship between the parents gave the kids many opportunities to play together. First rolling and crawling around on the carpet, then later, going to pre-school together followed by lower school, middle school and high school, where they had suddenly again encountered the urge to roll around on the carpet together.

Both decided that college was an extravagance too expensive for a newly married couple of seventeen. Franklin joined the Army in hopes of getting a practical education and building up enough credit to qualify for tuition assistance after he finished his hitch. Cindy took a job working for a young state senator who had visions of righting all the wrongs that the White establishment had heaped on the minorities. He was actually only concerned with Blacks, but he was smart enough to know he needed a broader coalition if he was to stand a chance. Cindy became a basic campaign worker and then advanced up to administrative assistant, never making a great deal of money, but bringing home some fascinating stories from the front line in-fighting of the political wars.

Franklin chuckled and realized that state senator Reese Robertson accomplished what he wanted to. He'd done good for a brother. He became the Independent Senator from the state of Missouri and eventually was one of the founding fathers of the NCNWC. It seemed like eons ago yet at the same time, it seemed like only yesterday.

Reese Robertson won his election to the Senate on the day their daughter was born. Just before her birth, they had argued over names in a friendly sort of way, for almost three weeks before Cindy finally won the argument by saying that their daughters' name would be Shasa. She had no explanation other than she liked how it sounded. No, it wasn't the name of an old relative, or have some special meaning in Swahili. She simply liked the way it sounded, soft and feminine.

Jones interrupted Pierce's thoughts with the announcement that the java was hot and black, "Just like I likes my women". Pierce looked up to see Jones standing there, his arm reaching out with the metal cup of steaming coffee, laughing his ass off at one of the oldest jokes around.

Pierce, snapped back to reality of the moment by Jones' intrusion said evenly, "Lance Corporal Tyrone Jones." Which immediately made Jones wince since military formality of this nature was normally a lead into getting his ass chewed by a senior military type. "You have read my mind, my boy. I was just wishing I could have Cindy around here so I could jump them fine young bones."

Grateful the Pierce was in good spirits, Jones ventured further out on the comedic limb, "Yeah, with this here war and us being out here on the front lines gives one an excellent chance at getting a bad case of blue balls. Only in our case, Sarge, better make that black and blue balls."

Pierce looked at Jones, who was now rolling around on the ground, holding his sides, laughing like some school kid who just heard that one for the first time and said, "It's times like this that I wish that this here man's army issued side arms for us non-coms (non-commissioned officers), so I could put a poor dumb fuck like you out of your sorry assed misery."

This made Jones howl like a banshee, laughing so hard that Pierce's only course of action was to put his coffee down, get up on all fours and pounce on him like an older brother wrestles with a younger sibling. A few minutes later, Jones, looking like an overcooked pretzel, held in some ninja type hold that Pierce had placed on him, yelled "Uncle" and promised to only tell funny jokes in the future, and "Yeah, Sarge. Only if I ask permission first! Just let me go. Please!"

Sitting back down, huffing and puffing, Pierce picked up the journal and they started reading again.

Lieutenant Colonel Ralph Emerson had gotten word of the Claymore accident and stopped by to convey his condolences. He said that he had felt bad for not training us immediately and for not instructing us as to the proper method for handling ordnance such as the Claymores. We appreciated his comments but told him that we did not hold him responsible for the tragedy and were looking forward to the continued support provided by him and the Illinois National Guard. He assured us of this support.

Lieutenant Colonel Emerson gave us the following update on CW II:

The fighting in most cases was becoming more of a conventional battle. Needless killing of non-combatants by both sides was decreasing.

Though some skirmishes were still being fought in residential areas, most battles involved military or industrial targets. Residential areas were only involved when they got in the way of an army on the move.

NCNWC forces were in control of most of the countryside surrounding major cities. They were working to blockade these major population centers as opposed to outright attacks. They didn't have the forces to hope to win such battles and they also realized that our armies were tied to protecting the population centers and couldn't chase them around the rural areas. Thus a stalemate was developing.

Food & Medical supplies were getting thinly stretched but with proper rationing, would get us through the next couple of months.

Military supplies were limited. The world community had taken the unilateral initiative to place a moratorium on arms shipments to both sides involved in CW II. Some independent sources were shipping contraband weapons and armaments, but the supply was very limited. This has led to somewhat of a slowdown in the conflict since both sides were running low on ammunition.

Communications from NCNWC forces indicated they were preparing a list of demands, which they hoped could act as the basis for a negotiated settlement to the current hostilities.

Emerson said he would stop by tomorrow to hold the Claymore training class.

October 2 - Day Eleven

So far, this one takes the cake for best idea!

We were sitting around just after the morning meeting, pissing and moaning about the lack of fresh food when this perfect 'vee' of geese flies right over the subdivision, headed towards the golf course they built just down the road a few years ago. We all look at each other and the proverbial collective light bulb goes on. Hunting!

We've had geese around this area forever. Our subdivision was originally all farmland, mostly corn. There was a small stream running through it. As the development got under way, the geese were still used to flying by. It took a few years for all the homes to be built and during this time, some of the old fields still attracted the geese. The developers diverted a portion of the stream into a couple of decorative ponds, which held the geese.

Later, I guess back in '92-'93, some of the builders developed a golf course community about a half mile north of us, just off Pleasant Hill. Great place, they called it the Country Club. Put in eighteen holes, about fifty sand traps, a couple of tunnels under Pleasant Hill since the course was on both sides of the road. Planned on building about one hundred eighty $275,000 to $600,000 single-family houses.

During the development stage of the property, they also diverted the stream to form a series of ponds throughout the course; twelve altogether. Talk about geese. The property also held ducks, a few pheasant, even a deer or two.

I played the course a couple of times; tight and undulating. A real duffer's nightmare.

Then the roof caved in.

The course surrounded an old, abandoned asphalt plant. Stunk like hell. Naturally, the builders bought out the site and tried to clean it up. The initial ground tests by the EPA on both state and local levels gave everyone the green light to continue with the development. The acquisition went through, models built, about twenty-five homes up and sold and old Uncle Sam comes along. The Feds do their own series of tests and you'd think they found Love Canal the Second. Immediate injunctions to stop development. Carcinogenics and all that bullshit. Well, property values dropped like a lead balloon. People couldn't sell fast enough and the operation nose-dived. The Country Club golf course remained open, but they never sold another house.

Long story short, we decided to set up some hunting blinds near a couple of these ponds and take a chance at putting some fresh meat on the tables. Will the real Daniel Boone please step forward!

Wheaton, IL (Sandpiper Court subdivision)
2141 hours
October 2

TJ sat back, a small smile on his face. Instantly he was seventeen again and in central Wisconsin, at the summer cottage his parents owned on the Wisconsin River, seven miles north of Wisconsin Dells.

Ten years before, a neighbor of the Bender family had offered them the use of their cottage just outside of Wisconsin Dells. The Dells are a very scenic part of south central Wisconsin. The area was predominantly sandstone. Over the course of hundreds of thousands of years, the Wisconsin River had sculpted and shaped the sandstone sides of the river bank into some very dramatic figures and shapes. Granted, the 'figures' required one to have a strong imagination to see 'the face of the Indian chief', or the 'piano smashed on the beach when it fell from the ledge above the river during the fiery sermon of an old fire and brimstone preacher'. But, it was a cute idea, beautiful country and quickly became a tourist attraction; later, a tourist trap.

The Bender family had a blast that vacation. Everyone wished that they didn't have to leave. Mom, Dad, both brothers just loved it.

Talk about divine intervention, the family was walking down the road in front of the cottage they were staying at. They were passing the other nine or ten cabins also located on the same access road when they came upon this middle aged woman pounding a 'FOR SALE' sign in front of one of the buildings. Joe Bender, the father, walked over with the magic question and nearly fainted when the agent responded "Family tragedy. The owner was, had been, ain't no more, a lab technician at Argon National Laboratory, in suburban Chicago. He had been exposed to radiation levels far beyond critical during a reactor performance test where safety procedures weren't followed. He died within eight days of the accident and the family wanted out, real quick. The cottage needs finishing, put in the ceiling and floor tiles, wood trim on the doorways, stuff like that. So, you can have it 'as is' for $9,500," said the real estate.

The Benders put in the offer that afternoon and closed the deal three weeks later.

To say that the cottage was on the river proper was a little bit of an exaggeration. The river was typically about forty to fifty yards wide, reaching depths of over one hundred feet, though the average depth was only fifteen to twenty feet. As the river came around the bend just north of the cottage, a bowl like depression in the local topography created the appearance of a lake about a mile across, mile and a half wide. The far side of this lake was a massive rock outcropping that the locals called Louie's Bluff. The Bluff was a good two hundred feet high and a quarter mile in length. Virtually all sandstone with a few pines and shrubs jutting out of the top. When one got closer, you could actually see that these evergreens were growing right out of cracks and crevices in the rock itself, seeds having been blow into these tiny opening years before.

The 'lake' in front of the Bender cottage was only two to three feet deep for most of the year. From shore, some areas looked rather swampy, small islands with lots of vegetation. When you got closer thought, the bottom was sand and the vegetation mostly willows and wild rice. Waterfowl found this place extremely attractive, offering food, protection as well as remaining open and ice free during the winter due to the river's strong current.

Long before TJ was old enough to even consider hunting, fishing captured his attention and that of his brother, Mark. The river held small mouth bass, northern pike, catfish, walleye and plenty of 'sunnies'. Joe Bender and his wife 'Sis' never worried about the boys venturing out and about to play or fish. The water wasn't a concern due to its shallow depth and the cottage was far enough off the beaten path so that strangers and all of those unspoken fears were unwarranted.

Within the first few weeks of owning the cottage, the Benders ran out and bought a 16 ft. aluminum fishing boat from Sears. Real basic stuff. Three seats, two oars and an anchor. Even this small boat was too much for the two younger Benders to handle so a canoe quickly followed.

TJ remembered picking up the rods and walking out amongst the willow and wild rice islands, looking for likely spots where fish would congregate. If the islands didn't produce a strike, he'd wander over to the 'big bay' that was sprinkled with stark, bark stripped stumps. The stumps were left over from the logging operations up the river and had been pushed downstream over the years with the spring thaws and floods. The wood was bleached gray from the water, wind and sun. These miniature towers looked like a modern city's skyline, especially at sundown when Louie's Bluff played tricks with the last rays of the setting sun.

Catfish fishing was the best. You'd spend part of the day walking through the shallows, collecting fresh water clams. The boys placed the clams on the sea wall to 'ripen' under the summer's hot sun. Load up the boat just before sunset and row out to the bay, anchoring next to one of the skyscraper stumps.

The clams absolutely stank out loud when the boys forced apart the two halves of the shell to get at the meat. Stick that stuff on a number 1/0 hook and with a K-Mart special Zebco rod and reel combo, heave out about twenty yards on 12 lb. test line and get ready. The boys typically used an 1 oz. weight to add some resistance. They'd reel in the slack until the line to the hook was taut, the small weight digging into the soft, sandy bottom. Carefully placing the rods against the gunwales pointing skyward, TJ and Mark would lean back and wait.

Usually, within twenty or thirty minutes, the stink from this highly odoriferous bait would waft down the underwater currents and tantalize the whiskers of ol' mister cat. Instinct honed over a million years of evolution and a guidance system that would rival the best of Raytheon would allow the channel cat to find this little piece of slime amongst all the other pieces of everything and anything pushed along the bottom of the river by the current. As the boys gazed at their rod tips, one or the other would start to twitch. Cat come a knockin', knockin' on my door.

For some reason, it was usually Mark's rod that got the first nibble. He'd slowly reach over and pick up his rod, point it towards the general area where the fish was and reel in any slack, waiting for that next subtle tug.

Ready, ready, come on, knock one more...there she is, hit her, hit her hard.

Raring back on the rod and reel, driving the point of the hook past the soft tissue of the cats' mouth, taking in line, hitting her again to make sure the hook is set properly and the barb locked past.... the what? The boys were never sure if fish had lips. Did you set the hook in the fish's lips, or in the fish's mouth? But who the hell really cares when your fighting another 'Lunker T. Catfish'.

Most cats were between three and four pounds. Great tasting fish, at least out of this river. Cats are bottom feeders and if taken out of warm, stagnant water, have a pretty poor flavor. In this part of the river, aside from being stained with a tinge of tannic acid from all those old stumps and the logging operation upriver, the water was cold, clean and moving. Pan fried catfish made the effort worthwhile.

Then the real magic happened, happened every time they fished into the night. Sundown!

The top of Louie's Bluff would burst into brilliance as it captured, but only for a few moments, the dying rays of the day's sun. While this was happening, the boys would fire up the Coleman lantern.

The lantern was placed on the middle seat of the boat. The cone of light was only strong enough to illuminate a circle about twelve feet in diameter from the lantern. The boys could see each other, the boat and the tips of their rods. Everything beyond simply disappeared. Couldn't see the lights on shore, no headlights on cars and trucks moving down the highway, nothing at all laterally.

But my God! Look up and see the universe and all its glory. Millions, I bet'ya billions of stars appeared once their eyes adjusted.

The first time they saw it, Mark and TJ just couldn't find the words to describe it. They simply gazed upward for the longest time.

Later trips turned this time into the magic time. The surrealistic setting begged for ghost stories, future planning, if-I-were-king scenarios. But time is fleeting and special events rush by even faster and the boys started to grow up.

TJ had started hunting at about sixteen when the guy in the cottage next to the Bender's offered to take him out in his duck blind one day to get a feel for hunting. Talk about love at first sight. TJ couldn't get enough of it.

Joe Bender was never a hunter in his own rights. After that first solo season, TJ pestered his Dad so much about him taking up hunting that the older Bender signaled surrender and the closet was soon filled with two sets of waders, another pump-action shotgun, more decoys, extra wool socks. It started to look like Eddie Bauer gone crazy.

Joe Bender and TJ hunted for eight, nine seasons until poor health forced Joe to sit by the sidelines. Hunting seemed to fade from TJ's priority list since his hunting buddy had to hang up his call. Joe's eventual passing finally lay to rest all hope of rekindling those magical moments.

TJ missed hunting; he missed his father even more. Some memories are elusive. Memories of Joe, the canoe, a flock coming in over the 'deeks', of hunting with his best friend, were seared into the very essence of his being.

Some memories never fade.

To a man, the Scavengers jumped at the opportunity to help build the blinds and become the 'hunters'. Yeah, I know, LORD OF THE FLIES!

Anyways, we picked up some material for the blinds, 2x4's, chicken wire and stuff. We loaded everything into the back of a couple of cars and drove up Pleasant Hill to the Country Club. We decided to stick together with two acting as guards while the others worked.

Within two hours, we had set up two blinds, about six hundred feet apart. One was near the fourth fairway, the other across the pond near the thirteenth green. Both of these holes had some rather extensive ponds. We threw out about twenty or so decoys that I had at each hole, planning to wait a week before we started hunting to let the geese and ducks get used to seeing the decoys. We also decided to only hunt once every seven or eight days so not as to push the geese to find other places to go.

Keep your fingers crossed!

October 3 - Day Twelve

At times I amaze myself at how callous I've become. A couple days ago, a bunch of kids get killed because of my inability to do the right thing at the right time. We have funerals, bury our dead and another day dawns. More deaths, more funerals. And one short day later, I'm building duck blinds, reliving days gone by, actually feeling good.

When we arrived back at the subdivision yesterday, the Scavengers were acting like a bunch of kids, laughing and having a ball. One look into the eyes of Kathleen Granger changed all that. As we looked at her, bravely but unsuccessfully trying to hold back her tears, we felt her anguish at just having lost two of her three children to the Claymore accident. That anguish was burned into her eyes. We felt like fools.

She had met us to tell us that another accident had occurred. The rest of the younger children, who were the responsibility of Child Protection, had all gathered around for a game of hide and seek. Karen Stanley had slipped past the adults and had fallen into one of the window wells in back of the Granger house. Karen had a compound fracture of the left tibia. She was on the mend at Central DuPage Hospital. Kathleen was upset because she felt that had she been more in control of her emotions, she would have somehow been able to prevent the accident from happening. I immediately identified with her feelings, having faced a similar challenge a couple of days earlier.

You can't convince someone not to feel bad when they do. We finally managed after a time, to get Kathleen to calm down and acknowledge that sometimes, no matter how hard we try, things do go wrong. If fact, one will find that.....

Wheaton, IL (sandpiper Court subdivision)
1755 hours
October 3

The shrill screech of the siren startled TJ, causing him to pause and look up. The wailing increased and was quickly joined by a second, third, and then even more sirens. Something was definitely happening, and in a big way!

TJ was sitting at his desk in the study, often referred to jokingly by the family as the library, which he used as a place to find some peace and quiet when working on the journal. Dropping his pen, jumping up from the desk and running to the front door of his house, he looked out and saw lots of people running towards Falcon Street, the main road into the subdivision.

"What happened?" TJ yelled across the cul-de-sac to Ed Flanders, who had just come out of his own house.

"Not sure yet. Didn't you hear the explosion?"

"Oh, God. Not again. What the fuck could have happened now?" TJ yelled. Yet he sensed that the trouble was outside of the immediate area based on where people were running. They weren't moving to the areas where they kept the ammunition cached. Must be something else.

TJ caught up with Flanders and together they cut through some backyards and arrived at the defensive barrier where Falcon intersects with Geneva.

There, in the middle of Geneva, about one hundred yards east of the intersection was a huge, billowing plume of smoke and fire. Flashing lights all around the, what? You couldn't see for all of the commotion.

He could see police cars, a couple of fire trucks, three ambulances and several National Guard Hummers with flashing blue lights.

As he and Flanders got closer, pushing their way through the other subdivision residents, the carnage became more definable. A big bus, looked like one of those Frontier America excursion charters, was laying on its side, the front of it smashed in like some kid beat a toy with a hammer. Thirty feet away from in, sitting half in, half out of the street was the charred wreckage of an early '80s Lincoln Towncar.

TJ and Flanders continued through the crowd and approached the National Guard troopers who had cordoned off the area.

"Hey, what's up?" TJ asked.

"Sorry, sir. You'll have to stand back with the others and let the police handle this," the solider said firmly, but politely, moving a step closer to TJ, as his hand moved towards his .45-caliber sidearm.

"Whoa there, son. Just asking," TJ said to the young soldier. " I'm kind'a in charge of this subdivision and if there's anything I..."

"Listen, sir. Get back with the others," he barked in a much more direct and menacing manner. Drawing his gun from its holster lent credence to his sincerity.

Flanders started to move towards the soldier, clenching his teeth, determined to show this young pup a thing or two. TJ, sensing that any move could really set this kid off reached out and grabbed Ed by the shoulder saying, "Easy, Ed. There's the Colonel (it is military custom to refer to lieutenant colonels by the singular title colonel)."

"Hey, Colonel," TJ yelled. "Could we see you for a few moments?" And in spite of a ranking officer being called to mediate the confrontation, the young soldier still stood there, feet apart, both hands on the .45 in a classic shooting position, feet spread, arms out, aiming right at Flanders' barrel of a chest.

Lieutenant Colonel Ralph Emerson, standing near a group of other soldiers and a few policemen, turned when he heard his name called, not recognizing the voice at first. TJ noticed immediately the look of anguish on Emerson's face. For some reason the carnage was affecting him on a personal level.

Emerson turned back to say a few unheard words to those around him, then slowly walked over to TJ and Flanders.

As he approached the two of them, who were still being held at gunpoint by the young National Guardsman, Emerson said in a soft voice, "Private Pilsner, Colonel Emerson coming up behind you, son."

Pierce noticed that Emerson wasn't taking any chances in provoking an accident. Something serious was definitely going on. As to the what, Pierce and Flanders could only continue to speculate at this point.

"What seems to be the problem, son?"

"Well, Sir. These guys seem awful interested in what's going on here. Everyone else, why they're just standing off there in the distance looking and stuff. Not these guys. These guys come charging down here demanding to be let through. Looks suspicious, Sir. I got'a protect you, Sir. These guys could be in on it and I'm just trying to do my job and my brother and...," the rapid soliloquy died abruptly as the young soldier lowed his gun and looked over his shoulder at Emerson, a look of confused bewilderment on his tear streaked face.

Emerson reached out and gently patted the boy on the arm, "That's okay, soldier. You done well. I know these gentlemen. They're friends. Why don't you holster your weapon and see if you can help the sergeant? He's got his hands full."

Though the boy soldier gazed into Emerson's eyes he was clearly seeing something else; something Emerson could only guess at.

"Yeah, sure. Yeah, I mean, yes Sir," he stammered as he replaced the deadly .45 into the holster. Turning to TJ and Flanders, he offered in a whisper, "Sorry guys. You just can't be too careful. What am I going to tell mom? What can I possibly say to that poor woman? She expected me to watch out for him and now he's gone."

While this was happening, Emerson motioned to the sergeant to come over and escort Private Pilsner away.

When TJ, Flanders and Emerson were alone, Flanders spoke up first.

"Thanks a bunch, Colonel. That was getting out of control real quick like."

"Yeah, Colonel. What happened, and why did that guy jump all over us? TJ inquired. "We were just coming over here to offer our help."

"You know that most of the Guard is up from the Peoria area. I arranged for a weekly shuttle to run some of my people up and back to visit family, take a little R & R (rest and relaxation). The bus you see was just returning thirty of my troops back here. The car there," he said pointing to the wreckage, "was apparently being driven by a NCNWC suicide squad. The car was headed in the opposite direction and veered head-on into the bus. We're not sure what kind of explosives were in the car but between that and the gas, nothing left of the car and I lost twenty-one of my thirty troopers who were on the bus. Most of 'em killed in the fire afterwards. The only people to escape were the ones in the last couple of rows, by the emergency exit. They got out just before the bus was engulfed in flames.

"Private Pilsner there, well, his younger brother was on the bus, just returning from a visit to their mom. The private here was on one of the Hummers we sent out to escort the bus in for the last ten miles of the trip. He saw the whole thing happen. He got close enough to the back of the bus just in time to see his brother struggling to get out, but not making it when the gas tank went up." Emerson stopped talking, the pain of the experience registering on his face. He simply hung his head down and wept over the loss of so many good soldiers, soldiers who died on the battlefield without being given the opportunity to defend themselves.

Sensing that they really couldn't offer any assistance, and after expressing their condolences, TJ and Flanders turned and walked back to the subdivision.

Wheaton, IL (Sandpiper Court subdivision)
1905 hours
October 3

Sitting back down to complete the days' entry into the journal, Anthony Joseph Bender, reached over, picked up his pen from the floor and started once again to write.

Well, that sure as hell was something. Not only are the NCNWC trying to kill us, I almost get my head blown off by some pimple faced, weekend warrior who can't tell the good guys from the bad. To bad about his brother and the rest of the people on the bus but if Emerson hadn't come over in time, I think I would have caught a .45 slug in the head!

So you know what I'm talking about, a bus returning from central Illinois was rammed by a suicide squad. They had a bomb or something in the car and almost everyone aboard both vehicles was killed. The bus had a bunch of National Guard types who were returning home from visiting their relatives and friends. We tried to offer some help but this crazy National Guard private damn near shot me and Ed Flanders. Emerson said the guy just saw his brother get blown up in the bus, but what the fuck, he damn near killed us as well.

After the bus incident, I called a meeting of the Committee to discuss the whole situation and its impact on us. I realized that this subdivision has two exposed sides; where we border Pleasant Hill and Geneva. The houses we're living in backup to these roads. If suicide squads wanted to, they could drive cars or truck right through the backyards and into our houses. Also, our line of sight was limited by the number of houses, developed trees, landscape berms, etc. We were really in an indefensible position. After some discussion, everyone agreed with my assessment.

Flanders suggested moving to the Country Club, a golf course community just north of our subdivision that went bust. He argued that the clubhouse was located on a hill that was elevated about thirty feet higher than the surrounding land. The clubhouse and a couple of support buildings were also separated from other structures and heavy trees by the fairways and ponds. This natural 'fort' could be much more easily defended and our fields of vision and fire expanded to provide for extra measures of security. There were also some of the original builders' model homes very close that could be used for lodging.

We agreed to meet again tomorrow to work out the mechanics and then inform the other residents of our proposal.

October 4 - Day Thirteen

Seems like there is some truth to the saying that great minds think alike.

Lieutenant Colonel Ralph Emerson stopped by earlier this morning to tell us that the National Guard, with the full support of the mayor of Wheaton, was encouraging all of the people living in outlying areas to move into temporary shelters in the downtown area. The Guard felt that they were unable to continue to offer the same level of protection given that they had just lost almost 30% of their force. They had to abandon their original plan to patrol the boundaries of Wheaton and together with the Police, had arrived at a new defensive strategy.

Basically, they would establish the outer boundaries of Wheaton as a kind of 'no man's land'. Not to be patrolled, other than an occasional drive through by one of the Hummers. Residents living beyond this new line, about six hundred people in what used to be the outskirts of Wheaton and another couple hundred living in small, isolated subdivisions like ours, were encouraged to move into Wheaton central.

The targeted move date was October 16th. This date would allow the town to prepare adequate shelter, as well as give people enough time to pack and prepare for moving. The move was to be orchestrated by the Guard.

Personally, I didn't like the idea of moving into Wheaton proper. But, I didn't want to make the call by myself. This is clearly a decision for the Committee.

October 5 - Day Fourteen

I decided to use this entry to record a brief glimpse into an average day here in the subdivision. In fact, this is something that I probably should have done sooner so future readers would have a better mental picture of what really happened during this period in our history. Before getting into those mechanics though, I will describe some basic facts regarding the subdivision.

Sandpiper Court Subdivision, in the northwest corner of Wheaton, is a kind of transition point on the map. Just to our north is Carol Stream and to the west is Winfield, two communities who have had their sights on incorporating our subdivision into their tax base.

We really are unincorporated Wheaton. Thus, the DuPage County Sheriff's Department provides police protection, while the Winfield Fire Department handles the fire duties. We go to Wheaton or Winfield schools. About '92 or '93, the United States Post Office tried to use our Zip Code as a basis for saying we were Carol Stream. The assholes that made this stupid decision didn't have any idea that not only didn't anyone in the subdivision want to live in Carol Stream, such a move seriously impacted our housing values. It took several petitions, a bunch of meetings and a class action suit before we finally were returned to the preferred status of unincorporated Wheaton.

The land the subdivision occupies was originally the Schultz farm; two hundred sixty acres. The land was sold to three builders in '87 and the subdivision started in early '88. The original plan called for one hundred twenty single family homes. As of this writing, one hundred nineteen had been built. For some unexplained reason, the only open lot, which eventually became our little cemetery, just wouldn't sell. Nice homes on both sides and it's location right on MacArthur Lane would make you think it would sell in a minute; but it didn't.

Now, one hundred nineteen homes times an average of 3.4 people per family would lead you to believe that around four hundred people live in our subdivision. And if this is true, why are there only about seventy-nine residents in our group? Great question, super sleuth!

First of all, six spouses were on business trips. About eight homes were up for sale and are standing vacant after people already moved out. A few more families were out of town on vacations or whatever when the shit hit the fan. The rest of the people elected to either flee to Wheaton central, or attempt to travel to the home of relatives living in the area. The sum of all this was our small, merry band of seventy-nine souls, and because of the Claymore accident with the children, we now only numbered seventy-two.

There is a street in the subdivision called Sandpiper Court.. In fact, I live on it. No one really could say why the street had the same name as the subdivision, or what the significance of Sandpiper Court was in the first place. There were a few streets in the subdivision named after birds, but others, like MacArthur Lane, well, anybody's guess is as good as mine.

Anyways, me, Joyce and the kids moved into the subdivision in mid-'89, after having spent five years in Troy, MI, just outside of Detroit. We were all originally Land of Lincoln born natives. The only exception was little Jennifer, who was a Michigander by birth.

When you think about it, our brief life in Michigan should have tipped us off, or at least given us some insight into the developing problems between Whites and our non-White counterparts. For example, in the five years I lived in Troy, I made only two trips to downtown Detroit. The damn place was just about a war zone. Most every major business had fled the downtown business area over the last ten years and crack houses, burned out warehouses and plain old empty lots covered the area. This was segregation at its height. Detroit became the bastion of Blacks and the suburbs became the fortress of the Whites.

I can still remember the Fourth of July holiday during our first year. What a bunch of bullshit. On July 2nd, the day before Devils' Night, which is what the locals called, the Mayor of Detroit goes on local radio and TV programs, pleading for sanity and cooperation in containing the problems of previous years. Now I got to wonder what the hell is this guy talking about. Not being a native Detroit type, I was real confused.

On the night of July 3rd, I was looking south towards Detroit from the safety of my back yard and I see this red, ghostly glow illuminating the whole southern horizon. The next day, July 4th, this Mayor goes back on the radio and TV, thanking the community for the vast improvement over the previous years and complimenting the people for demonstrating that together, they can make a difference. It seems that this year, there were only four hundred twenty-seven cases of arson as compared to five hundred thirteen the year before and the record seven hundred three the year before that. It apparently was the tradition on Devil's Night to torch anything. Garbage cans, empty warehouses, old, hopefully abandoned houses, etc. The Fire Department, responding to calls, would often get shot at by snipers. I mean who the fuck is kidding who!

And the scary part is that this is true. Ask anybody who ever lived in or around Detroit. Ask 'em if you don't believe me.

Needless to say, we were thrilled when my company finally relented to my requests to transfer me back to the Chicagoland area. My original transfer to Michigan was to have been for three or four years. It lasted five. I left that company within months of my return to Illinois. They were a bunch of assholes anyways.

So we picked Wheaton, picked a subdivision, picked a model and built our dream house. The house was more than we needed or more than I could really afford on my salary, but my last job at the other company was as a commissioned salesperson and I made a bundle in a couple of years. Me and Joyce decided to plow it all into a house, which is exactly what we did. Fortunately, the mortgage is manageable enough that my current salary handles the monthly payments.

North of the subdivision is the Country Club golf development that I mentioned a couple of times. Nothing big here except that our northern boundary is a tree line and stream, which separates us from the course. On the east is another subdivision, James Place. Here, backyards backup to backyards. The real strange thing is that all residents of James Place decided to relocate to Wheaton central when CW II started, so, we basically live next to a ghost town. To the south, across Geneva Road, is the last piece of intact farm property in Wheaton. I guess it to be about four hundred acres. Actually, prime real estate. Some Baptists, or born again Christians or some group was going to build a retirement community, but for some reason, it never took off. So all that was there was open land and an old barn with a couple of other, smaller out buildings. West, across Pleasant Hill, is an elementary school, a couple of older homes and just a bunch of trees. All in all, we were pretty much isolated.

This location helped us in our defensive posture. By blocking a couple of access roads, MacArthur Lane and Falcon Street, we were able to cut ourselves off from easy access by NCNWC forces or other unwelcome visitors.

Now as to a typical day.

Food was stored in two central locations for protection and inventory purposes. We decided up front on a communal distribution of the wealth so to speak. A communal breakfast was held each morning at about 8:00 a.m. Lunch was typically served between Noon and 1:00 p.m., with dinner following at 6:30 p.m.

The Defense group made up a roster for guard duty with everyone fourteen and over participating with the only exception being Doc Furgenson, due to his always being 'on call', and Frank and Julia Farmer due to their age. Guard shifts were four hours on, twenty hours off, rotating throughout the day with midnight being the starting point.

My day would go something like this:

6:30 a.m.   rise
6:45-8:00   tour all defensive positions, general walk around the subdivision
8:00-9:00   breakfast

9:00-Noon   committee meetings (Food   & Medical and Defense)
Noon-1:00 p.m. lunch
1:00-4:00   committee meetings (Child Protection and Scavengers)
4:00-6:30   open time (usually trips to Wheaton center, training, catching up on journal entries, etc.)
6:30 -7:00   dinner
7:00-8:00   committee leaders meeting
8:00-Midnight guard rotation
Midnight   in bed

<u>Food & Medical day:</u>

Doc Furgeson and Susan Hollis pulled together a pretty comprehensive plan regarding their areas of responsibility. They came up with the idea of two central storage areas for Food & Medical supplies, thus allowing them to control dispersal as well as allow them to determine inventory levels on an on-going basis. Rationing was instituted right away and everyone was placed on a regiment of vitamins and fresh produce whenever available to help maintain health.

Doc decided to give quick, routine physicals to everyone once a week. These usually lasted about twenty minutes and though the physicals consumed a good part of every day, they went a long way in making sure he had his finger on the pulse of our health. It also helped him do sanity checks on all of us. We were living under some very stressful conditions and he helped a number of the residents, me included, deal with some rather tough issues.

Susan developed the meal schedule and worked closely with the other members of Food & Medical to make sure meals were done on time, that cleanup operations happened so as to avoid any health problems from developing due to unsanitary conditions, that sort of stuff. She continued to rely heavily on everyone's input looking for new and creative ways to either stretch food, or make it taste appealing.

Defense

Bruce Jamison and Larry Findler were charged with our defensive preparedness; no easy task given the exposed nature of our subdivision. They came up with the ideas of barricading the two access roads; MacArthur and Falcon. We blocked these with a couple of cars each and built up some earth works to act as bunkers for the guard detail. We also used cars to block some of the more open areas between houses. At first, a number of people complained that these cars could be damaged if we were attacked, but they eventually realized that worrying about the cars was a pretty silly issue given the situation we were all faced with.

Since a guard rotation was agreed to, most of the time Defense was concerned with maintaining and increasing our ability to protect ourselves. They developed a Security group that was mobile in nature; actually a couple of cars equipped with some extra rifles, ammunition, ropes, that sort of stuff. These were maintained centrally and could be dispersed to any part of the subdivision within a couple of minutes.

Defense also wired the Claymores to likely areas of approach. We had hoped of course that we wouldn't be attacked but with all that is going on in the western suburban area of Chicago, well, you never know.

Defense also set up and maintained two ammunition caches. One centrally located, the other in the north east quadrant, away from the hub of activity.

Child Protection

Frank Smyth and Janice Pedopoulos handled their one and only responsibility great, especially after the Claymore fiasco. Their job was simply to keep the children safe and out of the way. They rotated basements for protection during the daytime. Most of the time was dedicated to play and a little bit of continuing education. Reading, basic mathematics, coloring, just simple stuff.

They moved the kids around from building to building on the theory that this improved the odds against being hit by a artillery round, or some kind of a suicide attack. I'm not a student of probability so I'm not sure if this was valid or not, but it sure does makes us feel a lot better.

Scavengers

Bill Komanski and Ed Flanders have what is probably the riskiest set of responsibilities of all. Their mission in the grand scheme of things is to make sure we don't run out of essentials. Whether it's food, medical supplies, ammunitions, gas, batteries, clothes, whatever.

There were multiple sources for getting what we needed. The first option was to go to Wheaton central and buy food and medical supplies as needed at the few stores that had stayed open. In most cases, though, the stores weren't opened, so our second option was to break in and help ourselves, limiting what we took to what was really needed and not really trying to any cause extra damage. Quite frankly, most everyone has been stealing stuff this way from day three or four and most stores are pretty much bare to the walls regarding essentials. The third option was to accept supplies as furnished by the National Guard, however, the selection was extremely limited as were the quantities they would allow us to take The last option was to visit surrounding subdivisions that people had abandoned and again, take what we need without trying to do any real damage to property.

The Scavengers made it a rule to take extras if possible for bartering purposes, which came into vogue pretty quickly as the economy broke down.

We kept two jeeps, one van and a pickup truck permanently assigned to the Scavengers. Gas was collected and used to keep these vehicles running. None of the trips we took were more than ten or twelve miles in any one direction. We tried to minimize our exposure to risks from either NCNWC forces or marauding bands of thieves.

All in all, the Scavengers do a great job and take pride in providing for our needs. So far, we have everything we really need.

Except for the unexpected events, each day has pretty much settled into the above pattern. It took us about a week to arrive at an acceptable pace of activity. The first couple of days saw us rushing out trying to accomplish the impossible. The next several days saw us undoing a lot of things and doing them a second time, the right way. The committee leaders run their own committees the way they see fit. I try not to impose my feelings one way or the other unless conflict exists between two of the groups. The committee members are very understanding of everyone's needs and really do work together quite well.

That's a decent enough description of a typical day.

VIII

Philadelphia, PA
1830 hours
October 5

Simultaneously as TJ was putting down his pen and reviewing what he had just committed to the journal, another author, a tall, distinguished looking, fifty-two year old black man was mimicking those very actions. He, too, had just finished a major effort. He put his pen down near the old-fashioned oil lamp and reached up to remove his glasses. Rubbing the bridge of his nose, he pushed back his chair and picked up the final draft of his literary offering, **A Treatise: The Cessation of Hostilities and the Development of the New Order.**

Sitting back in the chair in a smallish bedroom of a tenement building on the outskirts of Philadelphia, PA, the black man started to read aloud.

"'When in the course of human events it becomes self-evident............' This proclamation, so eloquently captured over two hundred, twenty years ago by the founding fathers of what eventually became the United States of America is very apropos in view of the strife and conflict currently being experienced in what has come to be know as CW II, the second Civil War to be waged in these United States. The message contained in that proclamation, that imperfections in the then current social and political order required extreme and revolutionary actions designed to right the wrongs imposed by a misdirected and mislead political body, speaks to us again, today.

95

"The National Conference for Non-White Citizens was formed for the sole purpose of establishing a constituency of peoples harmed by the existing political structure and uniting these peoples in the face of said political turmoil to eradicate...

He paused and mulled the word 'eradicate' over several times before reaching for the pen, crossing it out and adding 'modify' in it's place.

"to modify the existing political structure to accommodate the divergent needs of a polarized society.

"Embarking on a bold and perilous journey, the NCNWC leadership marshaled forces sufficient to impress upon the current political structure the necessity to provide the NCNWC constituency with the political reform required to achieve a unification of the races based on unqualified equality.

"NCNWC leadership, determined to expunge past measures of intolerance and 'second class citizenry' that the current political structure had historically imposed upon the NCNWC constituency, hereby and forever more, declares and establishes now and forevermore, the formation of the NCNWC as a separate and equal co-inhabitant of the geography previously known as the United States of America."

The black man stopped reading and gazed off into space, reflecting on the great pains that had been taken and all of the energies expended in bringing the NCNWC to this point in time. Fifteen years ago, it didn't even exist. Today, the ol' US of A was on it's knees fighting for its very existence. A very heady thought indeed.

It hadn't been easy. In fact, it's amazing that it succeeded.

Starting as a small group of radical thinkers, the core of the yet un-named NCNWC leadership council numbered eight individuals. Eight people who used to sit around and dream of a new order. People who slowly became committed to the idea of making this new order a reality.

Starting small, the group developed a grass roots appeal in the intellectual community courting black politicians and academicians alike. Influential people willing to gamble all for the big payoff.

Approaching Black and Hispanic Army, Marine And Air Force leaders was a bold move. A calculated risk that these people, sworn to protect the interests of the United States, wouldn't turn into Uncle Tom's, kissing the white ass to protect their own fiefdoms.

Once the Armed Forces became committed to the idea of a new order, things really started to happen fast.

The Rodney King event was a godsend. The original jury's innocent findings allowed NCNWC agents to incite the riots in Los Angeles. Actually, in retrospect, racial tensions in the city of the angels were high enough that only a couple of sparks were really necessary to start that conflagration.

The World Trade Center bombing was a plan gone awry, especially since the plan was to level the whole fucking building. Fortunately, the cover story of the bombers held up to scrutiny and we did learn a great deal more about how and where to plant explosives for future events.

Even the Long Island train shoot-em-up was more effective that could be imagined.

Without a doubt, the riskiest operation during the formative stages was the so called 'Mexican peasant revolt' of late '93, early '94. In an effort to train one of Mexico's elite army commando units, federal prisoners were dressed up as peasants, armed and brought into obscure countryside locations. Once there, they were released and told to 'defend themselves', while the commando unit practiced their small unit assault tactics. This time, though, the practice included real bullets and the victims were really killed, not just identified through the laser light sensing rigs normally used in practice drills.

At the turn of the century, the plans of the NCNWC almost began to unravel as the US intelligence Agencies began to pick up humint (human intelligence reports) of growing, racial polarization. But then, almost as if a gift from the Almighty, September 11, 2001 happened and the intelligence community turned their main focus outward. Their only inward focus was on non-Americans thus the American borne NCNWC conspiracy once again disappeared into the background.

As he gazed into space he realized how lucky the movement had been. He realized that he had been pretty lucky himself. Here he was, fifty-two years old and almost at the pinnacle; *Right at the fucking top of the heap. The number two honcho of the NCNWC. Not bad for a dude from the St. Louis ghetto. Not bad for a guy without college, or a real job until he busted into politics in the late 60's. Not bad at all!*

Reese Robertson looked at the clock and seeing that it was past midnight, decided that the draft could wait until tomorrow to finish. Right now he needed to sleep.

IX

Wheaton, IL (Sandpiper Court subdivision)
0448 hours
October 6

The first explosion was rather muffled, if there is such a thing as a muffled explosion.

The next three or four explosions grew louder in rapid succession.

The fifth shook the whole house, scattering furniture and bric-a-brac everywhere, dust and debris drifting down from the ceiling where cracks exposed the rafters, which made up the floor of the rooms on the second floor.

TJ dropped the pen and looked up, startled.

Not knowing whether or not the artillery barrage had stopped, TJ threw himself on the floor and crawled under the table where moments before, he had been sitting, recording the events of the day into his journal.

A few minutes passed; no more explosions. No sound what-so-ever, just an strange, spooky silence.

TJ looked out through the hole in the wall where the window had been before it was shattered by the concussion and saw people running all around the cul-de-sac in a panic. Parents calling for kids; kids calling for parents. Some bleeding from wounds. Missing arms, exposed bones, blood everywhere.

Like a sledgehammer, the thought of his own family hit TJ hard. My God! They were all upstairs sleeping.

As he jumped up, he noticed a pungent odor in the air and heard a strange crackling sound flowing in from the foyer area. Running out of the room they joking referred to as their library because it contained a four shelf legal bookcase, the one with wood framed, glass doors that open up by sliding to the top, which housed their collection of paperback novels, TJ's worst fears came true. Looking up the staircase, he saw walls of deep, dark black smoke pouring out of the second floor rooms, blood red flames licking the top of the three story tall foyer ceiling.

He ran around to the base of the stairs, took a deep breath and started to ascend into this hell.

By the time he reached the fourth step, he could feel the heat. By the sixth step, it was getting damn hot. By the ninth step, the hair on his eyebrows and the back of his arms was getting singed. He was forced back to reconsider a course of action.

As he stepped back down the stairs, TJ heard the moans of, who? His wife? Daughter? Couldn't tell. Too soft; the flames making too much noise.

Then he heard a clear cut, high pitched scream. A frighten, pained scream as his youngest son cried out in agony, the flames apparently reaching out and embracing his young body.

Redoubling his efforts, TJ charged back up the stairs, staying low, trying to hide from the flames.

He finally managed, how, he'd never know, to reach the landing on the second floor, laying prone, hiding from the flames and that deep, dark black smoke that billowed upward.

He started to crawl towards his youngest sons' room when the smoke, descending upon him like a blanket, caused him to become disoriented. He was entangled by the smoke. It grabbed on to every part of his body and refused to let go. TJ couldn't tell where on the landing he was, couldn't even feel if he was face up or face down. He was lost in a curtain of blackness, still hearing the agonizing screams of fear and pain as the fire sought for and eventually found all four member of his family.

First, his youngest son, Rich. Then Jenny, his daughter. Joyce, his wife screamed the loudest, out of pain from the fire and the pain of knowing she was losing her family in the inferno.

And finally Joe, the oldest.

He lost his family, lost them to the flames, lost them to the deep, dark black smoke.

TJ closed his eyes in an attempt to wash away the agony; the memory.

He felt a wetness. A dampness. A strange feeling of what? Body fluids expanding, becoming gaseous because of the heat generated by the intense flames? Sweat pouring out of every pore, every opening? No pain now, no feeling now, no sounds except the sound of his own rapid breathing.

TJ opened his eyes, surprised he still had lids to open and expected to see heaven, for he had just visited hell.

He saw the writing desk in the library. He looked down and saw the journal, and the pen where it had fallen out his hands when he dropped it. He looked over and saw the window, the glass unbroken.

He looked up and saw that everything was in its place, nothing askew, nothing broken or laying on the floor. Even the ceiling didn't have any cracks.

TJ jumped up and ran into the foyer. He took the steps two at a time and hit the landing on the second floor hard, moving quickly to the kid's bedrooms.

Rich and Joe were asleep.

TJ rushed over to Jenny's room. She looked like a Christmas angel, laying curled up in a fetal position, her favorite doll gripped tightly in her left hand.

Anthony Joseph Bender walked slowly to his bedroom and saw Joyce just starting to awaken. He came over and sat on the side of the bed.

"TJ. You startled me. You just coming to bed? You look like shit."

TJ looked over at Joyce, tears streaming down his face.

"Hold me honey. Just please hold me."

"What's the matter, TJ?" Joyce asked, looking up, reaching out to wipe away the perspiration that had accumulated on TJ's forehead.

"The dream. It's that fuckin' dream again. It just won't leave me alone."

X

Glen Ellyn, IL (NCNWC bivouac area)
2054 hours
November 7

Pierce closed the journal and looked over at Jones.

"I've heard an old saying that tells you not to judge a man until you've walked a mile in his shoes. Now I never wanted to be no white man, Ty, but I don't think I'd want to be this here white man."

"Sarge, you took the words right out'a my mouth. This here war ain't no fun for any of us, but this TJ guy, man, he's not even a soldier. Be he's got to worry about all of the same shit. Even more. At least we got the LT to take care of the important stuff," Jones said, quickly thinking he may have said the wrong thing to Pierce, making it sound like you have be a lieutenant before you have to make important decisions.

Pierce didn't seem to notice this faux pas, or at least decided to let it slide, apparently knowing what Jones really meant.

Jones was relieved that he didn't get the Sarg upset. The Sarg could be a mean motherfucker when his dander was up. He remembered the time, just before the battalion landed at O'Hare on the surprise raid, when a couple of the older members of the squad, Brown and Williams, were fucking off and not paying the LT proper respect. Pierce called them outside of the mess tent right after dinner that night and proceeded to teach them niggers some manners. By the time he was finished with the lesson, both Brown and Williams had a new appreciation for the LT, and a deeply found, fear-induced respect for Master Sergeant Franklin B. Pierce.

Yeah, that's one brother you just don't want to piss off.

Glen Ellyn, IL (NCNWC bivouac area)
0430 hours
November 8

"Zebra Fox-trot," whispered the shadow down by the big oak tree, which was framed in a muted light by the starry night. "Zebra Fox-trot."

"Echo Romeo, Zebra Fox-trot," replied Jones who had drawn the crappiest shift for guard duty, 0230 hours through 0630 hours.

"Coming up, Ty," Pierce said, as he moved in a crab like crawl, inching up next to Jones.

Guard duty was never fun. You were expected to keep your eyes and ears open, your attention focused and your mind from wandering. Maybe you could do it during the day when there were things to look at, but at night, suck duty.

Shadows seemed to take on a life of their own, especially on a star lit night like tonight, with the wind pushing along a scattered cloud cover. Shadows actually moved, or at least they seemed to. You couldn't risk firing and giving away your position, especially if it turned out to only be a shadow. Now on the other hand, you'd look pretty stupid if one of these shadows crawled up to your position and stuck a bayonet up under your rib cage and plunged it deep into your heart. So the basic instinct to survive caused you to grit your teeth, put your finger on the trigger and get the sights on the, there it is again.

I swear the fucker's moving. No wait. Just the clouds. Man, I hate this shit.

"How's it going, TY?"

"Just great. Just fuckin' great."

"My, my, Lance Corporal Tyrone Jones. Do I detect a note of dissatisfaction with your assignment? Do you have a duty that's not to your complete liking? Well, well. I will have to ask the LT to plan on talking to you first from now on before we draw up the guard duty roster. No sense in you having to do something you don't like. You know of course, that we're here just to please you, don't you?" Pierce said softly, but firmly enough for Jones to realize he stepped outside the bounds a little.

"Come on, Sarge. You know what I mean. I don't mind no guard duty. You know that. It's just, well, it's scary being outside here, all by myself."

"Jesus Christ, Ty. How long we've known each other. Don't you know when I'm pulling your chain?"

Even though Jones couldn't ever figure out whether or not Pierce was joking, he said "Sure, Sarge. I knew you was kidding me. I was just, you know, playing along."

"See anything tonight?"

"Nothing. Bunch of noise kind'a northwest of here. But haven't seen anything yet."

"Keep your eyes open. I've got'a check on the other positions. Be coming back through here about thirty minutes from now; on your left. You shoot me, boy, and I'll be one pissed off Master Sergeant."

Jones' face was close enough to Pierce's that he could see the sergeant's smile.

"You just kidding. Right, Sarge?"

"Yeah. Just stay awake, and make sure you don't shoot me," Pierce whispered back hoarsely as he crawled away, moving over to the next position set up on the perimeter, about thirty yards left of Jones' position.

Pierce quickly moved out of sight in the darkness and Jones returned his gaze out in front of the position once again.

There, goddamit. The fuckin' thing moved again. That ain't no shadow. Or is it? Man, I hate guard duty, especially at night!

Glen Ellyn, IL (NCNWC bivouac area)
0710 hours
November 8

Jones dragged himself through the overnight campsite, walked up to the coffee pot and poured himself a cup of steaming hot java. He looked terrible, though four hours of guard duty, especially the late night/early morning shift, will do that to even the best of them.

Pierce, seeing this from across the campsite, got up and walked over to Jones.

"Say, Ty. Grab some shuteye. Nothing planned until this afternoons' reconnaissance stroll through the bush."

Jones looked up at Pierce. Smiling, he offered "Sarge, I'm to damn keyed up to go to sleep now. I think I'll just sit under a tree and grab me some time to unwind. How about we look at the book and see what ol' Mr. TJ is up to?"

Pierce nodded in the affirmative and they both walked over to Pierce's tent to get the journal. After selecting a big shade tree and getting comfortable, Pierce opened up the journal to where they had left off.

October 6 - Day Fifteen

A sad and unusual discovery was made during the day today. No one remembered seeing any members of the Dalton family during the day and we organized a search party at about 4:00 p.m. in the afternoon after the youngest Dalton son, John, didn't show up for guard duty. The grisly discovery was made about fifteen minutes later when several members of the Defense group found the entire family dead, still in their beds.

Roger, the father, Mary, wife and mother, Jeff and John were all stabbed in the neck. No sign of a struggle. They were all just lying in their beds, almost looking like they were just sleeping. Their blood had pooled, thickened and turned dark in huge amounts. They looked peaceful, in spite of the cruelty of their deaths.

When we started to talk about it, Larry Findler, who actually found the Dalton's, told us that the front door had been locked, but that the back door had been jimmied open. When I went to see for myself, you could see the scratches on the door frame where someone had inserted a screw driven, or knife or something to pry open the lock. We could only guess at the time and circumstances of the deaths. We looked around outside the house and found some footprints. They weren't very sharp because the ground was wet and we lost track of them approximately fifty yards away from the house. The tracks were headed toward the eastern perimeter.

Doc estimated that they died sometime during the middle of the night given the dried blood, probably around midnight. At that time of night, we have guards posted on the perimeter, but none of them reported seeing anything. I decided to call a meeting to review the guard posting schedule and establish some new rules for the perimeter defense.

The Dalton's were laid to rest in the subdivision's cemetery on MacArthur. As usual, everyone showed up and it was quite moving. We all recognized that the cemetery's population was growing quickly, much too quickly. First, the seven kids from the Claymore accident; now, the four members of the Dalton family. Eleven dead and buried already out of seventy-nine.

Anyways, I called the heads of the committees together for some serious planning regarding defense.

Typically, we posted two guards on each major compass direction, and have two floaters. The guards were therefore, on the north side, east side, west and south. The floaters usually just walked from guard station to guard station. The guard posts were about nine hundred feet away from each other, cutting each side of the perimeter into thirds. We had a couple of walkie-talkies that we used so the guards could communicate with each other, one on each side and one unit with the floaters. Guard shifts were six hours each starting at midnight. Everyone over the age of fourteen pulled guard duty. Kids and women pretty much handled most of the day shifts. The floaters and the night shifts were always handled by the men. Chivalry at its best!

We figured a NCNWC commando, or some thief, had crawled through the outer perimeter during the night and worked his way through the subdivision, picking the Dalton house at random. We didn't have enough people in the whole group to provide a completely tight perimeter, so we talked about increasing the number of floaters to eight, but discovered that that was impractical. Eight on the sides plus eight floaters equaled sixteen people. Take out the kids, and we didn't have enough people to handle four separate shifts of guard duty. We would have needed sixty-four; we only had fifty-two souls over fourteen years old now that the Daltons were dead.

We finally decided to keep the perimeter guards at two per side, and increase the floaters to four during the night. The members of the Defense group would pull double duty, along with a couple of the guys from the Scavengers if necessary to make this happen.

The initial thought was that this plan was manageable. The floaters would have one person walk the perimeters from post to post, while the other three would patrol inside of the subdivision.

The subdivision is one hundred sixty acres and contains one hundred nineteen homes. Large lots, a couple of rainwater containment areas and several parks. This leaves us with a rather large perimeter. People continue to live in their own houses and with the planned move to the Country Club on the 16th, we figure we can tough it out for another couple of weeks. A couple of the families have decided to move in together for mutual protection and we did recommend that families consider staggering their sleeping hours a little so someone is awake during most night time hours. We'll keep our fingers crossed.

Wheaton, IL (North Avenue and Gary - bivouac area))
0710 hours
November 8

Pierce looked up and stared into space, wondering, trying to image what had happened to the Daltons.

Jones, sensing that Pierce had stopped reading, said "What's up, Sarge?"

"Oh, nothing really. It's just that the way those folks were killed. Well, it sounds like a professional job. Maybe we did have some commandos working this area."

"Yeah, I guess. But why sneak into a civilian area to off a family? Don't make no sense. Why not hit the military targets? Like the National Guard, or the mayor or someone important?" Jones queried.

"My point exactly. There's more to this than meets the eye. Besides, the more I think about it, this must have happened before we hit O'Hare. I'm sure we didn't have no troops this far west back then," Pierce offered as he turned the page to the next entry.

October 7 - Day Sixteen

Fortunately, the events of the pervious day were not repeated. No new dead bodies. Everyone accounted for, several times over!

But I got to tell you, people are sure running scared. Almost everyone was walking around looking like death warmed over. Except for the real young kids, I bet no one got a wink of sleep last night. Shit, I know I didn't. I guess it was around midnight when Jim Stantree caused the biggest commotion of the night. Afterwards it was pretty funny, but when it was going down, we were all pissing in our pants.

It seems Jim was on western guard post duty just about midnight when he heard some rustling in the bushes across Pleasant Hill. There was enough moonlight out to allow him to see about a hundred yards out. Not real clearly, just shades of gray and black. Anyways, this bush about forty yards out across the road and just past the culvert starts shaking. A little at first, but more and more. Ol' Jim figures its the midnight killer come back for another victim and takes aim and fires of ten or twelve rounds into the bush. Sees a bigger commotion, hears a screech and then silence. By this time, people are gabbing their guns, diving to the floor, hiding under the beds, whatever.

A few of the Defense bunch show up, surprise Jim who's fixated on the bush, almost give him a heart attack and almost get themselves shot in the process.

They finally calm Jim down enough and decide to move across the road and see what's up.

In moves that would have made John Wayne and the Marines proud, these guys move forward, setting up flanking maneuvers and all, and finally surround the bush. They all fire about fifty shots into the bush, and then charge.

As it turns out, Jim had killed a big, buck deer, who was simply bedding down for the night.

The score for the night; good guys 1, deer, 0!

October 8 - Day Seventeen

There's an old saying that offers that if it wasn't for bad luck, I'd have no luck at all. Another saying suggests that when it rains, it pours.

We lost George Davis today in a freak traffic accident. Jason Waholik, who was with George at the time of the accident, suffered a broken arm and a number of cuts and bruises.

Jason and George, both members of the Scavengers, had taken one of the Jeeps and driven to downtown Wheaton to talk to the food committee about our weekly allowance. After the meet, the guys were heading back to the subdivision when they got a flat tire. They were changing the tire on the side of the road when another vehicle skidded out of control and crashed into the back of the Jeep. It had been raining a little and the roads were slippery. As luck would have it George had been leaning over the back bumper to pull the spare out of the back of the Jeep and got crushed between the two vehicles. Jason was in the process of pulling off the flat and got hit when the Jeep fell off the jack. We decided to wait until tomorrow morning for George's funeral. We took Jason to Central DuPage Hospital where they placed his arm in a cast and taped up his ribs.

This hit all of us hard, especially after just losing the Dalton family, and the Scavengers (John Dalton, Joe Bender, Danny Davidson, Steve Kornat, Ed Flanders, Bill Komanski and Jason) and I decided to hold an impromptu Irish wake on behalf of lost comrades. Ed and Bill got a couple of cases of beer and we all sat around getting hammered, at least a little. Telling stories and dreaming dreams.

Purely by coincidence, Ed, Bill and I were all in sales. We swapped a bunch of stories about being on the road, going to airports, stuff like that.

Ed told the story about a trip he had taken a few years back. He had scheduled a two day trip that took him from Chicago, IL to Allentown, PA for a meeting, leaving for Washington, DC to spend the night. The next day had him departing DC early for a meeting in Atlanta, GA with a return trip to Chicago later that second evening.

Ed's Washington meeting was apparently canceled during the course of the day so he had the travel agent arrange for a connection through Washington so that he could arrive in Atlanta late that night, thus saving him an early wakeup call the next morning.

Ed finished his meeting in Allentown, made the Washington flight without problem and connected through DC to Atlanta, arriving at about ten o'clock at night.

The travel agent had originally prepared a travel itinerary for him, which listed his flights, hotels arrangements, rental cars, etc.; a very handy tool. When Ed finally arrived in Atlanta, he walked towards the kiosk, which has direct telephone connections to local hotels, but saw that it was packed with people. Every line was being used and more people were waiting. Being a tried and true road warrior, Ed said "Fuck that noise!" and scurried over to a pay phone. He picked up the receiver, entered his calling card number, and looking at the travel itinerary, found the number of the hotel and dialed, requesting that a shuttle van pick him up.

The person on the phone told him to go outside and stand under the sign marked 'Delta Arrival'. Ed did this and twenty minutes later was back on the phone requesting the shuttle. The woman on the other side, the same one he spoke to before, told Ed that the driver drove by, didn't see anyone and returned to the hotel. They were sorry, and Ed would see the van in about twelve minutes.

Thirty minutes later, no van and ol' Ed's really starting to get pissed.

Well, he tells us, he's on a mission now. He could have taken a cab, or gone to a different hotel but Flanders is determined to extract his pound of flesh. He couldn't believe a national chain hotel would put a customer through such nonsense. Someone up the hotel's chain of command was going to get a poison pen letter of complaint when this evening was over.

Again he calls, this time using an outside pay phone right by the 'Delta' sign and speaks to the same woman. Flanders tells her that no van came by, that he's the only jerk standing on the curb at what is now eleven o'clock at night and he's really starting to get mad. Ed gives her a piece of his mind, not that he's got a lot to spare, about the jerks they have driving their shuttle buses and demand to be picked up immediately. She apologies again and tells him the van driver had parked by the curb, saw no one and once again came back to the hotel. She said that she would maintain radio contact with the van while he made the next trip.

So you got to picture this. There's Ed, on the phone, talking to this woman while she's also talking to the shuttle bus driver on the radio. The driver informs them that he's arrived. Ed tells the woman, actually by this time he was calling her a fuckin' bitch, at least when he was telling us the story, that there's no fuckin' van here. The driver swears he's at the curb, supposedly twenty feet away from him. Ed tells this poor gal that there's no damn van parked at the curb. The driver swears he's there and doesn't see anybody. Ed tells her to tell him to flash his lights and he'll find the asshole himself. She says he's flashing his lights while Ed keeps yelling on the phone that there ain't no goddamn van with flashing lights when she asks him what city he's in. Now Ed's in no mood for jokes and says "Atlanta! What the hell city do you think I'm in?"

"Sir, this hotel is in Washington, DC." Then she hangs up.

Now we get into a debate about what's worse; doing something this stupid, or being stupid enough to tell people you did something so stupid!

Bill, not to be outdone, offered his experience at a restaurant. He says he'll never forget the first big dinner of his then fledgling sales career. He was the host of an evening attended by three of the decision makers at a company to which he was attempting to sell some services.

They had a round of drinks and had moved on to appetizers. Well, Komanski, who just happens to be Polish, selected herring in sour cream, which for some reason he claims is a delicacy amongst his people.

During the course of eating their appetizers, Bill was describing all of the services that his company could offer their company. He described the history of his company, the depth of the organization, all that great sell stuff. While this was going on, he was eating bits and pieces of the herring. As he did this, he must have been pushing the plate closer and closer to the edge of the table. He never noticed until he tried to pick up another piece of herring on the fork and proceeded to upend the plate, with most of the sour cream and onions, as well as a fair amount of herring, flying right into his lap, which, by the way, just happened to have been covered by his new pants, part of the new suit he had purchased especially for this important meeting.

Once the laughter subsided, his guests helped him get cleaned up. Unfortunately, the restaurant was one of those old clubs with dark mahogany walls, high backed leather chairs, waiters in tuxedos and very low lighting levels. Cleaning up was a little bit of a challenge as he tried to contain the disaster to the immediate group without alerting the other patrons to his clumsiness.

Dinner came, was finished, desert, check, payment and they decide to go to a bar for a nightcap.

Well, Bill and his guests walked out into a beautiful Chicago night and everyone noticed as soon as they came under the first bright street light that his suit still contained gobs of sour cream, onions rings and a couple of pieces of herring stuck to his pants at mid-thigh level. Not only did his dinner party start laughing again, but about twenty complete strangers on Walton Street were pointing and whooping it up!

Then he starts to tell us what happened when he got home, his suit all mussed up and him stinking like fish. His wife, Mary, asks he what happened. Bill was pretty loaded by the time he gets home and thinks of a line he thinks is funny and says, "Honey, I screwed my way up one side of Michigan Avenue and then turned around, and did the same thing coming back down the other side!"

The way Bill tells the story, for some reason, Mary saw absolutely no humor in this, started thinking that sometimes something said is jest is true, and gets all pissed off at him.

By this time, we all had three or four beers and we're rolling around on the ground laughing our asses off.

When it was my turn, I offered the time I was calling on a prospective client in New York. I offered to buy lunch. He said, "Great, how about sushi?" I had never had the stuff before but was intent on making the sale and said "Perfect".

We walked down the street to a little corner sushi bar, sat down in front of a counter of raw fish and my eyes didn't believe what I saw. People really eat this stuff?

I had no idea what to order so I took my guests' lead and ordered a 'sampler' and a Kerin, a great tasting Japanese beer. After a few minutes, the waiter placed a 8" x 12" small wooden platform in front of me. It was full of what, sushi, I imagined. No forks, no knifes, only chopsticks, which proved to be the second challenge of the day.

I picked up the chopsticks, looking out of the corner of my eye to watch my guest nimbly manipulate the wooden sticks and tried to match his movements. At the upper right hand edge of the wooden platform was a glob of green stuff. My limited dinning experiences resulted in me thinking, good, I recognize that. I like guacamole, and I proceeded to pick up the entire green glob on my chopsticks and shove it into my mouth. A couple seconds later I realized that this was a horseradish of some kind; a incredibly hot horseradish. My mouth exploded in pain and tears ran down my cheeks. I quickly reached over for my beer and took a long pull from the neck, wondering if I would live to see the end of the day.

Seeing this, my guest looked over and said "Gees, you must really like that stuff." All I could do was nod a feeble 'yes'!

Well, the guys start whooping it up again, this time at my expense, when my son, Joe, asks, "So, did you get the sale?"

When I responded "No", they started laughing again, which made me wonder if Joe's loving mother could've somehow put him up to asking a question like that in public.

We start to calm down a bit when Ed leans forward and asks us if we all know about the Weary Road Warriors' Pervert's Club. We all look at him with questions in our eyes and respond "No".

He starts telling us this story while we're all sitting there around him, likes scouts at the campfire.

He tells us that he lost his virginity at an early age to Rosie Palm and her five daughters. As soon as he says this, I glance over at Joe who's getting a look of embarrassment on his face. I'm pretty sure he's whacked his wiener a few hundred times but this is probably the first time he's been in a public discussion about the subject in front of his old man. He looks over at me, our eyes meet and I simply smile and return to watching Ed who's going through some rather deliberate and obscene gestures to add some graphic spice to the tale.

Anyways, Ed tells us that eventually, he goes beyond Rosie and the girls and gets his first real live piece of ass. Now he decides he likes it and lives a very randy lifestyle until he meets his wife, Kathy, and they decide to get married.

Ed pauses here and starts to cry. We figure it's just the beer when we all realize at once that Kathy was one of the subdivision people who weren't here when CW2 started. In fact, we haven't heard a word about her. She had been on a business trip down to Arlington, TX, a suburban area of Dallas. Well, Dallas got nuked and we just don't know.

Ed finally regains his composure and proceeds with the story.

With his wild life behind him since he got married, Ed bit the bullet and decided to remain faithful to Kathy. Yet, like a normal male, still wanted to find, how shall we say it, a physical release from time to time and when he was on the road, his faithfulness caused him to rely on Rosie and the girls.

So he'd bought a Hustler, or Playboy, or watched the 'X' rated movies at the hotels and motels he stayed at to assist him in the self-stimulation exercise. But at $5 bucks a mag, and $12 bucks for movies, he was going broke.

So he tells us that he checks into this hotel for a three day stay one time, starts putting his clothes away in one of the drawers in the dresser and hears some scratching sound when he closes the drawer. He opens and closes it a few times and still hears the noise. So he pulls the drawer completely out and there, under the drawer wedged above the bottom support shelf of the dresser was a copy of some skin magazine. Well, he had his pleasures for the night and saved $5 bucks to boot.

On his next trip, thinking that the finding of the magazine last time was a fluke, he looked under the last drawer and found--nothing.

But the idea had been planted. Every time he traveled, he checked. He told us that about 25% of the time, he found something. A couple of times, he found Polaroid shots of people and several times he even found women's panties, complete with soiled crotch panels, of which he says that a sniff and a lick is almost as good as the real thing!

Ed was hooked. He also realized that a whole bunch of other guys were in the same boat because he found this stuff all over the US. From Los Angeles, to Dallas, to New York to Orlando. He decided to join the unofficial club and now every time he's does buy a T & A magazine, or finds some panties or pantyhose that some gal left under the bed or in the back of the closet, he leaves it under the dresser drawer, kind of like paying dues.

When he finished, we were all just sitting their, staring at him. Not sure if he was telling us the truth, or not. Great idea though, and I think we all made the mental note to check the next time we went to a hotel or motel.

Well, all good things must come to an end. We toss back one more toast to George, said good night and went to bed.

Glen Ellyn, IL (NCNWC bivouac area)
0740 hours
November 8

Pierce closed the journal and looked over at Jones, noticing a mischievous expression forming.

"Hey, Sarge. You think I could borrow the journal for a few minutes? Need to take a crap and could use something to read," Jones asked with a smile on his face.

"No way, TY. No fuckin' way. If I give you the journal, I got a strange feeling that I'll be getting it back with a couple of pages stuck together. Not a chance.

"Besides," Pierce continued, "we got to leave on patrol at 1200 hours. You got'a get some shut eye. So if you're gon'na take a dump, get to it, pronto like, and then hit the sack."

Wheaton, IL (Sandpiper Court subdivision)
2348 hours
October 8

It was approaching midnight when the figure, dressed entirely in black, crept through the shrubs separating the two houses closest to the northwest corner of Falcon Street and MacArthur Lane. Stealing through the night like a shadow, the figure moved closer to the window well at the back of the house located at 46 W 221 Falcon Street.

This particular window well was the emergency basement exit. As such, the well was about four feet deep and three feet wide, almost completely obscured from view, even during daylight hours, by a large, decorative mulberry bush.

The figure slowly rose to his hands and knees, dropping a leg over the edge of the well. He gingerly picked up and brought in his other leg, finally squatting down low in the well to catch his breath. Exertion wasn't the sole cause of the gasps for oxygen. Moving around alone in enemy territory was more than cause enough.

With the instincts of a cat burglar, the man carefully, silently, opened the escape window. For ease of removal in an emergency situation, the builder has selected exit windows that were held in place by two simple metal snaps. By pushing the window away from the frame and depressing the snaps with the end of his combat knife, the man was able to release the catches and remove the window, being careful not to make a sound and call attention to his covert activities.

Once the window was out, he was able to gingerly let himself down through the opening and into the basement. Knowledge of the layout of the basement helped him maneuver himself to the foot of the stairway, which led up to the laundry room on the first floor.

46 N 221 Falcon Street was a three-bedroom ranch with the standard study, living room, family room and kitchen compliment of living space. The house was owned and occupied by the Stantree brothers, Bob, and his younger brother, Jim.

The midnight intruder crawled down the hallway connecting the bedrooms and came across the bedroom that was Jim's. The door was open and the man glided across the floor until he was right next to the bed, the only sound the soft, rhythmic breathing of Jim, who was fast asleep.

Reaching down to his webbed belt to extract the combat knife from its sheath, the man slowly stood up and with catlike grace, clamped his left hand over Jim's mouth while his right hand, the hand with the razor sharp honed combat knife, drove the blade into the side of Jim's exposed neck. Drove it in deep with a swift, powerful thrust, twisting the blade clockwise when the steel hit bone.

It happened so quickly that Jim never had a chance to cry out or struggle. It happened so quickly that Jim didn't even know what was happening as the life rapidly drained from his body.

Pulling out the knife in one deft movement, the man wiped the blade on the blanket, returned the knife to the sheath and once again assumed a prone position on the floor. Then he crawled out, in search of his next victim.

Death came just as quickly to Bob, who was in the next bedroom, also sleeping.

Having completed his mission, the man looked around and disabled the guns that the brothers had placed near their beds by removing the firing pins. Sensing that he had consumed the eight minutes he had allocated for the raid, the man retraced his steps down the hallway, through the laundry room and down the staircase into the basement.

Exiting through the emergency exit window, the man reached the relative safety of the mulberry bush. Collecting his wits, and with another deep breath, he crawled away into the darkness, his mission accomplished.

XI

Wheaton, IL (Sandpiper Court subdivision)
0545hours
October 9

TJ awoke early. Something jolted him from his sleep, rescuing him from the reoccurring nightmare. The fire, the family, unable to help them, losing them in the smoke.

He noticed he was wet with the remnant of a night sweat, brought on by the dream.

God, I hate that dream.

Pushing back the covers and swinging his feet over the side of the bed, he shivered noticeably as his feet hit the ice cold floor.

Jesus, it's cold.

He hobbled over to the window to look out and saw a Steven King morning dawning. An out-of-season cold front must have moved through the area during the night. Everything was covered in a thin blanket of frost, gently caressing buildings, streets, lamp posts, grass and trees; nothing escaping the shimmering dust.

As his gaze moved skyward, it encountered absolutely no horizon. The warmth of the previous day, captured by ground and man-made structures were giving up their ghosts. The curtain of fog flowed toward the heavens, only to be consumed by the clouds, which couldn't have been more than a hundred feet or so above the ground. The wind swirled the mist ghosts, forming rippling curtains of silver gray fog merging with silver gray clouds, with all this happening over a simmering, silver gray dusting of frost covered, earth bound elements, both manmade and natural.

It was as if Rod Serling, stirred by some supernatural force, had been beckoned back to life to direct just one more episode of The Twilight Zone.

Rod, find a small town. Find a small neighborhood in that small town and do something really scary. Make it look, spooky. No, that's not the right word, make it look, surrealistic.

Just use whites, and grays and silver. Don't give anything a definite shape. Yeah, make sure you can tell what everything is, but kind'a make sure it all blends together.

Rod, that's great, just what I had in mind. Now, have this guy waking up in a bed. It's cold you see and this guy, have him shaking and stuff because it's cold. And ah, have him walk to the window and have him, well, you know, just make it interesting, like a natural phenomenon or something. You know what I mean.

TJ was overwhelmed by the beauty of what he was witnessing. The scene started to change, first almost minutely, than more quickly. The rising sun was adding more light, more detail, more color. The magic was disappearing, the rabbit was out of the hat, and the magician was taking his final bow.

Show's over kids. Please come back and see us again, and make sure you tell your friends about us.

TJ was hit by a flood of memories. He could very vividly remember laying in his twin size bed in his bedroom in his parents' house on the southwest part of Chicago, head supported by one crunched up pillow, cracking the cover on one of his Christmas gifts; a book. He couldn't remember the exact title or the author, but the book was about Tom Corbett - Space Cadet.

The story happened in the twenty-third or twenty-fourth century. Kids didn't go to college or university, they went to the Space Academy, where seventeen and eighteen year-old boys and girls were learning how to fly spaceships. Great stuff to read for a nine year-old boy. Great because it sparked the imagination and in TJ's case, introduced him into the true pleasure that one can receive from reading.

No longer bound by this earth, TJ couldn't get enough stuff to read. First the Corbett series, move on to the Hardy boys, more science fiction, a war novel or two, but always back to science fiction. Isaac

Asimov, H. P. Lovecraft, the Science Fiction Book Club. Just couldn't get enough.

Then the Twilight Zone hits the tube. Star Trek, One Step Beyond, Outer Limits. Talk about dying and going to heaven!

Strangely enough, this move into reading and fiction helped TJ in school. He finally recognized that the disappointment he saw in his parent's eyes when he kept bringing home those shitty grades wasn't the disappointment expressed because they knew that their son was stupid. It was disappointment expressed because they knew he was capable of a lot more. When the light finally came on for TJ, he was in his first year of high school, coincidentally, going to a second rated parochial school literally in a near west side ghetto of Chicago because he hadn't scored high enough on the admissions test for the school he and his parents wanted him to attend.

Man, talk about a daily dose of reality. TJ was one of six white boys in a class of forty-two. Discipline ranged from getting punched by one of the Brothers (Irish Christian Order) to getting smacked by one of them wielding a belt or worse, the iron pipe, which they would innocently drop on your wrist bone, using gravity to make it fall. At first, when you watched them doing it to someone else, it almost looked like a love tap. But I'm telling you, when it was your wrist bone, and the two inch diameter, eighteen inch long pipe falls twelve or fourteen inches and hits your wrist bone, that fucker really hurts!

Long story short, that first year did two marvelous things for TJ. First, he improved his grades dramatically. In part because the pace of education was slower, but mostly because he needed a high grade point average to qualify for acceptance to the high school of his first choice for sophomore year. Second, he was able to make, for the first time, friends among what was commonly referred to then as the minorities; Blacks and Hispanics. He learned by being immersed in their culture that they were people. Sure, they were different and he didn't want to change places, however, he was able to call a few of them friends and he learned about the us and them people whispered about. He learned a great deal that would help him in his dealing with people later in life.

Another image started to crystallize in TJ's consciousness; all of a sudden, TJ was in the rowboat with his brother, Mark, sitting inside a cone of light surrounded by the darkest dark imaginable.

Snapped to the present by the voice, TJ turned and saw his wife sitting up in the bed, naked from the waist up, her lower half still tucked under the blanket.

"Didn't you hear me, close the goddamn window and get back into bed. It must be ten degrees in here," she said, her jaws clenched to stop them from shivering.

"Oh, sorry hun. It was just so beautiful and all....,"

"I don't care if it's heaven out there. Close the window and do it now, asshole!"

TJ quickly slammed the window shut, making the pane rattle with pain. "Okay, happy?"

"Now get in here and warm me up before I have to go out and ask for volunteers," she said huskily, pulling back the covers, exposing a blond tuft of public hair.

Watching her legs spread open invitingly, TJ grinned and sauntered over to the bed and got in, reaching out to give Joyce a big hug. She stretched out her arms and with palms on TJ's shoulders, pushed him down between her legs.

"I think I'll let you have a little breakfast first. Now remember what mommy told you. Make sure you play with your food before you eat it," Joyce commanded as she spread her legs a little further.

XII

Master Sergeant Franklin B. Pierce raised his hand to stop the patrol. He absolutely hated these four-man walkabouts. Didn't have enough firepower if they found trouble, or worse, if trouble found them.

Never understood why the LT insisted on small patrols, especially during daylight hours. Fuckin' suicide mission, that's what it was plain and simple. Nothing but a fucking suicide mission.

The men were deployed in a rough diamond shape. Pierce handled lead, about fifty feet out in front. Brown and Williams each took a flank, about forty feet right and left of center. Jones was back of center about twenty feet. The only benefit he could see in this arrangement was that a mortar shell or Claymore wouldn't take out the whole group at once, but what the hell were the two or three survivors supposed to do once the shit hit the fan? Nothing but pick up and run for their lives.

Pierce, his hand still in the air, extended a finger and moved it in a circle, indicating that he wanted the guys to form up on him.

After Brown, Williams and Jones huddled up, Pierce pulled out a map of the area and started to explain the plan for the balance of the patrol.

Pierce found their location on the map. The patrol was in a forest preserve area, know locally as the Danada Forest Preserve, on the far

127

southern edge of Wheaton. Being forest, it seemed like a good place to set up a forward observation post, which was the reason for the patrol. They needed to make sure that the area was not being patrolled by the National Guard, or the local police force.

There were several ponds in the preserve, one of which was at the bottom of a rather shallow hill. Pierce crawled up to the top and checked his field of vision to determine whether or not it would be high enough to use effectively as an observation post.

When he reached the top, Pierce peered over the edge and much to his disappointment, the only things visible were more trees and the edge of the Danada Shopping Center, and at that, they were over three hundred yards away. The hilltop offered very marginal potential. He reluctantly crawled back down to conceive a new plan.

The topology of the Wheaton area is very disappointing, at least for those in search of establishing a forward observation post. There weren't that many high spots provided by nature, and the man-made structures were all within the city limits making them impractical for use. Pierce decided that based upon on the LT's orders, we was to proceed west to the Arrowhead Golf Club as a secondary site. Arrowhead was about a half mile due west, which Pierce estimated they could reach in just over an hour, caution dictating a snail's pace since they were within range of the enemy.

Wheaton, IL (on patrol)
1152 hours
November 8

Pierce had been studying the course and it's building for almost twenty minutes through the camouflaged field binoculars. No one was in sight.

He hand signaled to Williams to move up on the left flank and take cover behind a large outbuilding, which he figured to be the maintenance shed.

Williams nodded his acknowledgment and belly crawled the hundred and fifty feet from his position behind a large elm tree to the large, aluminum shed.

Eight minutes later, Pierce motioned to Jones to move up on the right and find cover in one of the deep sand traps surrounding the sixteen green.

While his men were moving up, Pierce continued to look through the field glasses and once again, was pleased to find that the entire area appeared to be free for the taking. Yeah, maybe his luck was holding out.

Wheaton, IL (on patrol)
1245 hours
November 8

Sometimes the gods of war decide to take a break from the activities of waging war. They sit back and do whatever it is that gods do when they take such a break.

Master Sergeant Franklin B. Pierce couldn't believe his luck for here he sat, together with his motley patrol, in the clubhouse of the Arrowhead Golf Club, feet up on the table, passing around an old bottle of Mondavi Chardonnay that Williams had found in the back of the kitchen, hidden under some rags; probably squirreled away by one of the busboys.

Yeah, the war could take five while we did. Besides, what the fuck. Ain't no reason to worry. Ain't no one around.

The thought had barely crossed his mind when he heard the squeaky rumblings of an armored vehicle, rolling along Route 56, which paralleled the course on the north side approximately three hundred feet away from the clubhouse.

Using hand signals again, he ordered the men into defensive positions near the windows on the north side, across the dance floor, from where they could monitor the progress of the vehicle in an effort to determine its intent.

When they reached the windows, Pierce motioned to Brown to get the LAW ready for action. The LAW, light anti-tank weapon, is a small, shoulder-fired rocket capable of penetrating thin skinned vehicles. The weapon consisted of two small tubes, which were held one inside of the other, with the rocket being inside the smaller tube. When the tubes are pulled in opposite direction, doubling the size of the weapon, two small sighting rings, and a trigger appear, which allow the operator to take aim and fire.

Brown unslung the LAW and held it in front of him, preparing to extend the tubes on orders from Pierce.

Pierce was using the field glasses and monitoring the progress of the APC.

Through the binoculars, Pierce looked out at an M2 Bradley IFV (infantry fighting vehicle). The Bradley, weighing in at a little over twenty-two tons, is claimed to be the best IFV in the world. The Bradley is constructed of aluminum. It is also encased with a second, additional protective steel covering on the lower half of its front and under most of its bottom as added armament against anti-tank mines. Its two man crew consists of a commander and a gunner, who also occupies a position in the turret, which is located just right of center on the hull.

The Bradley's main gun is a 25mm M242 Chain Gun, a mean weapon capable of spitting out a sustained fire of either armor piercing or high explosive rounds at a rate of up to 200 rounds per minute. This weapon isn't much good against a main battle tank, but is devastating on the thin skinned troop vehicles such as trucks and APCs.

Should the Bradley encounter a MBT, the turret also contains an electronically aimed and fired twin TOW (Tube launched, Optically-tracked, Wire guided) anti-tank rockets.

Additional firepower is supplied by a coaxially mounted machine gun firing standard 7.62mm slugs.

The Bradley, in addition to the two crew members, offers sufficient space inside to carry a squad of seven fully equipped troopers, ready to spring to action when the rear door opens, with a top down motion.

Pierce watched the Bradley slow down as it approached the road leading into the parking lot and turn left, right into the main drive. The vehicle slowly moved up the drive and stopped dead in its tracks about seventy yards away, its turret traversing from left to right, training its weapons on the clubhouse as it panned the entire length of the building.

The turret stopped at the last window, the window where Brown was preparing to extend the LAW.

Pierce motioned to Brown to get ready for action when they all heard the rear door of the Bradley opening.

This is it. Get ready. The gods must have decided to resume the game. But, wait, what's he doing?. What the fuck's happening?

A National Guard Lieutenant, who must have exited through the open door, walks around the side of the Bradley, walking like he's out for a Sunday stroll. He's not even carrying a weapon.

Pierce signals everyone to freeze.

The National Guard Lieutenant walks about ten feet past the nose of the Bradley, spreads his feet about twenty-four inches, reaches down and, *What the fuck, he's pulling down his zipper.*

The motherfucker's going to take a piss.

A giggle escapes Lance Corporal Tyrone Jones' lips, but is quickly silenced by Pierce's 'if looks could kill' glare.

After shaking out the last few drops, the National Guard Lieutenant, sticks it back in, zips up, sticks his hand up in the air and signals the Bradley to wind it up.

The NCNWC men hear the door closing and watch in utter amazement as the Bradley executes a 180 degree turn, leaves the course and makes a left turn back onto Route 56, apparently continuing its patrol.

Wheaton, IL (on patrol)
1432 hours
November 8

"I'm not sure if I should cry or laugh," Brown says as he slings the LAW back over his shoulder. He glances over at Jones, who is sitting there, laughing his ass off.

"Keep laughing, Ty. Next time you're going to get your ass shot off."

"Not me, Corporal Brown. Not this here nigger. Don't you know I lead a charmed life. Why I had that honky's dick clean in my sights. Course, it would of been a tough shot with him being so small," Ty replied, barely getting the words out between his giggles.

"Okay. Enough's enough," Pierce interjected. "Let's get a move on before they come back this way."

Glen Ellyn, IL (NCNWC bivouac area)
1830 hours
November 8

"So you think Pierce's is really fuckin' TY. I mean, up the ass and everything?" Brown asked.

"Well, figure it out my man. Aren't they always sneaking off together? Huh? I mean it ain't natural. There they are again, sitting down under that tree. I don't know what they're up to but, it sure does look funny to me," Williams replied.

Brown looked up and sure as god makes little green apples, there was Pierce and Jones, sitting with shoulders and knees touching looking at something in Pierce's lap. God only knows what they're up to.

Across the compound, Pierce was opening up the journal to the next entry so that he and Ty could visit yet again with Anthony Joseph Bender.

October 9 - Day Eighteen

Today we gave the hunting blinds at the Country Club their first real try out.

Danny Davidson, Bill Komanski, Ed Flanders, Larry Findler and my sons Rich and Joe all left around 4:00 a.m. to get into position in the blinds. We felt nervous leaving the safety of the subdivision, especially with the midnight killer still roaming around and the sounds of the fighting getting closer every night, but what the hell.

We finally got into position in the two blinds about forty-five minutes before dawn, making sure the decoys we had left there were in the right positions. As we walked up to the blinds, me, my boys and Ed in one, Bill, Larry and Danny in the other, we did flush out a bunch of ducks and geese out of the ponds by the fairways. But, since they hadn't been disturbed before and waterfowl not being very bright, we figured they would start to return once the commotion died down.

Sure enough, at false dawn, about fifteen minutes before the sun actually breaks above the horizon, the ducks started to come back first.

We hear them coming long before we saw them. They were calling out their singular, steady, "'Quack', I'm looking for someone call". We answered with a few feeding chuckles of our own, which actually sound like a duck chuckling, and a few "Where are you guys" calls for good measure.

We let the first few small flocks land amongst the deeks to provide the rest with a feeling of safety. When we had about twenty in the water and another flock of twelve or so coming in, we stood up and emptied our guns in rapid succession. Like market hunters of old, we dropped about twenty ducks, well beyond the legal limit. But, looking around and not seeing the game warden, we simply helped ourselves. As we were collecting the kill, we heard the shots coming across the course where Larry, Bill and Danny must have been having an equal amount of success, at least judging by the number of shots fired.

After that double flurry of activity, ducks became mighty scarce for a while. Though they are stupid, they aren't stupid enough to keep coming back to be live targets. Some instinctive capability allows their smallish brain to send out danger signals. We knew that the survivors would be gun-shy for a couple of days at least.

We waited until 9:00 a.m. to give the geese time to return. Even though I've hunted for a number of years, I could never find out why geese tend to come back to the pond, or lake or river where they left from later than the ducks. Ducks had a tendency to fly at dawn and sundown. Geese tended to fly a little earlier, normally before legal hunting hours started, but tended to fly back around mid-morning.

Anyways, the geese came in and unlike the ducks, since geese are quite a bit more leery about their safety, we opened fire on the first flock of fifteen geese as opposed to waiting for more to fly in. Now geese are a lot bigger than ducks. Hunters have a tendency to open fire too soon because they're used to looking at ducks, which have a small silhouette against the sky and simply fire early at geese when their silhouette matches the size of a duck's body. The result is that the shot falls short. Another problem is that because a goose is so big, at least compared to a duck, geese appear to fly slowly when in fact they are really moving along. Thus many times, the shot is behind the geese, instead of being out front where they can fly into it.

And even if you overcome these hurdles, geese are just plain hard to knock out of the sky because they're covered with a rather thick coating of down feathers.

Most people who don't hunt don't realize that most geese, and even ducks for that matter, are knocked out of the sky because one or more pellets hits and breaks a wing bone. They don't fall because you've hit a vital organ, at least not too often. It's simply because they can't fly with a broken wing.

Another thing that most non-hunters don't realize is that even though a shotgun shell may have one hundred fifty pellets, the range of these pellets is only sixty or seventy yards, and they're losing power all along the way. Also, the shot pattern of these pellets is in the form of an ever-expanding cone and gravity starts the pellets moving downward. All of this means that very few of the pellets actually have a chance of hitting the target, especially on those long shots that are at the extreme end of the range.

Long story short, it's pretty hard to knock down geese. So we only added four geese to our bag of twenty ducks. Not bad and this is just my little group. The others added sixteen ducks and seven geese. A feast for all tonight!

Not a whole lot happened during the balance of the day. Lieutenant Colonel Emerson stopped by for a visit. Not much going on nationally in the war. Local activities are increasing and he's all in favor of our move to the Country Club for security reasons.

He told us that the regular army is sending a reinforced mechanized infantry battalion into the general area to setup a defense against the NCNWC forces, which are rumored to be gathering about forty miles southwest of Chicago. Army Intelligence, an oxymoron if there ever was one, felt that the Chicagoland area would be in for some serious fighting in three or four weeks.

October 10 - Day Nineteen

Lieutenant Colonel Ralph Emerson, Illinois National Guard, stopped by this morning with some startling news regarding the NCNWC. Apparently, our side intercepted some NCNWC intelligence reports, and coupling this information with some other data developed from interrogating captured NCNWC soldiers, they are able to develop a pretty good guess as to what their intended strategy and tactics are for the Chicagoland area.

Emerson told us that NCNWC forces were consolidating southwest of the Chicagoland area, massing for an attack, which the army feels will take place within the next couple of weeks. The enemy is reported to be of at least battalion strength, maybe more.

Emerson continued to tell us that they also developed some information that indicates that a force of unknown strength, is scheduled to attacked from the north at the same time, the purpose of the two-pronged attach is to cut the western supply routes in a pinchers movement. In response to this threat, the army as sent the 3rd Airborne Division close to the Illinois Wisconsin border, thirty miles east of Rockford. From this location, the army feels it can defend the northern approaches to Chicago.

Regarding south, the army has ordered the 67th Armor Regiment, supplemented by the 3rd Rangers battalion to establish South Holland as a base of operations.

Emerson continued to tell us that the army's plan was to blunt the initial assaults in the Rockford and South Holland areas, then fall back to the far northern and southern edges of the Chicagoland area and establish a second line of defense if necessary.

When asked about additional troops being sent to assist us, Emerson replied that the troops currently guarding Chicago were the only ones available and that between the National Guards, local Police departments and individual citizens groups, we would be responsible for defending our lives and properties. He went on to tell us that in his opinion, the strategy adopted by the army was shaky because it committed all forces to two relatively narrow corridors of approach. If the NCNWC forces obliged and attack were we expected them, it would be a slaughter. If they by-passed us somehow, then we would be the one's slaughtered. Great bedside manner!

Emerson continued and told us that in his opinion, the NCNWC forces would strike quickly and where we least expect them. If their objective was to cut off our western supply routes, then the battles would be fought in the western suburbs, not Chicago proper. Emerson reasoned that the NCNWC didn't have enough troops for the street to street fighting required by a purely urban war, and would try to disrupt the supply lines as far away from downtown Chicago as possible. If he's right, that means Naperville, Wheaton, Glen Ellyn, Carol Stream, Lombard, Glendale Heights and a bunch more western suburbs are in for it in a big way.

After Emerson departed, I called a committee meeting to discuss our plan of action.

We decided to move to the Country Club as planned on the 16th. We figured it would be easier to defend. We also decided that we would need to strengthen the defensive perimeter at the Country Club once we relocated and felt we could get Emerson to loan us the use of one of the Cat's to build some earthen berms around the new encampment for added protection. Two Caterpillar bulldozers were located in a construction area just outside of downtown Wheaton. They were being used by a construction company that was in the process of renovating City Hall when CW2 broke out. The National Guard had used them to block off a number of roads on the perimeter of Wheaton to control vehicular access. Additionally, earthen berms were constructed between some of the houses on the perimeter as well.

Glen Ellyn, IL (NCNWC bivouac area)
1903 hours
November 8

"You know," Pierce said as he looked up from the journal and found Jones' eyes, "that weekend warrior colonel was pretty damn smart. He saw right through the diversionary tactics and guessed that our only real shot was here in the west. Man, I'm glad he wasn't able to convince anyone that he had the answer. Can you image what would have happened if the bad guys were waiting for us when we hit the runway at O'Hare?"

"Shit would have hit the fan, Sarge."

"You can say that again, TY. No. Wait," Pierce added quickly with a smile as he saw Ty getting ready to actually say it again. "Figure of speak, man. Figure of speech."

Across the encampment, Williams hits Brown in the ribs with an elbow and adds, "See. What did I tell you. Look at them two fucks gazing into each other eyes, smiling from ear to ear to ear. Man, I'm tellin' you they're fags."

"Sure looks that way. Why I bet ol' Pierce is the daddy and little dainty Ty is the mommy."

Now it was Brown and William looking at each other and laughing.

Across the encampment, Pierce wondered what Brown and Williams are whispering to each other.

Probably telling dirty stories or something.

"Well, TY," Pierce says. "Sack time for me. See you in the morning."

Pierce got up, placed the journal in his haversack and walked to his tent.

XIII

Glen Ellyn, IL (NCNWC bivouac area)
0630 hours
November 9

The life of a soldier, especially one in combat, is never easy. You never know when a mortar shell is going to be lobbed in on your head, or a bomb dropped by one of the fast movers, as people in the military tend to refer to jet aircraft.

There are also a whole myriad of other little obstacles that can ruin your day; mines, tanks, machine gun nests, artillery, snipers, ambushes, in addition to the common every day accidents that can occur.

There is also something called 'friendly fire', which refers to those unfortunate accidents when someone on your own side accidentally shoots someone else on their own side.

Life in an encampment, especially one deep inside enemy held territory, breeds its own set of problems and challenges.

First, you're surrounded by the enemy.

Second, you realize that you're surrounded because someone who is sitting somewhere else decided you and your unit should go there and be surrounded by the enemy.

Third, you constantly worry about your supply lines. Are we going to have enough food and water? Will we run out of ammunition? Either you resupply from the stores captured from the enemy, making due with what you find. Or, you plan some elaborate supply delivery system with home base via helicopters, or dropped into your zone by parachutes.

Fourth, if the enemy doesn't kill you, the food that comprises combat rations surely will.

Actually, Lance Corporal Tyrone Jones, thought, *there's probably a million fucking reasons why there's better things to do with one's life than be a soldier.*

Here he was, an island in the middle of a sea of white, waiting to get killed. *Man, what a life.*

"Hey, Ty. How are you and your, shall we say 'friend', Sergeant Pierce getting along these days?" Corporal Willis Williams asks with a shit eating grin on his black as coal face. "You two guys been gettin' pretty friendly lately. How come your still using separate tents?"

"Why don't you go fuck yourself, Willie boy?"

"Whoa there, boy," Williams adds, his grim growing to stretch from ear to ear. "Seems I've struck a nerve here. Sorry there, Ty. Didn't mean to offend you and the misses, or, you and your hubby, or whatever arrangements you and Pierce worked out."

Seeing absolutely no humor in this line of banter, Jones jumps up to his feet and dives at full force into Williams' mid-section, not that one hundred thirty-seven pounds can do anything at full force, and almost succeeds in knocking the bigger man to the ground. Williams, almost twice the size of Jones, and still laughing, maintains his balance and pushes the small man away, knocking him to the ground.

Regaining his feet, Jones reaches behind himself and pulls out his combat knife, crouching down in a classic knife fighter's stance. As he sways from side to side, his eyes are staring directly into those of Williams, looking for an opening, looking for a chance to strike.

Williams, sensing that he has pushed the little guy too far, puts up his hands, trying to signal surrender. Jones, seeing the quick movement of his opponent's hands, dodges left, feints right, then charges straight ahead. Williams caught completely by surprise, lunges backward in an attempt to avoid the razor sharp combat knife, which Jones is swiping hard from left to right across Williams' chest.

Thanks to Williams' quick movement and Jones' short arms, the blade passes harmlessly through Williams' camouflage battle jacket, slicing the material without actually making contact with his flesh. Jones, sensing a miss, regains his footing, preparing for another attack.

Just as Jones starts his second assault, he is frozen in his tracks by the sound of three or four shots. Dropping to the ground he rolls and comes up, prepared to defend himself against the new intruder.

He looks up and comes into eye contact with Master Sergeant Franklin B. Pierce, who doesn't look real happy.

"Put the knife away, Ty," Pierce hisses, trying to maintain his composure. "Willis, get out' a here. I'll deal with you later."

Williams seems very relieved and after saying, "Whatever you say, Sarge" quickly disappears across the encampment.

Jones, in the meantime, has replaced his knife in its sheath and is just standing there, waiting for the wrath of God to jump down his throat. But, completely unexpected, he hears Pierce say, "I heard what that sonofabitch said. I'll glad you didn't kill him, but the motherfucker deserved it. Thanks for standing up for me."

Pierce gives Jones a quick smile and walks away, leaving Jones to count his blessings.

Glen Ellyn, IL (NCNWC bivouac area)
1111 hours
November 9

"Frank, I'm real sorry about the fight with Willie. I just lost my head. He shouldn't be talkin' that way 'bout you and me," Jones offers, his voice indicating true contriteness.

Pierce, sitting on his cot, looked up and said "Ty, I really respect you for being there to defend me and my honor. Ain't enough of that kind of friendship between people no more. Especially amongst us soldiers. We get so used to fighting and killing and looking out for ourselves that sometimes we lose sight of the fact that we're on the same side. I appreciate what you did for me and you don't need to apologize."

Jones, sensing that Pierce was really forgiving his indiscretion, simply smiled in return.

Pierce, knowing that ultimately he must maintain a certain distance from the men who report to him and that he is responsible for, quickly adds "And if you ever feel the need to defend me again against some unwelcome verbal attack, I hope you realize that you fight words with words. Not knives. Ain't you never heard that only sticks and stones, not words, will break your bones? Tell me you've heard this before Lance Corporal Tyrone Jones, and that you've learned a valuable lesson here today."

Jones flinched at the formal use of his rank and full name. He knew Pierce was really pissed off and had just given him a severe reprimand. He also knew that Pierce liked him and was trying to cut him some slack. He simply nodded his assent.

"Good. Now sit down here and we'll give them assholes something else to snicker about," Pierce said slyly as he reached over to his haversack and extracted the journal.

October 11 - Day Twenty

My dad asked me to make the record in the notebook today so I'm going to do just that.

My name is Jennifer Bender. I am 13 years old and nobody calls me Jennifer. Everybody calls me Jenny.

Things are not too nice around here anymore since the war started. I don't have a chance to see my friends because most of them went with their parents to stay in Wheaton so the Police and soldiers could protect them. I miss my friends and I miss school a lot. I was in the eighth grade at St. Michaels in Wheaton and was looking forward to a great year. I was planning on being a cheerleader and tryouts were a couple of days away when the war started. Now those plans are all out the window.

I was really sad when Jeff Dalton was killed. You may hear that we were boyfriend and girlfriend, but that's just not true. We did like each other a lot, but were just friends. I don't think just because you kiss a boy a couple of times, or let him hold your hand that everyone can say that you're boyfriend and girlfriend. But I do miss him.

There are many things I don't like now that the war is going on. I can't see my friends any more. The mall is closed. We have to eat this yucky food that we get from the army or somebody. You can't even take a walk around by yourself. Someone has to go with you and they're always carrying guns. I hate guns and I hate this war.

It was terrible when the kids got killed playing with those mines. Someone should have been hanged because someone should have known that those things were dangerous. The kids shouldn't have been allowed to get close to those things. I think someone should hang for that big mistake.

I work in the Food & Medical group, which isn't too bad. I really don't like the cooking and washing up stuff we have do to for the meals. But I do like the doctor stuff. Dr. Harry Furgenson is a great guy and always lets me help him when people get sick and need bandages and medicine. I think I'm going to be a doctor when I grow up. I really like helping people and doctors always make a lot of money and drive fancy cars.

Well, I have to go help get lunch ready. Goodbye.

October 12 - Day Twenty-One

We found another casualty of the Midnight Killer this morning. Steve Kornat, who was the 'floater' on the perimeter during the early guard shift, found Frank's body, stabbed to death. Frank was at his post on the perimeter defensive position and after Steve called me for help, I rounded up a couple of the other guys and we ran to the position. We didn't find any signs of a struggle, nor did we find any tracks or anything showing how the killer got there and then escaped.

Frank had a stab wound in the neck and as a result had lost a lot of blood. He looked like the rest of the people that were killed by this guy.

Our defensive positions were a series of garbage cans set up in a circle with a small space left open in the back, which faced the subdivision. These fifty-five gallon trashcans were filled with dirt to help stop bullets and mortar fragments. In addition to this, we pounded a bunch of boards into the ground between the cans to allow us to add some dirt between the cans for additional protection. The three cans that faced outward were placed in a small trench, which positioned them about eighteen inches lower than the cans in the rest of the circle and opened up a little firing window for the guard. We built seats into the middle of each of these circles. Planking was placed on top of these cans and dirt piled on top of providing overhead protection. The result was that each of these positions resembled a little turret.

When we started looking for clues, we didn't see any footprints at all out in front of the position. The only tracks we saw were those going in and out of the circle of cans and a bunch more leading back to the subdivision. We found some tracks moving left and right, but they were all messed up and seemed to be in the general area of where our own 'floaters' would walk when moving from position to position. We asked all of the other guards and no one remembered seeing or hearing anything. It was almost as if a ghost had somehow entered the subdivision, done the deed and then disappeared. In other words, no leads.

People were really starting to get pretty scared what with the killings and Emerson's report of this impending NCNWC attack on Chicago. A couple of fights broke out between people since everyone seemed to have their own ideas as to what to do next. We finally got some order restored and agreed that the move to the Country Club would help. No one seemed interested in moving to downtown Wheaton, which we considered doing. It seems everyone felt that moving closer to the population center, especially in view of the NCNWC attack, was simply inviting disaster since we all figured Wheaton would be a target if the fight hit the western suburbs. Being five miles away from the center of town, kind of out in the sticks so to speak, has its appeal.

October 13 - Day Twenty-Two

We had another successful day hunting geese down by the golf course. Six of us got up before dawn and under cover of darkness, worked our way down to the pond . We positioned ourselves in the blinds we had built a couple of weeks earlier. Our plan to hunt the pond only once a week seemed to be working well, even though we missed the seven day period by a couple. Just as the horizon started to lighten up with the coming day, the geese started flying into the pond. We let the first group land, to act as live decoys. We opened up when the second group came in on final approach. Grand total; twelve geese. A little later, we added five ducks and decided to call it quits for the day. It took us about forty minutes to work our way back to the subdivision. It's only about a mile away, but we decided that with the increased NCNWC activity, it wasn't worth the risk to rush any faster.

We cleaned the geese and ducks as soon as we got back to camp. We still don't have an effective way to keep food fresh, so we had to eat the stuff the same day, one day later at most. Had a pretty decent feast with everybody sharing in the good fortune.

Just about Noon, Susan Hollis came running up to me saying that nobody could locate her daughter, Sara. I immediately told her to meet me at the Committee meeting place (I still have a hard time saying 'Headquarters'). I gathered Frank Smyth, Bruce Jamison, Larry Findler, Ed Flanders and Bill Komanski. Susan met us there with a couple of the other mothers, Nancy Sawyer and Janice Pedopoulos.

We were able to reconstruct most of the morning and where Sara had been. She had eaten breakfast with the group, completed her daily chores for Food & Medical and then volunteered to help Child Protection. The younger kids were working on a Thanksgiving play and the Child Protection adults had asked for some extra assistance to help the kids learn their lines and the songs.

Sara's activities were traced up until 11:30 a.m. After that, nothing. Susan Hollis, Sara's mother, started crying. At first we thought from the concern of not knowing where her daughter was, but then she blurted out that Sara had probably slipped out again to visit her boyfriend, Brad Trapani. Brad lived in a small development off of the Prairie Path. The Prairie Path was about forty or fifty miles long and had been converted into a path for hiking, bike riding and that kind of stuff. I got to admit that as long as I lived in Wheaton, I never was on the path, not even once and am not even sure of what it was originally. Given its length though, I would guess an old railroad road bed.

Anyways, the same group of builders who built our subdivision built the Glen Oaks subdivision. It's just off the Prairie Path, about two miles southeast of our place. We immediately organized a search party and ventured out. I'll record what we found later when we return.

Wheaton, IL (Sandpiper Court subdivision)
0130 hours
October 13

"Okay, listen up. Everybody got food and ammunition for a two day trek, just in case we run into any trouble?"

TJ looked around as everyone used the buddy system to check everyone else's equipment and packs. Seeing agreement in the eighteen eyes that eventually looked back, he waved the group forward.

The shortest and safest route to hit the Prairie Path was to move south along Pleasant Hill for about a half mile. They had decided to walk instead of driving, thereby avoiding the risk of leaving a couple of cars parked along the side of the road. Not only would they waste gas for such a short trip, they would have had to leave guards behind to watch the cars, which would only have further reduced the number of men left behind for defensive purposes. You just couldn't be too careful.

They walked both sides of the road, each person separated by about twenty yards from the guy ahead and behind. The two columns were further staggered across from each other so that when each guy looked across the road, he had nothing off his shoulder except trees and abandoned buildings.

Just past the small strip mall on the east side of Pleasant Hill, they hit the Prairie Path.

"Bill, Ed. Stay back here at the road and let the rest of us get about fifty yards up," TJ said in a low voice to the men gathered around him.

"Danny, John, Steve - take the point. The rest of us will follow at twenty-yard intervals. Now listen up people, I only want to say this one time. Ever since we've had reports about NCNWC forces taking control of Bensenville, we've all heard the fighting going on. Fortunately, they haven't yet sent any patrols out to our area but sooner or later, they'll hit us, too. I want everyone sharp and on their toes when we go down the trail."

TJ continued, "Susan Hollis told me where this boyfriend lives. I figure it's just over a mile down the Path. It'll be on our left. We're in no hurry, so we'll work the cover as we move. Make sure you alternate sides as we go. No bunching up or any of that shit. We don't need to lose anyone and I sure as hell don't want to lose three or four of you guys because you decided to have a chat or take a piss together."

A nervous laugh rushed through the semicircle of men. Everyone realized that this was their first 'mission' and to a man they were all hoping it wouldn't be a baptism of fire!

"Okay. Let's go."

The Path was about fifteen feet wide, bound by trees, shrubs and an occasional backyard. The various towns and suburbs through which the Path ran were responsible for and did a great job keeping the Path presentable.

Very little litter was evident and lights were put in at every intersection where the Path crossed a roadway, though the lights didn't work since the power had been cut off.

When they arrived at their destination, TJ called a halt. He noticed that he was right on his mental estimate of one hour; a strange hour for no one had spoken a word, not one single word. Everyone had been too busy looking behind each tree, each shrub, each whatever for a NCNWC sniper, or tank or APC or whatever else ten active imaginations could conjure up from the depths of fear. Someplace within the first fifty feet of the hike down the path, each individual crossed the threshold from make believe to reality. From being at home to being out in the wilderness. From looking to stay alive to looking to get killed.

The command "Halt" caused everyone to drop down and hug the earth, looking for a place to be inconspicuous, to disappear into non-existence.

"Danny, Steve, Frank - come with me. The rest of you, take up defensive positions. Make sure you cover all approaches. Ed, you're in charge while I'm gone."

The four of them, with TJ in the lead, ran through the backyard of a nice, middle-class Tudor and dove under some big pine trees that separated the white and chocolate brown Tudor from its neighbor. Slowly crawling up to the front of the house along the east side of the structure, the other houses on the deserted street came into view.

No people, no animals, no sounds.

"Say here," TJ whispered as he jumped to his feet, ran across the street and fell to the ground under a big, sprawling evergreen bush in front of a blue-gray tri-level.

The other men fanned out in a semi-circle to provide covering fire if necessary.

Moments later, TJ, moving on all fours, scurried like a crab up the steps and up to the front door, which the others had noticed was open.

Seeming like five hours, TJ emerged five minutes later and trotted back across the street.

"Nobody home, " he announced. "Let's head back."

"We've come this far, TJ. Why not keep looking?" asked Danny Davidson, at twenty, the youngest of the group.

"We can't take the risk. We don't even know if the kid came here. Susan's just speculating. We just can't take the risk. Besides, where would we look?" TJ responded in a soft, concerned voice. He was just as frustrated as everyone yet had to maintain some semblance of composure.

"Let's just head back, okay?"

The four reached the six and all ten men repeated the three first, five staggered, two back procession through the valley of darkness back to their little sanctuary in a country gone mad.

Glen Ellyn, IL (NCNWC bivouac area)
1142 hours
November 9

Pierce reached over and turned the page.

Susan Hollis took the news, or rather lack of it, very badly. Not only hadn't we gotten any news about her husband, Frank, now her only daughter, Sara, is missing.

I immediately convened a meeting of all residents and instituted a new rule. Effective immediately, no one is permitted to leave the boundaries of the subdivision alone. Preferably, the groups will be a minimum of four people with at least two of the members carrying arms. If a group does leave, they are responsible for telling one of their group leaders. If a group leader leaves, they are to tell me. I will tell at least three group leaders when I leave.

Glen Ellyn, IL (NCNWC bivouac area)
1224 hours
November 9

Pierce stopped reading, his mind reliving the events of a night three, four weeks earlier. He couldn't be exactly sure. Such was the nature of war. But he wondered.

October 14 - Day Twenty-Three

Just after midnight, Ed Flanders had reported that the guards on the southern perimeter had heard screams, like a young girl screaming. Then they heard moaning, which lasted about ten or fifteen minutes, then nothing. Ed decided to do nothing. You couldn't very well go walking around in the dark looking for sounds. After he reported this to me on the morning rounds, I pulled together a group to go see what we could find. Susan Hollis insisted on going with. We said it was okay. We were only going out a couple of hundred yards down by the old barn by the only farm, non-operating, left in Wheaton, just across Geneva.

We found Sara Hollis, dead. We guess she had been raped, tortured and finally, mercifully, she eventually died. Susan, her mom, got hysterical for a few moments and then fainted. As we were covering Sara's body up with an old blanket we found lying next to the barn, we heard sounds coming from inside the barn. Inside we found a NCNWC soldier, drunk and passed out, apparently left behind from some night patrol.

Glen Ellyn, IL (NCNWC bivouac area)
1238 hours
November 9

Pierce stared off into space for a split second. This was making more sense. He clearly remembered reporting to the LT. that Sergeant Johnson was missing. He had gone out with Brown and Williams to return a girl that had 'interrogated'. Only Brown and Williams came back from the trip. Again he wondered.

David A. Bragen

We took the soldier, along with Sara's body, back to the subdivision.

We tied up the soldier and interrogated him for a while. He swore that he didn't know anything about Sara Hollis. He said he was on a patrol and just fell asleep. We continued the interrogation for about ten minutes and then threw him into one of the basements under lock and key.

Wheaton, IL (Sandpiper Court subdivision)
0945 hours
October 14

"Get in there, asshole!" Danny Davidson yelled as he shoved the NCNWC soldier down the stairs into the dark basement.

"Fuck you, man," said the soldier. "I'm just a fuckin' scout. What the hell you giving me all this shit for?"

"Because you killed Sara, you bastard!"

"I told you, I don't know what you're talking about, man. I don't know any Sara. I didn't do nothing to nobody!" he yelled at the closing door, the basement turning a dark shade of gray.

After a couple of moments, the soldier got up on his knees, his eyes starting to adjust to the low light level.

What the fuck! Why did I have to drink so much and pass out? And that fucking nigger, Brown. How could he leave a brother behind? Why when I get back, his ass is mine. His thoughts were swirling like a maelstrom as he glanced around the basement, taking in his surroundings.

In the corner, he saw a lump, a lump that had a head, arms and legs. A lump that was starting to get up on all fours.

He stared in disbelief as the lump crawled closer and turned into an old, what was he, Mexican? Spanish? Whatever he was, he was a fellow prisoner.

"Hey, man. You look like something the cat dragged in."

The old man, looking to be about seventy years old, sat back on his haunches and said to the NCNWC soldier, "You don't look so good yourself, amigo. You hurt or anything?"

"No, they roughed me up a bit and it hurt like hell when that one fuckin' honky shoved me down the stairs. Ain't no big thing."

"I'm glad you're here. I'm was getting tired of sitting here by myself."

"Well, asshole. I'm sure not glad I'm here. Whad'ya think they'll do with us?"

"I've been here about six days. My name's Rico, by the way. I was just passing though and stole some food. These old legs couldn't get me away fast enough," he laughed, with a twinkle in his otherwise dreary eyes. "At least they feed me now. I heard them say they're going to turn me over to the National Guard tomorrow. I even been hearing that both sides are starting to exchange prisoners. Too hard to take care of them," he added hopefully.

"Food I could do with, Rico. By the way, my names Johnson."

"Glad to meet you Senior Johnson. How did they caught a fine young soldier like you?"

Johnson reacted like he'd been slapped in the face.

How the hell did he manage to get caught? That fuckin' Brown and Williams. Their ass is grass, man!

"We were having a little party. Found some young sweet piece of ass. Me and a couple of brothers were supposed to get rid of the bitch after it was all done. She started screaming as we got close to this place. Just decided she wasn't worth the effort. Just killed her, man. Just fuckin' killed her. Man, Rico, what a sight. What a fuckin' sight."

"Well, Senior Johnson that is your concern, not mine. I'm more interested in the War. Who's winning?

"Rico, you should be old enough to know that no one wins in war. Not bad, huh. Maybe I'll run for public office after this shit's over. Whad'ya you think?"

"It is my privilege to place in nomination for the President of the, what should we call it, the NCNWC Confederation, the honorable Senior Johnson," Rico ad-libbed, struggling not to laugh as he offered the pronouncement. Looking quickly at Williams, the ancient Mexican was relieved to see a smile spread slowly across the soldier's face.

"I likes the sound of that, the honorable Senior Johnson. Yeah, I likes that a lot," proclaimed Johnson solemnly.

"As far as winning, it's pretty much a stalemate now. Honkies ain't giving in to our demands so we've concentrated our forces on a couple of key areas. Chicago's one, San Francisco's another. Few more I'm not sure of. We're going to cut the supply channels into these big cities and starve Whitey into acknowledging us as a separate, but equal governing body.

"Our guys are doing okay here. We came in with about eight hundred guys in our battalion and lost about thirty percent so far. But we captured the objectives on schedule. You can't ask for more than that can you?"

Rico nodded his agreement.

Johnson continued, "Me getting caught, man, that was just plain stupid. Except for the bullshit with the young gal, we were just out on a patrol. Nothing fancy, just a walk through the woods. Then we finds us that young bitch and decide to have us some fun. You know, this soldiering's tough duty, man."

Johnson was puzzled that Rico didn't understand the humor in what he was saying. Well this old fuck's probably too old to remember his last fuck, the thought of which made Johnson laugh even more.

Rico did something strange, something unexpected. He whistled. Not a song or anything, just a long shrill, single note whistle.

The shaft of light, followed by rushing sounds startled Johnson. He looked up the stairs and saw three or fours guys coming down quickly.

The big guy when over to help Rico to his feet.

"Well, Juan. What did he give you?" Danny Davidson asked.

Juan Hernendez, resident of Sandpiper Court subdivision, member of the Food & Medical group, known as Rico to Johnson, got to his feet saying softly, "He was one of the group. In fact, he bragged about killing Sara. He also gave me some stuff about their plans that we should share with the National Guard."

"You motherfucking spic! How could you...." The rest of Williams words were captured by the darkness that shrouded him after Danny Davidson smacked him in the back of his head with the butt of his rifle.

TJ walked over to the limp form on the basement floor, and gave it a quick, hard kick to the small of the back, right where the kidneys were located.

"Give him to the women, Danny," he said, a disgusted look on his face. "Give him to the women."

Glen Ellyn, IL (NCNWC bivouac area)
1630 hours
October 13

Pulling up his zipper as he walked into the tent, Jones, with a grin on his face said "Hey, Sarge. You should try some of that stuff. Sure is good."

Pierce looked up from his cot. He was in the middle of writing a letter to his wife and daughter, both of whom he hadn't seen since the outbreak of hostilities. Actually, since he was a career soldier, he realized as he was writing that he's been away more than he's been home. It seems like just yesterday that he was dating Cindy, and now their daughter, Shasa, was a few weeks away from sweet sixteen. Time sure does fly.

"Huh?"

"The boys got us a sweet young thing. The whole squad's taking turns."

As Jones was talking, Pierce became aware of the background noises outside of the tent. Laughing, some yelling and a small, waif-like moan every once in a while. With a disgusted look on his face, he swung his legs over the edge of the cot, sat up and asked Jones what was going on.

"A couple of the boys on patrol found this gal wanderin' around the ruins. Brought her into camp. Asked her a few questions, stuff like that.

"Ol' lover-boy Wilson took a shine to the gal and tried to get her to suck him off. Well, she bit him and that ol' nigger slapped her around so bad she begged him to let her suck his big, black snake. After that the boys took turns. Man, Sarge, that gal took it all ways. Front door, back door, in the mouth. Why a couple of the guys even had her eating out assholes. Me, just the normal man on top routine. That's the way I likes it best. Boy, that bitch was still tight."

Pierce, having already decided to put a stop to this insanity, stood up, and picking up his M-16, started to walk out.

"Hey, Sarge. The bitch's giving it away. You don't need no fuckin' gun," laughed Jones.

Turning around slowly, Pierce took deliberate aim and drove the butt of the gun squarely into Jones' smile.

As he walked to the scene of the gang-rape, Pierce, thinking about Jones lying unconscious on the floor of his tent, remembered hearing at least two of Jones' teeth breaking; three if he was lucky.

By the time he arrived at the sight of the impromptu gathering, most of the squad was lying back on the ground, satiated, gathering steam for a second go.

"What the fuck gives?" Pierce shouted. "What the fuck do you think you're doing here?"

He glanced over at the young girl, who winced at his yelling as if she felt she were being scolded. He noticed a couple of ugly, discolored bruises on her cheeks and also saw that the few strands of her just sprouting pubic hair were matted with fresh blood and drying semen.

"Cover her up and get her out of here." Some of the fury had left his voice, but every one realized he was very upset.

"Ah, Sarge. I...ah, I didn't get my turn yet."

Pierce looked at the youngest member of the squad with enough hatred in his eyes to kill.

In a whisper that could hardly be heard, yet commanded everyone's full and complete attention, he said "Cover her up, walk her back to where you found her and put an end to this. If anyone in my squad ever, ever does anything like this again, he's dead. No ifs, ands, or buts."

Brown and Williams, the two oldest members of the squad, picked up the girl and helped her back into her tattered clothes. Then they, along with Sergeant Johnson, picked up their weapons and led the girl out of camp.

A couple of minutes later, Williams came back and picked up a big stick. He said that the girl had fallen and twisted her ankle. Johnson had sent him back to get something for a crutch. He then walked over to his tent to retrieve his haversack and then ran back out of view.

Pierce thought that maybe there was hope for this group yet. After all they were at war. Sometimes things get out of control in a war.

Glen Ellyn, IL (NCNWC bivouac area)
1317 hours
November 9

Pierce read the next paragraph.

I didn't want to get involved in the justice that the women were administering to the soldier. For the record, by the way, he was wearing a name badge, Johnson. We didn't bury him....we just dumped his body on the communal garbage heap near the Prairie Path.

Glen Ellyn, IL (NCNWC bivouac area)
1318 hours
November 9

Pushing the thoughts back down into the recesses of his memory and looking back at the diary, Pierce wondered if the waifs' name was Sara.

This time when Pierce stared into space momentarily, all of the pieces came together; it all made sense.

Pierce continued reading.

Anyways, I did make it a point to inspect the body after they were finished. They must have literally hacked him to pieces, extracting their revenge. They had him gagged, which explains the absence of any screaming. His male member was missing, as were his eyes. Cuts and gouges all over his body. It was really grizzly.

About 6:00 p.m. tonight, Susan Hollis stood on the fresh grave of her only daughter, Sara, who we had laid to rest earlier that afternoon, put the barrel of a .38 caliber revolver to her right temple and pulled the trigger.

Glen Ellyn, IL (NCNWC bivouac area)
1319 hours
November 9

Pierce stopped reading and closed the journal, wondering if he could have prevented the three deaths. Would Johnson, Sara Hollis and Susan Hollis be alive today if he had acted faster? If he had put a stop to the gang rape sooner?

He now understood how Anthony Joseph Bender must have felt when the children were killed by the Claymore mine.

XIV

Wheaton, IL (Sandpiper Court subdivision)
0530 hours
October 15

Anthony Joseph Bender awoke early; his internal alarm clock once again rescuing him from the reoccurring nightmare, a nightmare that he was starting to feel truly represented his destiny.

Rising slowly and quietly so as not to disturb Joyce, TJ maneuvered out of the bed and made his way downstairs to the kitchen.

Since they had interrupted the natural gas flow a few weeks back, he had to use a Coleman stove to heat up his morning coffee. After getting the pot and coffee grounds ready, he fired up the portable camping stove, placed the pot on the burner and sat down at the table, awaiting his morning ration of hot coffee.

As he sat at the table, his mind raced from memory to memory, amazed at the rapid passage of time that represented his brief stay on this earth.

Though only forty-five years old, TJ's appearance gave most people the impression he was probably seven or eight years older. His gray hair and somewhat overweight frame lent credence to those impressions. He had tried dieting and exercise, but to no avail. He finally decided that he was what he was, and the rest of them could just go fuck themselves.

Forty-five years, sixteen thousand, four hundred thirty-five days including leap-years, almost four hundred thousand hours, over twenty three and a half million minutes and at least a billion dot four seconds.

No matter how you sliced it, he'd been around a long time and yet, sitting there in his kitchen waiting for his morning coffee to percolate, TJ just couldn't believe that all of that time had slipped by. And maybe slipped by is the wrong way to look at it for there were uncountable good times along the way. Yet, he felt a nagging sense of frustration that if he were honest with himself and viewed his life in the light of day, he'd probably have to acknowledge that for every good time, there had been a bad time. Actually, a fifty/fifty split would be okay. He suspected that the true ratio was probably closer to forty/sixty, with the good times losing out.

Realizing that he was quickly becoming enveloped in a blanket of melancholy, TJ gave one last, though feeble, attempt to resist a self-flagellating trip down memory lane, but decided that he was entitled to some well earned self pity. The only problem now was, where to start the journey and where to stop along the way.

There was nothing in this whole wide world more important to TJ than family. Throughout his entire life, the family was rather self-contained. Sure there were jobs, friends, other events and life in general; however, the driving force behind TJ's very existence was his family.

Everyone is a product of their environment and TJ was not an exception. His family life as a child was great. He always had the safety and comfort of his family, no matter what other adversities he encountered outside; outside in that cold, cruel world.

At home, he lived surrounded by love, warmth and safety. His parents were supportive, almost to a fault. His brother was a friend. Their grandparents were built in baby sitters, an extension of the immediate family.

Years later, TJ had his own family that included his wife Joyce, the kids, even a cat and dog. And once again, he attempted to cloak himself in the cocoon of family, except that somewhere, somehow, the magic had disappeared.

When it first happened, or at least when he first noticed that it had happened, he couldn't explain it. Things just didn't feel right.

Eventually it dawned on him that the difference was called 'responsibilities' and that with responsibilities, especially those of a having a family, came all of the problems of life; the problems of having to grow up.

Right after he and Joyce had gotten married he clearly remembered the shock of opening up his underwear drawer and finding nothing. Not one goddamn pair of briefs. That never, ever happened at mom's! *What the hell kind of woman did I marry? Doesn't Joyce know what her responsibilities are?*

That coldwater dose of reality added some zest to their early years of marriage as similar events occurred, which only cemented the fact that he had to grow up; that life with mom and dad and brother was a thing of the past.

Enter kids and more problems. TJ absolutely loved being a parent yet parenting wasn't all that it was cracked up to be. Actually, it was damn tough!

The biggest problem with kids, or as Joyce to this day constantly reminds him, goats have kids, people have children, was feeling their pain when they're feeling pain. No matter how protective and watchful you are, eventually, your children experience pain. It may be the emotional hardship of a dead pet, the physical pain of a broken arm or the mental anguish in realizing that they, too, are growing up and expectations are not always satisfied.

TJ was never able to watch one of his children struggle or get hurt without feeling a sympathetic pain of his own. Physical, mental, emotional; he bled with them, cried with them and got angry with them.

The trip down memory lane was interrupted by the gurgling sound of coffee coming to a boil.

TJ stood up, wiped the tears from his eyes and poured himself a cup of joe. Today would be a busy day. Today we would prepare for the move over to the Country Club.

Wheaton, IL (Sandpiper Court subdivision)
0730 hours
October 15

Standing up on the plank he had placed on top of the cinder blocks, TJ gazed out at the crowd that had gathered before him. Everyone in the subdivision had been called to assemble so that he could inform them of the details of the move to the Country Club.

As he raised his hands to call the group to order, TJ noticed that his neighbor's expressions ranged from apprehension to concern to anger to just plain tired.

"If I could have everyone's attention for a few minutes," he yelled, "we'll get done with this in short order. You all know how I hate making speeches."

A general chuckle ran through the assembly who recognized that just the opposite was true.

"Okay, thanks. Good morning."

"Good morning Mr. Bender," the crowd sang in unison, which only caused more laughter.

"Come on. Settle down and let's get this over with," TJ said with a grin as the crowd gathered itself and started to pay attention.

"Sorry to get you up so early but today's going to be a busy day and we best get it started."

Finally commanding their rapt attention, TJ scanned the faces briefly before continuing.

"As you all know, the situation in the western suburbs is getting desperate. Since we learned that the NCNWC has plans to interrupt the supply flow into our area everybody on the military side figures that the western suburbs will become the main battle area. Lieutenant Colonel Ralph Emerson, estimates that a coordinated attack by NCNWC forces will begin sometimes within the next two weeks. Clearly, we don't know the details of the tactical plan they will use, but make no mistake about it, they're coming.

"Our subdivision is just too large to defend adequately with the forces we have available. We've all participated in the debates as to whether or not we should move into Wheaton central. We have all agreed that would just put us into greater jeopardy as we all think large population centers will become primary targets.

"The committee has explored the options available to us and the recommendation came back to move to the Country Club. We will occupy the main club house and the builders' models. This is an area that is isolated and defendable.

"We intend on moving everyone tomorrow. The people in the Defense Group will go over first to establish defensive positions. The Scavengers will pick up the defense responsibilities here at Sandpiper, as well as assist people during the move.

"All kids will..."

"You mean children, don't you honey?" Joyce yelled, her hands cupped megaphone style around her mouth, causing the crowd to laugh and ease some of the tension.

"Right you are, honey," TJ said, emphasizing the 'honey' rather sarcastically.

"Anyways," he continued, "the children will be the last ones to move over.

"The basic idea is to move into the Country Club without making it too obvious that anyone is living there. We hope that by camouflaging our presence, we will increase our chances of avoiding a fight if the NCNWC moves into this area. This will, out of necessity, require some hardships.

"First of all, everyone will be limited to move only food, clothing, firearms, and medical supplies. No family heirlooms or favorite artwork or any of that stuff. We need to travel light and not be burdened with a lot of (he wanted to say 'junk' but said) non-essential items.

"Second, we will all live the lives of hermits. No walking about outside unless you have a specific purpose. We will live invisibly. We cannot afford to broadcast our being at the Country Club. Calling attention to ourselves will only invite disaster.

"And finally, we will have some very strict rules regarding leaving our new home. I'll fill you all in on this later, after the relocation

"Until then, thanks for your cooperation. Please see your individual committee leaders if questions or problems arise."

And with that, the preparations for the great exodus began in earnest.

XV

Philadelphia, PA
0830 hours
October 15

Fifty-two year old Reese Robertson, second in the chain of command of the NCNWC, stopped reading the battle plan that was in the manila file folder he was gripping so tightly. After a slow, deep breath, he closed the folder and placed it in his lap. He reached up, took off his reading glasses and said aloud, "Sweet Jesus. I can't believe we're going to do this. I just can't fuckin' believe it."

The ruling council of the NCNWC movement, realizing that a purely military solution to the conflict at hand was destined for defeat, had been drafting various peace proposals for the last couple of weeks. Numerous ideas were presented by the various constituencies, no two of which seemed to capture enough of the common elements that would allow for a consensus to be agreed upon. The result was clear. They were simply spinning their wheels. And while they did, their military forces were being decimated and their dwindling supplies being consumed at an alarming and irreplaceable pace.

All previous peace overtures that had been funneled back channel through the Canadian government to Paul Fitzpatrick, the Speaker of the House who became acting president of the United States Government after Washington, D.C. was destroyed on the opening day of the war, had been rejected.

As a result, Keshum Aguawada, the head of the NCNWC had called an end to the peace process, deciding instead to up the ante for the so called United States of America. He planned to ease off fighting in most parts of the country, and concentrate one devastating attack on a middle American city. After much debate, Chicago was selected as an appropriate site to demonstrate the unrelenting commitment of the NCNWC to their sacred principles of separate but equal.

Aguawada felt that by forcing President Fitzpatrick to once again witness the resolve of the NCNWC movement, an acceptable and accommodating peace could be negotiated.

The battle plan in Robertson's manila file folder was ambitious beyond belief. It called for leaking the news that NCNWC forces would spring a sneak attack on the Chicagoland area, their objective being to cut Chicago's supply lines to the west. This two-pronged offensive would start seven days hence. The information had been leaked three days ago through various means including several NCNWC soldiers who volunteered to be 'captured' so that through interrogation, the secret would unfold.

Preliminary intelligence reports indicated that the U.S. Army forces charged with guarding Chicago had swallowed the bait and had deployed their forces north and south of Chicago to act as a defense buffer against the anticipated NCNWC attack.

The plan was barbaric in its simplicity. Two Boeing-Vertol CH-47 Chinook helicopters would each deliver one 155 mm howitzer, along with a special crew of six soldiers, to an area adjacent to the U.S. Army troop emplacements east of Rockford and at South Holland, on the south side. The surprise; in addition to the howitzer and squad, each helicopter would also deliver two, 10 kT (kilo-Ton) nuclear tipped shells. Ten hours before the planned NCNWC assault, the two squads would deliver their deadly payload.

The two-pronged attack was comprised of a regimental sized unit attacking from the southwest and an airborne battalion landing 'behind' enemy lines at O'Hare airport.

With luck, also know as the fog of war, the troops would arrive at O'Hare undetected, or if detected, the ground controllers would assume that they were replacements arriving after the devastation at Rockford and South Holland. Phony radio transmissions sent by the NCNWC pilots would aid in the charade.

Maybe he's right with the tactical nuclear solution, thought Robertson. *Sure would show Fitzpatrick we aren't just fucking around.*

Glen Ellyn, IL (NCNWC bivouac area)
1830 hours
November 10

Returning late from an all day patrol, Pierce unlaced his muddy combat boots, pulled them off and gave his feet a well-deserved massage. He'd heard it said that if you take good care of your feet, your feet would take good care of you. He wasn't sure if that was true or not. What he was sure was that his poor old dogs were barking loudly.

Laying back on the cot, Pierce wasn't sure what was worse, being here embroiled in combat, or being here without his family. The thought caused him to reach inside of his combat flack jacket, open an inside pocket held closed by Velcro, and pull out something precious.

Looking at the badly creased picture of his wife, Cindy and his daughter, Shasa, Pierce cringed. God, though he'd never tell Cindy, he really hated the name Shasa when she first suggested that was what they were going to call their first and only born. Didn't ask him, didn't seek his counsel, didn't debate the issue, just pronounced that her name was Shasa. Shasa?

Jones start to walk in through the canvas door of the tent, stopped quickly and said, "Oh. Sorry, Sarge. Didn't mean to disturb you."

Looking up as he pushed the worn photograph back down into the safety of the inner pocket in his flack jacket, Pierce, with a strange grin on his face said, " Why Lance Corporal Tyrone Jones, do come in and take a load off."

Jones walked in, wondering what was going to happen. Formal greeting with full rank included usually spelled disaster.

Pierce waited as Jones moved slowly across the confined floor space of the tent and sat down on his footlocker.

"So tell me, Lance Corporal Tyrone Jones, have you been a good boy today? Would God and country and your mama be proud of you today?" Pierce queried, the silly grin still on his face.

Jones, having absolutely no idea where this journey would take him replied meekly, "Yes, Sergeant. I was good today."

"Well, well. That makes two of us. Not only were you a good boy today, I, too, made God and country and my mama proud."

Jones was really starting to get an uneasy feeling. The second shoe had to drop any time now. He was just hoping it wouldn't land on him.

"Lance Corporal Tyrone Jones, please get up and drag my footlocker over here," Pierce asked as he swung his legs over the side of the cot and came to a sitting position. He watched as Jones dragged the heavy box across the six feet that had separated them.

"Use the chair, Lance Corporal Tyrone Jones," Pierce said as he worked the combination lock and after opening it, pushed up on the lid of the footlocker, obscuring Jones' view as to what was happening behind this impromptu curtain.

That's the third time he's called me Lance Corporal Tyrone Jones in less than two minutes. Either I'm in deep shit or the fucker's lost his mind, Jones thought as he watched Pierce rummage around in the footlocker. And sure enough, Pierce pulled out a holstered, pearl handled .45-caliber automatic.

The sonofabitch has flipped out and he's going to shoot me!

Jones mind raced as he sat frozen, unable to move. He was completely consumed with fear as Pierce dropped the .45 on the cot and went back into the footlocker, saying, "Ah, here it is."

As he watched Pierce close the footlocker lid, Jones felt a wave of relief surge over him for there sat Pierce, a bottle of Pinch scotch in his right hand, two old jelly jars in his left.

"I don't know about you Lance Corporal Tyrone Jones, but I sure could use a belt right about now," Pierce added as he placed the jars on the lid of the footlocker and poured each of them three fingers of scotch.

Reaching one out to Jones, Pierce said, "Ty, here's to us. Here's to our survival."

As both men drank, they felt a bond between them that separated them from the horrors of war. Under different circumstances, they could probably be good friends, maybe even best friends. But this was war and this was the army and they were in the chain of command. There would always be an invisible wall between them, but for these brief few moments, the walls were down, the stripes on the table and they were just two friends, sharing a moment's rest from an otherwise shitty day.

Pierce reached under his cot and pulled out his haversack. Opening up the restrain clips, he extracted the journal, waved Jones over to the cot and together they continued their on-going experience with Anthony Joseph Bender and the other residents of the Sandpiper Court subdivision.

October 15 – Day Twenty-Four

Time sure does have a way of flying by!

It seems like just yesterday that there wasn't any war and here we are, preparing to move the entire population of our little enclave to the Country Club. The area of the Club we are moving to includes the club house, which was next to the parking lot on the south side, sandwiched in between the seventh fairway on the east and the eighteenth green on the west, and about two hundred yards away from a cul-de-sac that held the original six builder's models on the northern perimeter. It was a great area for defense. The area was surrounded by hills and sand traps. The approaches were out in the open thanks to the fairways. This position gave us excellent fields of fire.

I got to tell you, this move was really a pain in the ass. Every single asshole, even the assholes I call my family, wanted to take every fucking piece of shit they owned. It was like no one bothered to listen when I spoke to them this morning. Some people even came up to me and said they needed five or six trips in the cars to get all their stuff over to the Country Club. These are the same people that were told to take food, clothing, guns and medical supplies. And they're over here with sewing machine, recliners, paintings and every other goddamn thing they own.

Anyways, it's now about 11:00 p.m. and we finally got every thing in order for the move tomorrow. I got to get some sleep.

October 16 - Day Twenty-Five

Well, the move to the Country Club is over and thank God!

From the crack of dawn until the final setting of the sun, what a bunch of bullshit.

It all started early when a certain red headed member of our subdivision, who will remain nameless, started bitching about the whole move. She couldn't understand why we had to move at all. And she wanted us to leave her and her husband at the subdivision and get this. She wanted us to protect them from over at the Country Club. She felt like she was entitled to this protection. I'm telling you, I was ready to pull out a gun and shoot the bitch right there because by then I had had it up to my eyeballs with that broad.

It really started over seven years earlier. Joyce and I had moved into the subdivision with our three kids. This nameless bitch and her wimp husband lived just down the block from our house. We tried to make friends with these people, but it was a real case of oil and water.

Anyways, we were kind of loud what with three young kids all feeling their oats and maybe we did leave some toys and bikes and shit in the drive way, but like who really cares. We paid for the house and what the fuck, we wanted to live the way we wanted to live. We had heard that they were unable to have kids of their own and I suspect she felt that if she couldn't have them, no one else should as well.

Well this uppity bitch thinks she's god's gift or something and keeps doing shit like yelling at our kids or when the wind blows some paper or something on her property, she picks it up and tosses it over the fence out back into someone else's backyard whether or not it even belongs to them. Talk about nerve.

And take the fence for instance. You know why most of the neighbors eventually built fences? Because they got tired of her bitching about seeing all of the junk in everyone's yard. And the junk; baseballs, bats, kid's toys. Nothing big or rusty or obnoxious. She's just a bitch.

Or, the time the kids were bringing home some discarded lumber from one of the new houses being constructed so that they could build a clubhouse in the tree line out back, they walked across her backyard or something and this bitch comes flying out on her broom yelling and threatening the kids. Well, Joyce hears the commotion, looks out the window and runs out to help the kids. This bitch stops yelling at the kids, turns and grabs Joyce, starts yelling at her and pushes her to the ground.

If it wasn't so damn strange, it would be funny.

This gal ain't cute or nothing. And she ain't no doctor or lawyer or anything. And they live in the same kind of house like the rest of us. So who the fuck does she think she is?

Though in all fairness, she does have one redeeming quality; her ass.

I got to admit I just love it when she out there in the summertime on all fours, pruning her garden. She's usually wearing a two piece bathing suit that doesn't leave anything to the imagination And she always got this little concave arch in her back when she works and she slowly sways back and forth, like she's just looking to be mounted. And after a while, she's kind of glistening with sweat. Man, I can still picture the mental image that tightly stretched bikini bottom...... But I digress.

I ended up telling her and her hubby to fuck off and we just left without them. About 5:00 p.m., they finally dragged their sorry asses into the Country Club and I didn't have any more trouble with them. And that was just the start of the day. All day long, people were complaining and moaning about what they couldn't take, why they couldn't go next in line, why they had to live with this family or that family, and on and on and on.

Even my son, Joe, got into a pissing match with me over some stupid box of souvenirs that he wanted to bring along. We argued for a few minutes before I lost control, yelled "No!" for the last time and told him to grow up and get to work.

In retrospect, that probably wasn't the right way to handle him but I couldn't very well make exceptions for my own kids. Could I? What the hell kind of leader takes advantage of his power? Yeah, I know. Stupid question. They all do!

Anyways, we finally complete the move around 8:00 p.m. There are only six homes plus the clubhouse. There are sixty-three of us. Talk about confusion.

I'm not going to bother detailing the housing arrangements here. They're really not to important other than to say that this unorthodox situation is placing a strain on us all.

Glen Ellyn, IL (NCNWC bivouac area)
1918 hours
November 10

Noticing that Pierce had stopped reading and moved his gaze upward off the page, Jones asked, "Lost in thought, huh, Sarge?"

"What? Oh, yeah. I'm not sure if this here soldier's lost in thought, or just plain lost."

Ty shook his head in agreement. "I sure do know what you mean."

Together, both men started to read once again.

October 17 - Day Twenty-Six

Today was a slow, lazy day for relaxing. People spent most of the time indoors, honoring the request to remain invisible to outside eyes. Everyone was pretty tired from the pack and move bullshit and they enjoyed the rest. The only people really working were the Defensive group, who were being assisted by the Scavengers. They were in the process of establishing defensive positions around the perimeter. We basically built the same type of bunkers out of dirt filled garbage cans, but this time, we went out of our way to incorporate them into the surrounding scenery as much as possible so that from a distance, they seemed to blend right in. I have no real good way of calculating the perimeter of the subdivision where we moved from. The area we were now living in though is probably one fifteen the space. This reduction in territory gave us a great deal of security in terms of establishing perimeter guards posts and feeling like we could prevent another infiltration by whomever killed the Dalton family, the Stantree brothers and Steve Kornat, the perimeter guard.

We ended up establishing a roughly triangular perimeter. One guard station was positioned at each corner of the triangle, with another position in the middle of each leg. This arrangement gave us good fields of vision and fields of fire.

The builder's models were not representative of the lot sizes that were offered in the development. Most were well under an acre. The models were on a cul-de-sac, which permitted prospective customers to park, and walk from model to model with ease. This

ended up being a blessing for us in terms of minimizing the area
that we needed to defend.

October 18th - Day Twenty-Seven

Once again, the day ended up without major problems. One thing that did surprise us and I feel pretty stupid for not checking this out before moving the population to the County Club, was that we didn't have any electricity. Somewhere in the quarter mile distance from our subdivision to the Country Club, the wires were down. In this new development, much of the wiring was underground and we couldn't have fixed anything even if we knew where the break was. As a result, people weren't really happy about this revelation.

We ended up going into Wheaton and argued strongly enough for the National Guard to give us an old generator to help power a couple of refrigerator for medical supplies and perishables. Additionally, we used it for a couple of lights that we used at night, especially when we had committee meetings.

Other than that, not too much going on. As we looked at our defensive perimeter, we decided to place our supply of Claymore minds mostly towards the corner of the triangle by the builders' models. This approach was fairly flat and open and we felt that this was the 'weak link' in our defense.

Other than that, the Scavengers also made a food run to Wheaton when they picked up the generator. We ended up with enough staples for about three days. This was disappointing in that just 2 week ago, our rations usually were enough to last six or seven days.

When we questioned Lieutenant Colonel Ralph Emerson, Illinois National Guard, he told us that the NCNWC had sent in some advance forces to start disrupting the supply lines. They really weren't directly causing a great deal of damage yet, but no one was taking any chances. The supply convoys were demanding adequate extra protection, which simply resulted in a slower flow of supplies. The NCNWC plan was working and they weren't even required to fire a shot. Just the mere threat of an attack was helping them accomplish their goals.

Colonel Emerson said he expected the situation to continue until our forces met and crushed their forces in battle. He reminded us that troops were taking up defensive positions east of Rockford and in South Holland to bunt the expected NCNWC attacks from the Wisconsin and Indiana borders.

We invited Emerson to visit us in the next couple of days to review our new stronghold and offer comments on the effectiveness of our defensive positions.

Wheaton, IL (Country Club)
0220 hours
October 19

In spite of being the leader of this merry band of scared shitless subdivision residents, Anthony Joseph Bender was just another name on the list when it came to guard duty. Sitting in the dirt filled garbage can bunker on the north corner of the triangle, TJ had a tough time keeping his eyes open. His shift ran from midnight to 4:00 a.m. and here he was, just over half way through and he could barely keep his eyes open.

What the hell am I going to do for the next one hundred and six minutes?

Just as he was starting to dose off, he heard some footsteps crunching dirt and then a voice whisper, "Guard two, this is Rover one. Guard two, this is Rover one."

Pushing back the cobwebs, TJ gripped his rifle tighter, moved around to aim it in the general direction of the voice and responded, "Rover one, name it."

When he didn't receive the immediate and expected response, he clicked off the rifle's safety mechanism and prepared to fire, realizing that while he didn't know where his target was, the sound of the shot would result in his fellow guards providing some desperately needed assistance.

Taking a deep breath, he picked out a shadow on the horizon and started to gently squeeze the trigger, but that motion was interrupted by the words, "Ah geez, dad. I forgot the password."

Sonofabitch, I almost blew my own kid away! TJ's mind screamed as he put the safety back on and whispered rather loudly, "Get in here. I damn near shot your head off, Joe."

Moving away from the small entranceway, TJ went back to looking out over his assigned area as his eighteen-year old son, Joe, crawled into the bunker on hands and knees, moving over next to his father.

"Sorry 'bout that. Kind'a forgot the words."

"How the hell could you forget 'Chicago Bears'? Huh? This ain't no fuckin' game out here. There's a goddamn war going on and...."

His tirade was interrupted as a sharp, shrill scream pierced the night, a sound in a voice that sounded uncomfortably like his wife's.

Rushing out of the bunker, gripping his rifle tightly and followed a moment later by Joe, TJ sprinted back towards the house that the Jamisons, the Komanskis and the Flanders were sharing with his family. As he got closer, his ears picked up the sounds of a general commotion. He could hear voices, but at this distance, the words were still indistinguishable.

Finally, he was close enough.

"Stop him. Get the sonofabitch!"

"It's the midnight killer, stop him!"

The sound of rifle shots, more screaming and yelling, someone rustling through the bushes coming this way.

TJ dropped to one knee and brought up the rifle. Joe, on his fathers' heels, mimicked the action and together, they prepared to face the assailant.

He yelled "Bill, Ed. I've got the front. Flush him."

The response was several more rifle shots and the bushes erupted as a figure came tumbling out, not more than twelve feet in front of father and son.

Startled by the sudden appearance Joe fired, but missed wide right. TJ, also caught flat-footed, swung his rifle around towards the figure that by now was only five feet away and moving quick, and fired off a quick round without aiming. The figure moaned, continued running past TJ and stumbled, falling down face forward.

TJ stood and chambered another round when Ed Flanders came running up, a flashlight in his hands, illuminating the back of the prone figure who was moaning and rolling, his hands wrapped around a small hole in his thigh, which was pumping blood.

TJ rolled the figure over, and when the light illuminated the face on the ground, TJ's spirits sank as he said, "God, Juan. I'm sorry. I heard Joyce scream and the shots and all. Then you come running out of the bush. Jesus, man. I'm sorry. I though it was the 'midnight killer'."

All Juan Hernendez could do was moan and groan. The bullet hole pumping so much blood that the bullet must have hit an artery.

"Juan, I'm sorry," TJ started to said again, his voice quivering with sorrow, "I just didn't know."

Just then, Bill Komanski and Joyce arrived, carrying another flashlight. When they got close, Joyce said in a hollow voice, "It's Juan Hernendez."

"I know. I accidentally shot him. He just came running out of the bushes. He's pretty bad shot up. Somebody get Doc Furgenson," TJ responded quickly.

"TJ, I mean that's the man who attacked me," Joyce offered in a quite, though disgusted tone of voice. "Juan was the guy in the house and he tried to kill me."

TJ, a look of disbelief on his face, transferred his gaze from Joyce to Juan Hernendez and noticed for the first time, that Juan was dressed entirely in black. He also noticed that he had streaks of black across his face as well as the backs of his hands. He also noticed that there was a large combat knife dangling in it's sheath secured to Juan's waist by a webbed military belt. And the light finally came on. Here, before them, was Juan Hernendez, resident of Sandpiper Court Subdivision, friend and neighbor, and killer. In addition to his own blood, Juan's hands were immersed in the blood of the Dalton family, the Stantree brothers, Steve Kornat and if not for some unexplained stroke of luck, TJ's family's.

TJ stood up, told everyone to move back, and said, "Juan Hernendez, by the power invested in me and for crimes against society, I sentence you to death."

Anthony Joseph Bender calmly brought the rifle up to his shoulder and cheek, aimed at Juan Hernendez, not even caring to hear what had driven him to kill his neighbors, and pumped a .303-caliber round squarely into the middle of Juan's forehead.

Glen Ellyn, IL (NCNWC bivouac area)
1927 hours
November 10

Pierce turned the page to the next entry.

October 19 - Day Twenty-Eight

Today was the hardest day of my life. I have never before killed a man and my execution of Juan, though maybe justified, really upset me. In hindsight, I'm not sure if this was the best course of action to take. Everyone here supports my actions, but still, I have the nagging feeling that I may have overstepped the boundaries. I know I will never be the same guy again. I'm not yet sure how I'll be different, but you can't kill someone without it having some affect.

But it's strange. While I feel bad, I don't really feel remorseful. There is a certain inner peace. I mean he did kill seven people and almost killed my family. Yet the peace has a strange, bitter taste to it.

And the problem was only worsened since Juan also had a family in our midst. Were Rosa and Rita Hernendez involved? Were they accomplices? Should they pay for the crimes committed by their husband and father?

I was surprised that a number of the residents wanted them executed on the spot. The racial prejudice that had lain dormant within our little community erupted with a fury that seemed unquenchable.

I finally decided to take Rosa and Rita to Wheaton and place them in the custody of Lieutenant Colonel Ralph Emerson, Illinois National Guard.

I ended up simply washing my hands of the whole situation. What's done is done.

October 20 - Day Twenty-Nine

We tried hunting again this morning with little luck. All totaled; two geese and three ducks, all mallards.

I'm not sure why the hunting was so bad. Very little flying. Could be other groups got the same idea and though there are no other blinds anywhere near us, the waterfowl could be getting some hunting pressure from other areas. We have heard gunshots from time to time, but no telling what they are.

Maybe next time will be better.

Glen Ellyn, IL (NCNWC bivouac area)
1943 hours
November 10

"Well, that's about it for me."

"Yeah," Jones said as he stood and stretched his lean frame towards the top of the tent. "I'm pretty damn tired myself."

"Goodnight, Sarge," Jones offered as he walked out of the tent.

Pierce, replacing the journal into his haversack, simply grunted in return and after laying back down onto his cot, was asleep in a matter of minutes, dreaming he was home again with Cindy and Shasa.

XVI

Galena, IL (abandoned farm field, eight miles west of town)
1650 hours
October 21

The two NCNWC Boeing-Vertol CH-47 Chinook helicopters stood under camouflage netting on either side of the ramshackle barn. The Chinook is a massive helicopter having lift capabilities in excess of 27,000 pounds. The Chinook was designed to be the mobile workhorse of the armed services. Capable of carrying forty-four fully equipped soldiers, the Chinook could also be configured as a flying hospital transport. In the medical mode, capacity was limited to twenty-four stretchers held in place by a customer frame arrangement to prevent movement during flight.

The twin rotor helicopter derived its power from two, massive Avco Lycoming turbine engines. Having a flight speed approaching one hundred twenty miles per hour when carrying its maximum payload, the Chinook has proven its value time and time again.

The NCNWC maintenance squad had just finished final preparations for the covert mission scheduled for 0945 hours tomorrow morning. Next to each helicopter was a 155mm howitzer, also hidden under camouflage netting. Next to each howitzer, was a wooden crate measuring three feet by three feet by forty inches. Contained within each of these crates were the two, deadly, tactical nuclear tipped shells.

Each howitzer was capable of launching the ninety-eight pound shells approximately nine miles, thus providing the gun's crew with a sufficient margin of protection from the low yield nuclear explosion.

The 10 kT tipped shells were set to airburst at one thousand feet above sea level. The airburst would assure maximum effectiveness in terms of the destructive potential of this small, tactical nuclear weapon.

Ground zero, a point directly under the initial explosion, would be completely vaporized within microseconds of the explosion. This destructive circle would eventually expand to encompass an area having a diameter of approximately three quarters of a mile. The next concentric circle of destruction, reaching for the next mile of so, would contain enough destructive force to kill or main an estimated 95% of the troops stationed in the blast area. Beyond this ring of death, the survival rate increased dramatically to over 50% with most of these injuries being due to force of the explosion as opposed to the heat wave generated by the nuclear detonation.

Each six-man squad assigned to each howitzer was given the instruction to bracket the target area and commence firing at exactly 0945 hours on October 21st.

The first shell was to be aimed at a point one mile to the east of center of the 3rd Airborne Division headquarters near Rockford, IL. The second shell would be fired one minute later, aimed at a point one mile west of center. The combined destructive power of these two tactical nuclear weapons was estimated to reduce the strength of the 3rd Airborne Division by just over 75%. This loss ratio as well as the shock of the attack would render the Division combat ineffective and useless.

At the same time this was happening, the howitzer assigned to the South Holland, IL raid would be firing its shells at its target. In this case, the destruction would fall on the heads of the 67th Armor Division, which had been reinforced by the 3rd Rangers Battalion. Once again, destruction of man and machine was estimated to be in excess of 75%.

In order to coordinate the attacks, the first Chinook would depart for South Holland from the abandoned farm at 0730 hours, thirty-five minutes earlier than the second. Their payloads, howitzers, shells and six man squads, would be on the ground by 0910 hours. The squads should have the howitzers ready for action by 0930 hours. Their firing mission commencing at 0945 hours and ceasing at 0946 hours, the six man squads had been instructed to leave the howitzers in place, after first disabling the firing mechanisms, and rendezvous with the main NCNWC attacking forces.

The maintenance sergeant, a veteran with almost thirty years of experience, wiped the sweat from his forehead with an oil-stained rag. Reaching up, he closed the communications access panel on the helicopter commonly refereed to as 'Mable', turned and walked towards the barn, his contribution to the mission completed.

Glen Ellyn, IL (NCNWC bivouac area)
0645 hours
November 11

Over a breakfast of watery, reconstituted powdered eggs, Pierce and Jones poured over the Journal, the reading of which was becoming an obsession. They each found themselves living vicariously through the action of TJ, admiring the man while at the same time feeling the same fears and anxieties that he must have felt.

October 21 - Day Thirty

I guess I've become jaded to the point where nothing surprises me anymore, though a lot that happens around here now would have surprised me if times were 'normal'.

Take today for instance. My wife, Joyce, and seven or eight of the other women come to me and demanded that they be given instructions in handling and shooting firearms. We did have some real basic training for them a few weeks back when out of necessity it became obvious that the women and older kids would have to pull guard duty, but admittedly, it really was basic stuff. But now here was this entourage demanding that they be given detailed, step-by-step instructions.

Okay, I guess it makes sense. The Hernendez affair caused quite a stir and the anticipated attack by the NCNWC is making everyone nervous. These things I can understand. But these women wanted to be educated because they wanted to go out on patrols and ambush the bad guys. I mean actually go out, set up an ambush and kill some NCNWC types.

Needless to say, we had some interesting conversations about this one for a period of time before I finally relented. Not to the patrol bullshit, but just to the education stuff. I sent Komanski into town to let the Police and National Guard know that we'd be having this instruction period so they wouldn't be concerned about the gunfire.

Our ammunition supplies were pretty decent. We allocated each woman ten rounds each of a .38-caliber pistol, .303-caliber rifle and 12-gauge shotgun. The instruction period was handled by Danny Davidson and Bruce Jamison. Verbal instructions lasted over three hours.

They started from scratch and went over everything including a number of 'dry fire' exercises several times before passing out any live ammunition. After the firearms instruction, Danny and Bruce spent a hour talking strategy, tactics and reviewing our defensive posture.

The women finally had the chance to show their stuff on the various targets that the guys set up in one of the fairway bunkers and I'll tell you, everyone including the women, were surprised by the accuracy of their results. Now I'm not talking bulls-eyes, but they threw the lead close enough to be effective.

The hidden benefit in all of this was that in addition to feeling more secure in their role as daytime guards, we honestly could use the additional firepower in case it hit the fan. Now I'm not a chauvinist or anything, but I didn't think the women had it in them. They surely proved me wrong.

Galena, IL (abandoned farm field, thirty miles west of town))
0730 hours
October 22

At precisely 0730 fours, the first Chinook lifted off on its deadly mission. The cables attaching the cannon to the belly of the helicopter strained at the weight of the 155mm howitzer, stretching taut to the point of breaking before the heavy gun finally gave up its hold on the earth. Within three minutes, the helicopter was out of sight behind the tree line on the eastern horizon.

Galena, IL (abandoned farm field, thirty miles west of town))
0808 hours
October 22

Running three minutes behind schedule, a time that the pilot knew he could makeup on the ninety minute run to the landing zone, the second Chinook departed.

Immediately after lifting off, the maintenance crew began storing all of their gear, expecting their own evacuation by helicopter at 0830 hours.

Rockford, IL - South Holland, IL, (landing zones)
0910 hours
October 22

Arriving on schedule, both chopper pilots carefully, but quickly, lowered the howitzers down to the ground and disengaged the cable hooks holding the cannons to the belly of the Chinooks. Immediately after, they flared twenty yards away, set down and as the doors opened, the Chinooks disgorged the six man squads and their wooden crates of tac-nuk shells.

Twenty minutes later, both crews were awaiting the commands of their lieutenants to fire the first shells at the distant targets.

At precisely 0945 hours, the two lieutenants issued identical orders to the two howitzer crews; "Fire".

Both guns barked and the crews scrambled to reload. Twenty seconds later, the order "Fire" was obeyed a second time and all twelve men, wearing specially darkened goggles flung themselves on the ground and awaited the coming of Armageddon.

Rockford, IL - South Holland, IL (nine point two miles east of the landing zones)
0947 hours
October 22

By the time the second atomic airburst rained destruction over the US troops, eighteen thousand, three hundred, seventy-eight soldiers were killed outright, another twelve thousand, six hundred ten were maimed or seriously injured and another three thousand, twenty-six injured sufficiently to demoralize them completely. The Army and Airborne groups lost enough materiel to reduce their combat effectiveness to zero.

The surprise nuclear attack also opened the front door and back door to phase two of the ambitious and deadly plan of Keshum Aguawada, the head of the NCNWC: the plan to place a stranglehold on Chicago and force President Paul Fitzpatrick to the bargaining table.

Wheaton, IL - (Country Club)
0948 hours
October 22

The rapidly rolling roar came out of the northwest like a fast moving, runaway freight train. Seconds later, like some hideous echo, a second roar cascaded down upon the subdivision from the southeast; followed by a third, then a fourth. Thus were the former residents of the Sandpiper Court subdivision, current residents of the Country Club, informed of the destruction of the U.S. forces assigned to protect Chicagoland.

What was still unknown at this early hour, was that NCNWC forces were preparing to land a battalion strength force at O'Hare airport as a further diversion to cover their regiment sized attack from the southwest. Within a couple hours of the nuclear explosions east of Rockford and in South Holland, an estimated forty-three hundred NCNWC troops and sixty-seven MBTs and APCs would be approaching from the southwest, near Morris. Their goal; link up near Wheaton in order to cut the western supply routes into Chicago.

October 22 - Day Thirty-One

The two pronged attack, nuclear in nature, completely took us by surprise. We were all shocked at the start of CWII when NCNWC detonated the nuclear bombs in Dallas, Seattle, Cheyenne and Washington, D.C., though in hindsight, it seemed like a reasonable strategy to get our attention, let us know they were serious and attempt, successfully, to cut the head off White America thus causing confusion, which help offset the imbalance between the size of their forces and the size of ours.

No one in their wildest dreams even considered the possibility that once again, nuclear weapons would be used in our own country. Clearly, the government forces have the same weapons, but have restrained themselves from launching missiles or dropping additional nuclear bombs on America soil.

Apparently, the NCNWC felt that this was the only way to continue the struggle, which the news reports had been saying was winding down, that victory for white America was just over the horizon.

One very critical piece of information that was introduced in the news reports of the early afternoon was the shocking results of the attack. The 3rd Airborne Division, the 67th Army Division and the 3rd Ranger Battalion were effectively wiped out with losses estimated to be well over 75%. Reports criticized the Army's plan of concentrating the troops such that the four explosions were sufficient firepower to take out so many soldiers at one fell swoop. The report went on to say that under normal circumstance, a division sized force would normally have an operating area under battle conditions of five to six mile across its front and run troops back as far as two miles. If this had been the case regarding the troop deployment near Rockford and South Holland, the report estimated that while over 30% of the troops would still have been killed or put out of commission through injuries, the remaining forces could have been used to help in the ground war. The reports were saying that someone was calling for an investigation and all the usual bullshit. Our little band of suburban commandoes were less concerned about what could've, would've, should've been done, and more concerned about what we had to do to protect our ass.

The news reports concluded with some rather bad news, as if it wasn't bad enough already, that NCNWC forces throughout the U.S. had once again stared to mount attacks and raids. Nothing too significant, but clearly an attempt to tie down other U.S. forces from coming to the aid of Chicago.

October 23 - Day Thirty-Two

The shock of the nuclear attack was still the topic of conversation at the Country Club. We were in a panic.

Lieutenant Colonel Ralph Emerson, Illinois National Guard, stopped by early in the morning to tell us we were on our own. He needed to dedicate his forces to protecting downtown Wheaton and the majority of the population. He was kind enough to bring along a few more weapons, another dozen Claymore mines, some food and water. He told us to go on strict rations. His men would deliver food once a week. He apologized for seemingly leaving us on our own, but told us that his opinion, the NCNWC wouldn't bother with such a small group as ours and that if we maintained a low profile, the whole battle may just move past us without stopping on our doorsteps. Right!

So, we're really on our own. I called a meeting of the committee heads to inform everyone about Emerson's comments and to develop a plan.

We decided that if the fight came to us from the north, east or west, we'd fight a delaying action and try to make in back into town. If the fight came to us through Wheaton, we'd move out to the east and try and link up with people in Chicago proper.

Emerson had also told us that a battalion strength NCNWC unit landed at O'Hare, somehow taking everyone by surprise. That meant an estimated eight hundred NCNWC soldiers as well as support equipment including howitzers, APCs, trucks, and Hummers were on the ground within thirteen miles of us as the crow flies and that their mission was to move south, pretty much through the Wheaton area, to tie up with a regiment of NCNWC troops moving northeast from the southwest. We were definitely going to get fucked in this deal and no one even offered to buy us dinner first!

So we spent the balance of the day digging in deeper, reviewing our defensive perimeter, assigning positions and fields of fire in case an all-out attack happened, that sort of stuff. But these events really got me thinking about this whole war and why we were fighting it in the first place.

I got to admit that while some people may consider me a closet bigot, I really don't have an ax to grind about Blacks or Hispanics or anybody. Now I don't particularly want one of them living next to me, even though that has happened over the years and we did become friends, my preference would be to live with my own as I'm sure most people would prefer. On the other hand, there are a lot of White folks I wouldn't want living next to me either.

I tried to discover why I feel like I do. I've always heard that you are the product of your environment, yet I know that neither of my parents were bigots. Like me, or more correctly, me like them, felt that separate, but equal, was good. Everyone should have the same chances and the same opportunities. What bothered them and bothers me, is that it seems like Uncle Sam always expects me to pay for someone else's problems. Now I guess you could argue that's what a democracy's all about, but I can't buy that argument.

Personally, I'm tired of people who say they're simply entitled to this or entitled to that. I'm not talking about the person who tries and fails for I think that person deserves help. I'll talking about that asshole, whether he's Black, Brown, Yellow, Red or White, who sits back and says "I want what you got".

Well, fuck you buddy, I ain't going to give it to you unless my old Uncle Sam makes me do it because it just ain't right and even then, it's just not right.

Everyone deserves a fair shake and an opportunity. But I'll be damned if I support everyone throwing what they got into the pot and divvying it up equally.

I suppose if you go back far enough in time, everyone will agree that the Whites fucked every other color there is. Hell, we'll even fuck ourselves if we have to!

I read somewhere that somewhere around ten million Blacks were brought over from Africa into slavery. Don't know if that's an accurate number or not, but the fact remains that we fired the first shot. It's equally true that we took the Red man's land away from him at the muzzle of a gun and the point of a sword. When slavery was outlawed, we felt no pangs of conscience in bringing over our Yellow brothers to work the mines and build the railroads. Double standards at it best, or should I say worst?

There is no doubt in my mind that we got what we asked for. Push someone, anyone, far enough and eventually they'll push back.

Is this some Darwinian force at work here, trying to correct the social order deformities that have resulted from man's inability to co-exist peacefully?

Glen Ellyn, IL (NCNWC bivouac area)
0725 hours
November 11

"You believe that shit. That fucking honky don't know what he's talking 'bout. Them fucks been sticking it to us for hundreds of years and that asshole don't even know what's going on," Jones said with conviction.

Looking up from the pages of the journal and moving his gaze over to Jones, Pierce asked, "Ty, how many White people you know?"

"I don't know. A bunch. Why? What's the difference?"

"I'm just trying to figure out if you know what you're talking about or if you're just reciting the gospel according to the oppressed."

"Whad'ya mean, Frank?"

"The way I see it, you and me are a lot like this here TJ guy," Pierce said softly and seeing that he had Jones' rapt attention, continued. "He's right, you know, about people being the product of their environment. But you also have to look at what that environment is to be able to determine if your environment is truly representative of what the environment teaches you to believe."

"You're losing me, Frank. What are you talking about? I know what my environment was. It was shit. I grew up in the slums of East St. Louis, IL. I never knew who my daddy was, my mom was always strung out on drugs, I joined a gang when I was twelve and the White man ain't never done nothing to help me. So what's your point?"

"My point is that the only thing you know about White people, or Brown or Red or Yellow for that matter, is what you was told when you was growing up. You don't know any White people so how can you say you know who they are or what they think or what they will or won't do for you?" Pierce said.

"People don't bother to find out the truth no more. Everyone believes what the hear on the street or watch on the TV. People have to start getting to know each other."

"What the hell for?"

"What for?! Are you kidding me?"

"No. I'm not kidding. What the fuck do I got to get to know mister Whitey for?"

"Because, TY, someday this war's going to end. Someday, soon I hope, we're going to lay down the guns, admit that this fight was a great big fucking mistake and try to put this country back together. There ain't no way we can live in this country, divided the way we are. You got all kinds of people living in all parts of this country. How are you going to get along we can't find a way to get along?"

"You know, I never even considered that. The war ending I mean. Just what are we going to do, Frank?"

Pierce just stared into Jones' eyes, not answering.

"Frank? You hear me?" Jones asked.

"Ty. I hope to God someone's thinking about that question because I sure as hell don't know."

Pierce turned the page and started reading, glancing up to see if Jones was also reading, realizing that someone definitely had to have the answer if this war was ever going to end.

October 24 - Day Thirty-Three

Things are moving pretty quickly around here. We've been hearing a lot of artillery fire during the day and at night, both the northern and southern horizons glow with fires.

Regular Army troops moved into the forest preserve south of town and brought in a battery of large bore, tracked howitzers. Ever since, they have been regularly firing shells up over our heads into the NCNWC troop concentrations about ten miles north of us. In return, the NCNWC batteries have been responding in kind, though they must have smaller cannons since a number of their shells are falling short, hitting Wheaton. In fact, a salvo hit our old subdivision and destroyed a couple of houses. Good thing we moved.

Well, got to run. We heard a lot of commotion last night and I think the NCNWC have patrols out. We've increased the night guard shift and now have twice as many people on the perimeter as before.

Wheaton, IL - (Country Club)
0645 hours
October 25

The sun had been up for approximately forty-three minutes and was welcoming in a beautiful day. Hardly a cloud spoiled the brilliant, deep blue sky. A gentle breeze was causing the slightest movements of trees and shrubs as they seemed to wakeup and stretch away the stiffness of a good night's sleep.

Ed Flanders, stirred to activity by the sheer beauty of the dawn, placed his rifle up against the inside wall of the garbage can bunker and tried to standup to stretch, his efforts being restricted by the five foot, three inch ceiling height. Yawning and half stretching, he gazed through the portal of the bunker and saw movement on the horizon about a thousand yards across the golf course just along the tree line at the northeast. Reaching for his binoculars, Ed knelt down by the firing port and used the earthen barrier to help steady his shaking hands, trying to bring the movement into view.

Sure enough, people. People wearing camouflage had just scurried across the fifth fairway and dove into one of the deep sand traps the surrounded the fifth green. Four of them appeared with one on point, two on the right flank and one on the left. They moved with precision, though never moving at the same time.

First, the point man would move up fifty or sixty feet. Then, he would throw himself prone on the ground to provide support fire for his comrades if required. Then the two right flank soldiers moved in unison, mimicking the movements of the first. This was followed by the soldier positioned on the left flank position performing the same ritual, which only served as a command to start the process all over again. This caterpillar like movement was bringing the patrol directly to the Country Club. Unlike two ships passing in the night, Ed Flanders realized that these two ships were on a collision course.

Flanders reached over and shook Bill Komanski's shoulder until the big burly guy sat up with a start, ready to punch out whoever had the nerve to disturb his sleep when he looked over and saw the anxious fear on Ed's face. Realizing that something was wrong, he crawled over to Flanders and peered out of the opening, seeing the movement on the horizon first hand.

Five minutes later, when the patrol had moved up to a point only six hundred yards away from the bunker, Ed was able to distinguish that the faces half hidden by the helmets and combat flak jackets were black.

Leaving Komanski to keep a lookout, Flanders knew he had to spread the word.

Scrambling from the bunker, Ed half crawled, half ran back to inform someone, anyone, that the NCNWC was moving in for an attack, or at least a reconnaissance effort. At the rate they were moving, they would be upon the Country Club proper in ten to twelve minutes.

Running into Danny Davidson who was fulfilling the role of rover that morning, Flanders told him about the patrol and rushed back to his bunker.

Within three minutes of his return to Komanski's side, the ambush was being prepared. Fifteen Sandpiper Court residents were on the front line ready for the patrol. Word was still spreading back through the rest of the encampment to prepare secondary lines of defense just in case. All of the meetings, discussions, training and practice were reaping a huge dividend as every single person knew their position, their task and knew exactly was expected of them.

The fifteen people on the north point of the defensive perimeter arranged themselves in classic ambush deployment. Looking like the letter 'L' laid on its left side, nine work-a-day people, people who just over a month before had been salesmen, or lawyers, or mid-level managers or accountants, lay prone behind a small ridge of dirt constructed to obstruct the enemy's view and provide the defenders with some modest element of protection. The other six formed the short leg of the rotated 'L'. In theory, the enemy forces would walk into the fields of fire of the nine, supported by enfilade fire from the six fields of fire on the defender's right flank. In theory, this ambush was designed to not only prevent the enemy from penetrating the defender's positions; it was designed to stop the assault with deadly force.

Anthony Joseph Bender was position right in the middle of the long leg of the rotated 'L'. The plan was to remain in position, motionless, awaiting the command to fire. The interlocking fields of fire were designed to throw up a wall of lead that few, if any, would survive.

The NCNWC soldier on point had just completed his get up, move fifty feet and drop routine, when he thought he noticed something up front, about sixty yards just left of center.

What the hell?

As he held up his hand to motion to the two soldiers on his flank to wait, he turned his head to see if they had seen his command. The two soldiers had in fact already started to get up, and seeing the command to stop stopped death in their tracks, standing there out in the open. Before the point man could yell and tell them to drop, the fusillade from the ambush slammed into his body and both of the soldiers who were standing up, looking like target range silhouettes to the defenders.

The fourth NCNWC soldier, seeing his comrades cut down in a flurry of gunfire, panicked, fired a quick burst of eight or nine shots from his M16, the bullets flying harmlessly over the heads of the defenders, his aim distorted by raw fear as he jumped up to run back to the tree line. Before he had managed his third step, several bullets had raced the seventy-two yards from the 'L' to his back and he was dead before he hit the ground; dead before he realized that he had really fucked things up royal.

A deadly silence fell over the battlefield even before the echo of the reports had faded. The fifteen men forming the 'L' had all been in school. Had all read about Gettysburg, Stalingrad and Waterloo. They had seen movies and watched men die on TV. They had read newspapers, and books, and magazines. And just like the visions seen in those movies, or read about in those stories, here before them was yet another battlefield. A new battlefield covered with four dead bodies. Bodies who only seconds before had been living, thinking, breathing human beings.

But never before had these fifteen individuals created a battlefield. Never before had this small group of people been involved in something so significant, so final.

TJ was the first to stand up and slowly start walking towards the figures lying lifelessly before them on the seventh fairway. After he had walked about twenty, feet, Flanders and Komanski started coming in from their position on the short leg of the 'L'. Then, all fifteen men, with looks of confusion on their faces, were wandering over towards the bodies.

As they stood around, seeing the carnage that they had created, no one spoke, no one moved. It was as if each man had for the first time viewed death firsthand. A death that they had inflicted upon another man, a death that each had had a hand in causing.

A distant rumble disturbed the silence of the moment as if God himself was opening the heavens in order to see clearly who had committed these abominable sins.

But this was no act of God. This was no heavenly apparition for as the sound grew louder thirty eyes seemed to find the source of the disturbance at once and what they saw would have made the appearance of God himself pale by comparison. For there, on the horizon, not more that eight hundred yards from where they now stood, came a tank and two armored personal carriers, crashing through the small pine trees and fairway junipers that separated the golf course from the open fields beyond.

As thirty eyes watched in terror, fifteen minds gelled into one common, fear filled realization that the NCNWC soldiers that they had just reduced to lifeless heaps had been the advance patrol for these behemoths, which were clearly beyond the limited defensive capabilities of the Country Club citizen soldiers. For those who live by the sword, die by the sword, and some old shotguns and rifles wouldn't be of much use against trained soldiers headed this way in armored vehicles. Judgment day had arrived and the grim reaper had a list in his hand, a list with fifteen names on it written in blood.

XVII

Wheaton, IL - (Country Club)
715 hours
October 25

In unison, the fifteen men ran back to their defensive perimeter positions, each realizing how feeble their protection would be against the firepower of a tank or APCs.

They all dove for cover as the first sharp report sounded on the horizon, followed a second later by a huge explosion twenty yards short of their positions. When the dust and dirt settled back down to earth, a crater three feet deep and ten feet in diameter remained as stark testimony to the power of the big gun.

Moving forward to the front of the three-vehicle task force, the tank fired again, disappearing in a cloud of white smoke as the propellants left the end of the canon tube, throwing the deadly projectile on its way to the defensive perimeter. Landing twenty yards over their heads, showering the first builder's model with shrapnel, the defenders knew that their ineffective positions were bracketed and that they were doomed.

Looking like a flock of geese flying in 'vee' formation, the NCNWC tank was flanked on either side by one of the APCs, each one being twenty yards right or left of center and twenty yards further back. TJ noticed that the turrets of the APCs were swinging left and right as if searching for another ambush, or in search of other targets of opportunity. In a second, it all became crystal clear in TJ's mind. The NCNWC sent out the four-man patrol to investigate this small cluster of houses, the houses TJ and the group now called home. Whoever was in command of the enemy force must have figured it was a better investment to risk four people running into a trap as compared to sending in his armor and falling victim to whomever or whatever might be hiding within the structures. Then the brief firefight and the NCNWC commander waited and watched. Watched as a group of *Civilians?* came stumbling out of dirt filled, garbage can bunkers. Knowing now that he didn't face regular army troops or even national guardsmen, the NCNWC commander ordered an immediate frontal attack having complete confidence that victory was at hand.

In the micro-seconds that it took for TJ to have those thoughts, he could see the tank maneuvering in for the final shot, the shot which would snuff out his life within the next few seconds. Behind him, a strange buzzing noise reverberated, growing geometrically louder with each passing second. Was this fear coming to perch on his shoulder?

Before he could even turn to look, he heard a strange "whooshing" sound, watching as a peculiar looking white line appeared before his eyes. He followed it and saw it reach out to embrace the tank in a huge fiery explosion. As the APC on the left rotated its turret, already spitting a hail of bullets from its 25mm chain gun, their path highlighted by tracer round, which glowed a deadly red even in daylight, TJ watched as another smoky, white line reached out, pointed and consumed the vehicle. A few moments later, the process was completed a third time as the second APC disappeared in a muted explosion, followed quickly by the enormous fireball as its internal fuel bladder erupted and burst into flames.

As these events were unfolding before him, the buzzing noise became oppressive, literally driving him into the ground. He felt a huge downward pressure, pushing him closer and closer into the dirt, or was the dirt rising to meet him? He was engulfed, as if the earth opened up and sucked him into its bowels. Struggling to regain his senses, TJ raised himself to his knees and watched as the huge insect flew overhead, dancing from side to side, in a 'dragonfly over the pond' motion.

Thirty feet above TJ, at the controls of the McDonnell Douglas AH-64 Apache, Captain John 'Bossman' Swift maneuvered the thirteen million dollar helicopter with the loving care one would show a virgin on that first faithful night. The three Hellfire ATGW rockets that his copilot/gunner, Lieutenant Deane 'Deeno' Fraser had launched at the NCNWC tank and two APCs, had worked beautifully.

On a routine patrol searching for NCNWC targets of opportunity since the bad guys landed at O'Hare, Bossman had noticed the brief puff of white smoke indicating the tanks' first shot towards the seemingly deserted structures. Charging across the open golf course, the NCNWC vehicles were not only targets too good to pass up, they maneuvered in such a manner that indicated they were unaware that the gunship was in the area. Acquiring the targets with their sophisticated equipment was easier than normal for the crew of the Apache as they flew nape of the earth to avoid direct detection. In one quick, head-on attack, the Apache took aim, fired, aimed, fired and aimed, fired in rapid succession, with the entire engagement lasting just under thirty seconds.

TJ watched as the insect became a helicopter. It slowly flew over to inspect each of the damaged vehicles, looking for survivors. Finding none, the helicopter rotated one hundred eighty degrees as it hovered. Slowly flying back towards the defenders, it stopped twenty yards short of the perimeter, waggled side to side in a friendly gesture of support, leaned right and accelerated out of view over the distant tree line.

TJ stood there for the longest time, thanking God for being alive, asking forgiveness for killing others.

XVIII

Glen Ellyn, IL (NCNWC bivouac area)
0645 hours
November 11

Settling down next an overturned HUMMER, a casualty of an earlier battle, with another one of Cookie's delightful battlefield dinners consisting of some brown, gray, watery stew, Jones and Pierce tried to relax after a long day patrolling the western suburbs of Chicagoland.

These were strange times. Here they were, a squad of a platoon of a company of a battalion smack in the middle of the enemy, an enemy that was disorganized and unprepared to fight a battle in their own backyards; literally.

The elimination of the regular army forces assigned to defend Chicago left the task up to national guard troops, police and local militias, this last category a stretch because they were in reality simple groups of neighbors with guns. Everyone wanted to defend their own and no more. Since no one would leave their home, or subdivision, or town to fight someone else's fight, Pierce found that he and his patrol could generally move around with impunity. In fact, vast, contiguous tracts of land were left open for exploitation, allowing his patrols to often proceed without fear of being spotted. This meant long patrols, trying to gather as much intelligence as possible.

Long patrols also meant tired feet and aching backs. Humping around for hours carrying over fifty pounds of shit in your sack wasn't for the faint of heart.

"I'm telling you, Sarge. This is fuckin' horse meat," Jones croaked as he forced down another mouthful. "That fuckin' buddy of yours is feeding us a fuckin' horse. I'm telling you I know because I just ate the fuckin' saddle."

Grinning at Jones, Pierce added, "I do believe you're teasing me, Ty. Why my ol' buddy Cookie would do no such thing. A horse is a beautiful and intelligent creature. Not some animal God meant to grace a man's table. If anything, this is rat meat. Had it once in Kuwait. Yep. If it's anything it's rat meat, pure and simple."

Coughing up a mouthful of whatever it was, Jones laughed so hard he started to cry. Before you could say 'rat meat or horse meat', both men turned their plates over and scrapped them clean, each believing that the other might in fact be right.

Washing their mouths out with lukewarm coffee, Pierce reached deep into the haversack and extracted the journal. Motioning Jones over, both men once again saw life through TJ's eyes.

October 25 - Day Thirty-Four

The shit hit the fan today!

Just after sunrise, we spotted a small NCNWC patrol making its way towards the Country Club. We setup an ambush and took the four of them out just as they spotted us. Our relief was tempered with the knowledge that we took the lives of these guys without true provocation. Yeah, they were the enemy, but they were people, just like us. Probably had families, probably didn't like the war and just like us probably wanted to have the whole goddamn mess be over with.

We didn't let them fire first. They were heavily armed and were professionals. We hit them first and we hit them hard.

Moments after this battle, we were surprised by the appearance of a tank and a couple of those APCs Man, talk about getting the shit scared out of you. These guys opened fire at about seven hundred yards with a fucking tank. Like what are we supposed to do? Shot back with a 12-gauge shotgun?

We were fucking dead when all of a sudden one of those helicopters you see in the war movies appears out of nowhere and mows down the NCNWC with rockets of some kind. Blew em' right off the map.

The pilot comes back, gives us some John Wayne salute by shaking his chopper from side to side and flies off. Talk about salvation. It's great to be alive!

October 26 - Day Thirty-Five

We spent most of the day trying to remove as much of the wreckage of the tank and APCs as we could. We figured that by making them disappear, we could once again remain invisible. We weren't sure if anyone in the vehicles got off any radio calls or anything telling other NCNWC forces that we were here. We hoped not but who knows.

It was pretty grisly when we first got to the wreckage. The two APCs must have been aluminum or something. They pretty much just melted away. Not too much left of the bodies. Enough to know they were bodies, but mostly charred bones.

The tank was different. The rocket killed everyone and there was a small fire towards the front of the turret where the rocket must have struck, but inside, well, it was pretty gruesome.

Bodies and pieces of bodies totaled probably four guys. Guts, arms, legs, brain. All kinds of shit all over. On the positive side, we were able to recover the weapons from the four soldiers we killed in the ambush and picked up some more stuff out of the tank.

After an hour or so, we figured it would be impossible to really make the wreckage disappear so we just shoveled a lot of sand on top and threw a bunch of branches over everything to at least conceal their silhouettes.

Lieutenant Colonel Ralph Emerson, Illinois National Guard, stopped by to find out what the fireworks the day before had been all about. He was surprised with the battle report, even more surprised that we had survived without taking any casualties. He didn't know where the helicopter came from or how it found us. All he knew was that he didn't call it, that without it we'd all be dead and that if it hadn't appeared, the NCNWC could have moved along all the way down to Wheaton proper. He said he respected and admired us, but I could tell that he really thought we were simply the luckiest bunch of assholes he ever knew. Other than this activity, the rest of the day was uneventful.

October 27 - Day Thirty-Six

We heard a report on the mid-day news that gave us all a little more insight as to what was going on in Chicago proper. I must admit that since the start of CWII, I've been pretty caught up in what's happening to us and haven't done a good job of capturing any information about the rest of the country, or even Chicago for that matter. I though I would use today's entry to rectify that situation.

I know I said in one of the early entries that there had been a mass migration of non-Whites out of the cities. And while this is true, you have to realize that this was a generalization. Hard-core members of NCNWC couldn't move out quick enough. But Joe average and his family couldn't just pick up and move. A large number of non-Whites remained in the major cities.

After the breakout of hostilities, the big cities like Chicago, found that a series of pockets had developed. Integration was never real big in Chicago. The south and southeast are generally Black as is the near west. Near north was predominately Hispanic as is the southwest. Chinatown is obviously Chinese. The far north and west and far southwest are pretty much White. After the first few days of the conflict, these pockets became islands within the island called Chicago. Various no-man lands developed isolating these pockets further.

Now I'll be the first to admit that every single Black or Hispanic or Chinese in these areas wasn't walking around carrying guns and shooting Whitey. In fact, most of these people were just as scared as the rest of us and stood an equally good chance of becoming a casualty.

But, fearful of each other, the races separated and didn't come into contact.

The Whites didn't trust anyone. The Blacks and Hispanics also had a history of conflict and while they may have joined forces in the combat areas and sided with each other philosophically, there was no love lost between them in the Chicagoland area. To each his own.

There weren't too many battles being fought in Chicago, or other major cities. Both sides had eventually adopted a tacit agreement to wage war against the warriors, not the public at large. NCNWC radio mentioned early in the conflict that the attacks of the first few days were part of their overall strategy to awaken America to the seriousness of their intentions and to force all parties to the bargaining table. Having failed in this approach, the NCNWC attacked the US Army troops near Chicago with nuclear weapons to once again demonstrate their continued resolve.

The fighting that did take place in the cities tended to be small groups fighting against small groups. A gang of Whites or Blacks or Hispanic or whoever would attack a gang of somebody else. Mostly snipers, raids for food or weapons, occasional rapes, that sort of stuff. Conquering and holding territory never seemed important and wasn't in anybody's best interest. It just stretched the assets used for defense.

There were some pretty large military type battles, however. The fighting in the southern and southeastern states tended to be very severe. Most of the military bases are in these parts of the country. Numerous company and battalion sized actions occurred as a matter of routine. The largest fights were reminiscent of the first Civil War in that the occurred in and around the D.C. area. Even though there was residual radiation left over from the initial attack, people viewed Washington as the seat of power and while no one tried to capture the city proper, or should I say the ruins of the city proper, that general area still had some appeal to it. Los Angeles was also a highly contested area because of the racial mixture there. A couple of cities like San Antonio, TX and Newark, NJ, where the racial mixture was skewed towards non-Whites that the White population was driven out, also had some rather large battles as both sides maneuvered for victory.

Glen Ellyn, IL (NCNWC bivouac area)
0722 hours
November 11

Just as Pierce was turning the page, a tremendous explosion picked him and Jones up about two feet and slammed them both back down, hard. Seconds later, before either soldier could even start to regain their balance, a second, then third explosion followed in rapid succession. And as fast as the fury hit, it stopped.

Squinting to protect his eyes from the dust that lingered in the air, Pierce got up on his hands and knees, ready to dive back to the relative safety of the ground if another shell hit their encampment. As he continued to look around, he noticed Jones lying on his stomach, no movement evident.

"Ty. Ty!" Pierce yelled as he crawled over to the prostrate figure, fearing the worse. "Ty. Can you hear me?"

Rolling Jones over, Pierce sucked in a deep breath as he saw blood streaking down the entire left side of Ty's face. Gently cradling the boy's head in his arms, Pierce leaned closer to his ear and whispered, "It's okay. I'm here, Ty. Ain't no one gon'na hurt you anymore."

As tears were starting to form in Pierce's eyes, Jones started to moan and move his arms. Slowly, moans turned into words.

"Frank, what the hell happened?.

"Not sure. Either art'y or mortars."

"Man, I feel like shit," Jones said as he first blinked, and then slowly opened his eyes completely. "How bad am I hurt?"

"Well, slugger. You ain't dead," Pierce added, a grin starting to spread across his sweat stained face. "But you sure had me scared there for a while."

"Now you know how I felt, Sarge, when you stopped that bullet with your helmet the day we found the journal."

All Pierce could do was to continue to smile, glad that Jones was still alive and apparently not hurt to badly.

"You know, Sarge. I didn't hear that one coming. Did you?"

"No. That's why I'm wondering why we're still alive. By all rights, we should be pushing up daisies. I guess that just goes to show you that there's always an exception to the rule."

Pierce gently laid Jones back down on the ground and reached over to get his canteen. Pouring some water into his left hand, Pierce wiped most of the blood away from Jones' face. The wound was near the hairline, just over the left eye. Surprisingly, in spite of the tremendous amount of blood, the cut was rather shallow. It was more of a scalping blow than a deep contusion. Reaching into his haversack, Pierce pulled out a field compress and secured the bandage to Jones' head.

With his sergeant's assistance, Jones was finally able to get to his feet and Pierce helped him walk to his tent, but not before he bent over and picked up the journal.

As they walked slowly towards the tent, they both had an opportunity to survey the damage. Three shells, probably 81mm mortar rounds, had landed just the other side of the HUMMER that Pierce and Jones had been using as a backrest while they were reading the journal. Without that vehicle as protection, the shrapnel from the exploding shells would have surely killed them. Fortunately for their unit, the shells had hit the camp just on the outside of the perimeter. No real damage to equipment or supplies, and only a few walking wounded, mostly cuts and bruises.

Settling down for a well needed rest, Ty quickly fell asleep. Pierce remained at his side until Jones began to breathe rhythmically. He slowly got up, walked to the end of the tent, turning once to look again at a friend who just stared death in the face and came away a winner.

XIX

Glen Ellyn, IL (NCNWC bivouac area)
1830 hours
November 11

Returning from the day's patrol, Pierce stopped by to check on Jone's condition. When he entered his tent, Pierce saw that Jones was sitting on the edge of the cot, his hands holding his head. The field compress bandage had been removed and replaced with a conventional bandage that wrapped a large portion of Jones' head like a mummy.

"So how you doing, Ty?" Pierce queried.

"Oh, hi, Sarge. Doing pretty good," Jones offered as he picked up his head and looked at Pierce, wincing from the throbbing pain. "Doc says I was mighty lucky. Eighteen stitches. Just like a fuckin' injun tried to scalp me or something. A fraction more and good-bye earth, hello heaven."

"You sure scared the hell out of me when I saw you face down in the dirt. Thought you bought the farm for sure."

"Gon'na take a lot more than some ol' mortar round to kill this here soldier."

"Just glad you're okay," Pierce said as he walked over and sat down next to Jones. "You know it's pretty hard to find good people up here at the front and I just about got you trained. I'd sure hate to have to go through the bullshit of turning some other private into a lance corporal."

Jones turned to look at Pierce. His suspicions were confirmed when he saw the smile on Pierce's face. Pierce's words were spoken softly, as one would speak to a friend. The smile lent additional credence to the fact that Pierce really liked him and was really grateful that he pulled through with only a relatively minor head wound.

"Frank, I appreciate all you've done for me. I know I've been trouble from time to time, but you always stuck by me. Thanks."

"Don't mention it, Ty. Just glad to see you up and around. When will you be able to return to duty?"

"Doc says a couple of days."

"That's all. You sure you'll be okay?"

"Absotively, posilutely, Master Sergeant Franklin B. Pierce."

"Glad to have you back, Lance Corporal Tyrone Jones."

XX

Glen Ellyn, IL (NCNWC bivouac area)
2005 hours
November 11

As Pierce was undressing for the night, he remembered that he and Jones had been interrupted by the mortar attack and never finished reading the events of October 27th in TJ's journal. Though he felt some strange sense of guilt in not waiting for Jones to join him, Pierce wanted to read the rest of that entry. He sat down on the edge of his standard issue military cot and reached into his haversack to retrieve the journal. He pulled it out and froze, noticing that a small amount of Jones' blood now stained the cover. Seeing the drops of blood brought back with amazing clarity just how close both men had come to dying earlier in the day.

Opening up the journal, Pierce started to read.

After the breakout of hostilities, the big cities like Chicago, found that a series of pockets had developed. Integration was........

Pierce turned the page after realizing that they had read this part.

The Whites didn't trust anyone. The Blacks and Hispanics also had a history of conflict ....

Read that, too, Pierce thought.

Now there were some pretty large military type battles. The fighting in the south and southeast ....

Read it.

A couple of city like San Antonio, TX and Newark, NJ, where the racial mixture was such that the White population was driven out, also had some rather large battles as both sides maneuvered for victory.

Ahh, here we go.

But the strange part of this whole war is that no one seems to want to be fighting it. There's a couple of hot heads on both sides, but the guy on the street just wants the fucking thing to end. It just isn't worth it. Egos are getting in the way of common sense. Both sides keep offering to talk peace, but both sides are also demanding that certain conditions be met before they actually get to the table. The result of this is that people keep getting killed for no good reason. These fucking politicians are playing a game of chess with you and me being the pawns. If that ain't bullshit, I don't know what is.

Pierce, turned the page, saw the entry start for the next day and decided to wait until Jones was present so that they could continue the journey together, just as they had started.

As he replaced the journal back into the safety of the haversack, Pierce reflected on TJ's words.

Who indeed would win, if such a thing were possible, in this conflict? Both sides have lost uncountable numbers. The initial strikes on September 15th, though designed to kill Whites, actually killed a number of non-Whites. NCNWC propaganda suggested that this was not true, that this was continued evidence that White America was attempting to deceive non-Whites. However, the NCNWC leaders and the NCNWC military forces all knew the truth before hand. They knew that the nuclear strikes would kill anyone and everyone without regard to race, religion, age or creed. Weapons of this type are not selective in their destruction.

Furthermore, the NCNWC leadership knew in advance of the outbreak of CWII that military victory was impossible. There just weren't enough soldiers, equipment and materiel to wage a successful conflict against a population that outnumbered them by more than three to one.

So if total victory was unachievable, why fight? Fight for the benefit of the masses? Fight for the benefit of the few?

The more Pierce wrestled with the questions the more he became confused, the only issue coming into focus was the utter futility of the armed struggle. In an instant, he stumbled on one of the truisms of war; there are no winners, one side simply loses less than the other side.

The enormity of this simple realization weighed heavy on his mind, his soul, his very essence. In that moment, he decided to dedicate his life after the conflict ceased to helping the country rebuild itself; to helping build the new order.

XXI

Wheaton, IL (Country Club)
0638 hours
October 28

"Pssst. Hey, Kyle. Pssst. You ready?" Jason Komanski, age eleven, whispered as he poked Kyle Granger, twelve, in the ribs.

"Yeah. I'm up. Did ya think I'd let you go alone?" Kyle whispered back in an angry tone.

"Come on then. Let's get out' a here before anyone else wakes up."

Jason and Kyle had been friends on and off for almost six years. They were close enough in age to play together around the house, but as soon as they started school, Jason, a year younger and a grade behind Kyle, first encountered the wall. An invisible wall that peer pressure had erected.

You can't expect a first grader to play with a kindergartner. Well, can you?

This made their friendship difficult because the boys really enjoyed each others' company, but the peer pressures of the school scene imposed these seemingly strict, almost caste-like rules. So they learned to exist in both worlds. Friends and compatriots while playing in the neighborhood ands arms length acquaintances in the other.

"Take your backpack, Jason. And don't forget to take the food."

"What are you? My mother?"

"Just do what I tell you and let's get out'a here," Kyle retorted, gathering his own gear.

The boys slipped out past the rest of the kids sleeping in the communal style kid's room, actually the basement of one of the larger model houses. They slowly crawled up the squeaky wooden staircase, hoping that the noise would go unnoticed.

Jason and Kyle were tired, damn tired, of being treated like the rest of the kids. Here they were in fifth and sixth grade and they were forced to go through all of that crap the babies and young kids were made to do every day. No baseball, no football, no running around. They spent most of the day time in the stupid basement listening to stupid stories about stupid fairies and stupid bunny rabbits.

The women who ran the Child Protection group spent all of their time on the girls and babies. Mr. Smyth, the only man involved decided he'd let the women do most of the work and he was always off doing something else. It was kind of strange because Mrs. Pedopoulos always seemed to be gone whenever Mr. Smyth was gone. The other moms talked about it a little, laughing when they were telling the stories, but every time the boys asked what was so funny, no one ever answered.

Reaching the first floor, the boys crept down the hall to get to the back door. Just before they left the house, Kyle reached out and grabbed the rifle that was leaning up against the doorjamb.

"I'll carry it," Jason whispered.

"I got it first so I'll carry it. Besides, you never held a real gun before. This thing's pretty heavy."

"Come on, Kyle," Jason said a little louder. "Let me carry it."

"Quiet, Jason. You'll wake up the whole house if you keep screaming like that. You can carry it when we get out in the woods. Now shut up."

Slowly opening the back door, the boys crept out of the house and ran over to the big hedges that separated the structure from the parking lot of the clubhouse. So far so good, since the guard positions were designed to face outward, no one had seen them so far. They had been planning this trip for over a week. They were just plain tired of being cooped up with the kids. All this action going on and they got to play 'patty-cake' and crap like that.

The ambush and fire fight between the helicopter and the tank was the last straw. If they were ever going to prove that they were men, capable of defending the women and children, they had to do it now.

The plan was really quite simple. Take a gun, sneak out of the encampment, hunt down some enemy soldiers and fight them. Fear of death, or the unknown didn't enter into the equation.

"Someone was trying to hurt us and our families and well, that's just not right. We have to show them that they can't do that kind of stuff. Besides, once we show the grownups that we can fight, why I bet'cha they let us pull guard duty and stuff like that," Kyle had told Jason. Seeing the wisdom in the older boy's logic, Jason readily agreed and the pact between the two boys was sealed.

Now that the first challenge, getting out of the house without getting caught, had been accomplished, the next hurdle presented itself. How to get across the defensive perimeter without being seen?

Crawling on hands and knees towards the edge of the row of high bushes, the excitement of what they were doing started to grow, almost beyond control. Maneuvering past one enemy to go out and fight another enemy. Cowboys and Indians. The North and the South. Schwartzkopf and Sadam Insane. Talk about grabbing life by the collar and shaking it for all it's worth.

"Quiet. They're going to hear you," Kyle scolded Jason. "Let's wait here a few minutes and see what's going on. I'm not sure how we're going to get past everyone. The minute we get out there on the course, or on the road, they're going to spot us."

No sooner than Kyle had uttered those words, the came a banshee scream out of the east.

Looking up, both boys finally spied the movement of a jet fighter as it streaked across the golf course at near tree top level, quickly followed by a second, then third plane.

Jason grabbed Kyle by the arm and yelled, "Now or never" as both boys grabbed their backpacks and ran across fifty open yards of fairway before diving into a culvert that paralleled the eighteenth fairway.

Hunkering down and catching their breaths, both boys smiled at each other, feeling even more confident of their capabilities. They would be boys for just for a little while longer. The glory of triumphal combat beckoned loudly and was impossible to be ignored. And like the moth to the flame, the adventure continued.

Wheaton, IL (six miles northeast of the Country Club)
0910 hours
October 28

Ending up walking northwest on the Prairie Path, the boys stopped for a short rest.

"You know, Jason, this ain't all that easy. Why don't you carry the rifle for a little while. The damn things gettin' pretty heavy."

"Really?! Sure, Kyle, I'll carry it," Jason replied as he stood up, walked over to where Kyle had leaned the rifle against a fence post and picked it up, admiring its weight. "Man, if I ever see one of them En-See guys, he's dead meat."

Jason returned to where he had been sitting and sat down crossed legged, holding the rifle in his lap, stroking the stock. As he was doing this, Kyle leaned over on his side, his left hand holding up his head, asked, "You think you really could? I mean, really shoot someone?"

"Sure."

"Come on. Really shoot someone? I mean shoot 'em dead?"

"Well, if they were hurting my mom or someone. Yeah. I guess I could do it. How 'bout you?"

"I don't know. I guess so. Yeah. Me, too. I'd do it."

And with that, both boys leaned back on their packs to rest a little while longer.

They had moved up the Prairie Path about five or six miles during the first couple hours of the adventure. Out and about for a walk down the trail; half the time looking for the bad guys, the other half throwing stones and telling jokes. They were resting in an open area just south of when the Prairie Path crossed Army Trail Road. After another ten minutes, they had recuperated enough to get on with the hike.

The plan was to move up the path another mile or so, and set up an ambush point. Great plan; two boys, one gun, seven miles from the closest known source of help and safety. Yet, ignorance is bliss.

They gathered their stuff, adjusted their packs and with Jason proudly lugging the rifle, once again started up the Path.

When they reached Army Trail Road, Kyle put his hand up like they always do in the war movies and said in an authoritative voice, "Halt."

"Yes sir," came the quick response from Jason.

"We'd better wait here a while and see if anything's goin' on before we cross the road," Kyle suggested, dropping to his right knee after seeking cover behind a large oak tree. "You watch on the right. I'll take care of the left."

Wheaton, IL (Country Club)
0910 hours
October 28

At the very same moment, Kathleen Granger, one of the mothers assigned to the Child Protection group ran up to Frank Smyth to report that her son Kyle and Jason Komanski were definitely missing. She and the other mothers had searched all over and didn't find them anywhere. They had looked everywhere within the confines of the Country Club with the same result. The unspoken fear that they all shared; a repeat of the Sara Hollis incident.

Immediately, a search party was organized, but where to search quickly became the problem. The boys could have gone in any of the four major directions. The decision was made to contact the National Guard and Police to alert them that the boys may be wandering through the town somewhere. Ed Flanders and Kathleen Granger took care of these communications.

The search party was divided into three teams of three each. The plan was to use cars to drive around the local streets and see if they could get an idea as to where the boys might have gone. Jim Sawyer, Brian Jenkins and Bob Pedopoulos headed east on North Avenue in one of the Jeeps. Bill Komanski, TJ and Rich Bender took the other Cherokee and were to first drive through the old subdivision just in case, and then head west on Geneva Road. Frank Smyth, Jack Furgeson and Phil Savatini, in an old, blue pickup, where charged with heading north on Pleasant Hill, then west on North Avenue.

Hand held radios would keep the group in contact for the first three or so miles. After that, they would be out of radio contact and on their own.

Wheaton, IL (six miles northeast of the Country Club)
0920 hours
October 28

"Come on, Jason. We've been sitting here at least ten minutes. Nothing's happening. Let's cross the road."

"Okay. Let's do it," Kyle said as boy boys jumped to their feet and ran across the deserted, four-lane road.

Reaching the other side, the boys dove for cover behind the front end of a late model Toyota Prius, which had crashed into a drainage ditch that ran parallel to the road. Looking around, half expecting the entire NCNWC army to be chasing them, they didn't hear anything, or see anything out of the ordinary. Not a sound. Not even a bird in the sky. Nothing, except for that terrible smell.

What the heck was that terrible smell?

Turning towards the windshield of the late model Prius at the same time, both boys became aware of the man sitting in the driver's seat, partially slumped over the steering wheel. Only it wasn't a man. Not really. Every man Kyle and Jason had even seen in their whole life had had a face. You know; two eyes, a nose a mouth, but not this man. This man had a big open hole where his face should have been. And the hole was moving, swirling with some strange, small motion. As the image burned more deeply into their very souls, the boys realized that it wasn't the hole that was moving, it was the bugs and maggots that had infested the huge wound, feasting on the corpse.

"Jesus Christ!"

"Ka--Ka--Kyle. Let's get out' a here," Jason stammered, feeling his stomach starting to react to the horrific scene.

Jumping to his feet, Kyle reached over and grabbing Jason by the back of the shirt, directed both of them up the trail. Looking back as they were running, both boys encountered something soft, yet hard with their feet and went down in a tumble.

Kyle, recovering first, looked back at what they had stumbled over and saw another body, this time a women. She didn't have any clothes on and her skin was a strange gray color. There were flies and bugs on her, too, but she did have a face. The only real damage seemed to be this big cut across her neck and some dried blood between her skinny legs. And there was dried blood all over the ground near her head. It had pooled near where she lay and it looked like a gallon or more.

Kyle turned to look at Jason, who had started to cry.

"Come on, buddy. Time to go," Kyle said gently and for some strange reason, probably just unconscious thought, steered Jason even further up the Prairie Path. Every step they took only added to the distance between them and the safety of the Country Club. The safety of mom and dad.

Wheaton, IL (six miles northeast of the Country Club)
1020 hours
October 28

"Goddamit. Where the hell are those kids?" Frank Smyth said out loud to no one, and everyone.

"God only knows, Frank."

"Yeah," piped in Phil Savatini, apparently in complete agreement with Jack Ferguson's' assessment. "No tellin' when they went or why. It'll be damn lucky if we ever see them kids again."

"I just can't believe they found a way to sneak out'a camp," Frank said, instinctively feeling guilty since these kids were under his charge. "I just feel so damn responsible."

"Take it easy, Frank. No one's blaming you."

"Yeah. Right. You didn't have to tell Komanski his kid was missing. I did. Though the guy was gon'na kill me or something. Went fuckin' ape-shit."

"Let's just keep looking."

Wheaton, IL (seven miles northeast of the Country Club)
1012 hours
October 28

Having hiked up the trail about one hundred yards beyond the up-ended car with the faceless man and the naked woman, Jason finally sat down and just bawled his eyes out.

"I've never seen no dead people before," Jason blurted between sobs. "I mean, they were just dead."

Kyle sat down beside Jason and in an instinctive, brotherly motion, wrapped his left arm around Jason's shoulders, "Yeah. That was something, wasn't it. The only dead person I ever saw before was an old uncle. He must have been eighty or ninety years old. That was pretty bad. But this stuff--did you see the guy? He had no face, like it got shot off or something."

"Kyle. I wan'na go home. I don't like it here no more. We're not soldiers. I just want to go home. Please, Kyle. Let's just go home."

"Sure. Just stop crying, okay? It was just a couple of dead people," Kyle cajoled, trying to keep his voice from wavering. "Let's go home."

Wheaton, IL (intersection of Army Trail Road & the Prairie Path)
1105 hours
October 28

By the slimmest of margins, an example of luck at its ultimate, Kyle and Jason came into view of the intersection just as the truck carrying Frank Smyth, Jack Furgeson and Phil Savatini slowed down and drove past the Prairie Path. Phil spotted the kids and yelled at Frank to slam on the breaks. The squeal of the screeching tires froze the kids in their tracks, not knowing what the hell was going on. Phil jumped from the car and yelled to the kids. Jason and Kyle, hearing a familiar voice, ran to the truck that was still partially obscured in the dust cloud that was generated by the sudden stop. Talk about a reunion. Everybody hugging everyone. The kids glad to be home, the adults grateful in finding the kids alive.

After a few moments of auld lang syne, the kids piled in the cab with Frank Smyth while Jack and Phil crawled up into the box at the back of the blue pickup.

Across the street, hidden from view by a knocked over billboard telling you to DRINK COKE, the NCNWC solider lined up the truck in the open sights of his LAW, pulled the trigger, launching the small rocket housed within the firing tube. In a fraction of a second, the rocket traversed the two hundred three feet between the muzzle of the LAW's tube to the left quarter panel of the pickup. The exploding gas tank immolated the passengers in the cab and the two men sitting in the pickup's box before the reality of what was happening had a chance to register on any of the five instantly deceased occupants.

Glen Ellyn, IL (NCNWC bivouac area)
0800 hours
November 12

Late wakeups are very rare in the army, especially in units involved in combat. Pierce searched his memory, still a bit groggy from a good night's sleep, but couldn't remember when the last time was that he had slept past 0500 hours, let alone 0800 hours. Well, someone or something is bound to put a stop to this. Good things don't last for long around here.

Slowly crawling out of his cot, standing to stretch and get the blood flowing to his arms and legs, still heavy from the glorious eight hour sleep, Pierce was jolted into the current happenings by the intrusion of his lieutenant.

"Sorry, Franklin. Didn't mean to startle you, but got some good news from HQ. The major says a cease-fire is being discussed. Supposed to go into effect immediately. If both sides reach final agreement, this whole fuckin' war could be over today, tomorrow. No one knows for sure," First Lieutenant Charles Rudderman said as he moved past Pierce and sat down on his cot.

"You're kidding, LT. You really think this things over?"

Not wanting to crush the hopefulness in Pierce's question, the lieutenant added cautiously, "Sure hope so. We've been ordered to stand down today. No combat activity, just security patrols. Same for the bad guys. Gon'na give Keshum Aguawada and President Fitzpatrick a chance to reach agreement at the bargaining table. They're actually meeting today to discuss the short strokes in person."

Master Sergeant Franklin B. Pierce, standing in the middle of the tent, and First Lieutenant Charles Rudderman, sitting on Pierce's cot, just started at each other, both hesitating to latch on to the great news just in case the negotiations went awry. Finally, Rudderman said, "Remember, no activities today. Just stand down and get some rest. Make sure you keep some guards on duty and check the defensive perimeter every hour. You know. Just in case. Got' a run and tell the rest of the platoon."

And with those final words, the lieutenant left Pierce alone with his thoughts.

Glen Ellyn, IL (NCNWC bivouac area)
1017 hours
November 12

"How you doing?" Pierce asked as he walked into Jones' tent and sat down on the footlocker that had been pushed up against the edge of the cot, table fashion.

"Not bad. Big fuckin' headache's all. But not bad."

"I guess you heard the news by now about the cease-fire?"

"Yeah. Think it's gon'na happen?"

"Sure hope so. Gettin' tired of getting my ass shot at."

"But what do you really think? I ain't never been in no war before like you have. Is this all bullshit or will we really have peace?"

"I guess the combat veteran part of me says that something will go wrong and that we'll be fighting again in a couple of days. I ain't no fuckin' politician. Them guys let their egos get in the way and then guys like you and me and the poor fucks we're fighting just become pieces on a chessboard..." Pierce immediately caught his breath and realized that while those were his true feelings, the were TJ's words. The words he had read in solitude the night before.

"Sarge, you okay?"

"Huh? Yeah. Just lost in thought. Like I said, sure hope this thing ends. Hey, Ty, let's you and me go for a walk, get a little exercise."

"Sounds great. Gettin' a little stiff just lying around here. Where to?"

Let's go over to that place where we found the journal. You know, the big house with the fireplace."

"Shit, Sarge. That's almost two miles from here."

"Don't worry, We're on stand down. Bad guys, too," Pierce said, catching his breath. Were they really the bad guys?

"Yeah, sure. Well, all I know is I'm bringing my gun, just in case."

Wheaton, IL (Sandpiper Court subdivision)
1120 hours
November 12

Sitting down, using the massive three story high fireplace as a backrest, Pierce and Jones got comfortable. Looking around, Pierce realized that a few weeks back, he stopped a bullet with his helmet just a few feet from this very spot. But that's war. He got shot in the head and he's okay while the poor slob who shot him stopped one and just plain stopped.

"Hey, Ty. I brought the journal," Pierce said, pulling the notebook from the inside of his combat jacket. "Let's read some more."

October 28 - Day Thirty-Seven

Tough day today. Real tough.

A couple of the younger boys, Jason Komanski and Kyle Granger skipped out of camp today to go hunting or something. Maybe they just got bored and were looking for some excitement. We organized a few search parties to go out looking for the kids. Jim Sawyer, Brian Jenkins and Bob Pedopoulos were one team. Another included Frank Smyth, Jack Furgeson and Paul Savatini. The third was Me, my son, Rich and Bill Komanski. Searched most of the morning without results. Went back out after checking out the roads close to us and decided to expand our search area.

By 3:00 p.m., Sawyer and his group and me and my group were back. Didn't see any sign of the boys. Frank Smyth and his people were still not back. We waited until 5:00 p.m. before deciding to go looking for them as well as the boys. Me, Bill Komanski and my son, Rich, were in the Jeep that found Smyth's pickup. They were on Army Trail Road. Looked like a tank or something got them. The whole truck was burned to a cinder. Found the bodies of a man and two boys in the cab. Two men were laying on the side of the road, thrown about sixty feet away from the truck by whatever caused the explosion. Their bodies were burned bad, but we were able to recognize them. We buried them in the empty lot in the old subdivision. No one had the heart to start a new cemetery here at the Country Club.

Just don't feel like writing anymore.

October 29 - Day Thirty-Eight

More bad news. We heard a lot of artillery fire last night. Real close.

In the morning we walked over to the old subdivision and found that a number of the houses, including mine, had been hit. From the destruction, it must have been some pretty heavy stuff.

Food supplies running low. We're really starting to ration more. Water holding out okay. I going to send out a hunting party tomorrow morning to see if we can get any geese. We'll take a run into Wheaton to see if any more food is available.

Wheaton, IL (Country Club)
0309 hours
October 30

Just after 0300 hours, Lieutenant Colonel Ralph Emerson, Illinois National Guard, walked towards the battery of 155mm howitzers. The three howitzers were arranged in a rough triangle, hidden below overhead camouflage nets that had been secured to some nearby trees. The barrels of the cannons protruded from the netting. From a distance, or from the air, the battery was virtually invisible.

Tonight's firing mission was basic interdiction and disruption. Reconnaissance flights over the NCNWC positions in western Carol Stream has resulted in the discovery of a truck park and POL (petroleum, oil, lubricants) storage cache in a grove of trees just off the Prairie Path. The coordinates were recorded and orders were cut to have Emerson's battery fire fifteen shells at exactly 0315 hours in the hopes of catching the enemy with their pants down. Destruction of the vehicles and POL supplies would severely hamper their effectiveness during the upcoming week.

The 155mm howitzers were capable of lobbing a high explosive round weighting in excess of ninety pounds almost fifteen miles. The distance from the battery to the target was twelve miles, well within he maximum range of the medium weight artillery.

As Emerson checked his map, he noticed that the coordinates of the target were such that the shells, once leaving the muzzles of the howitzers, would fly directly over the self-defense group that were using the Country Club as home. Emerson, however, wasn't concerned with this in that the Country Club was only three miles away from the battery. The high powered, high explosive shells coming from the howitzers would fly safely over the Country Club, probably two thousand feet over ground level. The muzzles of the 155mm's would be angled at approximately 58° to achieve the required twelve-mile distance to the targets' coordinates. The residence of the Country Club would hear the distance 'kaarummmp' as each howitzer fired as well as hear a brief overhead disturbance like a freight train in the distance. Time to target would result in an echoing explosion approximately twelve seconds later.

At precisely 0315 hours the three 155mm howitzers 'kaarummmped' in unison, throwing almost three hundred pounds of deadly explosive force towards the NCNWC truck-park and POL storage site. Twenty seconds later, after the breeches had been cleared and another three shells had been loaded, the guns barked again. The mission called for each howitzer to repeat the process five times, with minor elevation adjustments being made between each shot in an effort to blanket the area with a man and materiel killing hail of shrapnel.

Unknown to Emerson and the gun crews, the trucks and POL cache had been moved just prior to midnight thus their shells were falling harmlessly into a now empty grove of trees.

Harmlessly, except for the last shell fired from the #2 gun.

After firing its fourth shell, the crew of #2 emptied the breech and inserted the next and last shell in accordance with standard operating procedures. What they didn't know, and couldn't have known, was that the last shell through the barrel of the canon left a six ounce sliver of metal wedged into the rifling grooves, which put the 'spin' on the shell as its hurls through the barrel. A defect in the shell had resulted in this sliver being thrown off of it as the tremendous power of the initial explosion of the propellants hurled the shell out of the muzzle onward towards its target twelve miles away.

When the fifth and final shell was in the breech and the "fire" command given, the gunner engaged the firing mechanism, which triggered a series of events, happening in rapid secession.

First, the firing pin struck the shell, which ignited the propellant charge. The build up of gaseous forces between the locked breech and the shell resulted in the forward motion of the shell, a classic example of the 'for every action there is an opposite and equal reaction' theorem. The rifling of the barrel placed a spin on the shell to aid in its accuracy during the flight to the target, much like a football thrown with a 'spiral' spin flies farther, and more accurately. than one that wobbles.

As the shell and the expanding gas behind encountered the six once metal sliver that was wedged into the barrels' rifling, the normally perfect balance of the gas to shell to barrel relationship was perverted. The uneven pressure build up by the small obstruction in the barrel caused the barrel on the opposite side of the sliver to experience failure. The barrel bulged, then cracked and then burst open like an exploding balloon, showering the surrounding area with small, deadly pieces of shrapnel. Fortunately, through some miracle, none of the National Guard troopers were hit. The barrel was obviously no longer functional and the crew immediately started to grumble. They would have to replace the barrel, a rather time consuming, heavy manual labor type of activity.

The shell, still being pushed along by the reduced pressure of the propellant gases after the failure of the barrel, left the business end of the howitzer on a relatively straight line towards the target. With a great deal of the pressure released by the bursting of the barrel, however, the shell was not moving anywhere near as fast as it needed to be traveling to go the full twelve miles. In fact, it had only received enough kinetic energy to travel a little over a mile and a half before gravity worked its immutable power and pulled the shell towards the ground.

Six seconds after the shell left gun #2, it slammed into one of the model homes at the Country Club that the Sandpiper Court residents were using. The shell hit the back of the house right were the ceiling of the first floor becomes the floor of the second. The shell hit with deadly force, killing nine people who were fast asleep. Nine people who thought they were out of harm's way. Nine sleeping people who would never again wake up.

Wheaton, IL (Country Club)
0830 hours
October 30

Anthony Joseph Bender walked with a noticeable stoop to his shoulders, the weight of the senseless slaughter of the early morning hours extracting a tremendous toll. He walked over slowly to meet Lieutenant Colonel Ralph Emerson, Illinois National Guard, who had just arrived in one of the HUMMERs.

"Don't know what happened, Colonel. Big explosion last night damn near wiped out the whole building. Lost nine people, six hurt pretty bad. I just gettin' so damn tired of burying my friends."

"TJ. We need to talk. Let's go for a little walk."

TJ looked up at Emerson, struck by the unusual words that the colonel had used. Something was in those words, a message of some sort. The colonel was trying to say something, but what?

Looking into Emerson's eyes, TJ saw the pain and the sorrow and in an instant, somehow knew that the colonel was involved in the early morning events. In that same instant, he knew that Emerson was somehow responsible.

"It was one of ours?" TJ said, hoping that he was wrong in his snap decision, yet sensing that the question was really a statement of fact.

"Yes. A fire mission gone bad. Tube exploded on one of the howitzers. The shell didn't receive its full kick. Dropped short," Emerson said in hushed tones.

"You're telling me this was the result of 'friendly fire'?"

Drawing in a deep breath, Emerson nodded his head, not sure that he could even say a simple 'yes' without losing control of his emotions.

"My God, Colonel. What am I supposed to tell everyone? How can I say that our own guys killed all their neighbors?" TJ asked softly, knowing full well that there was no acceptable answer to the tough questions he threw at the colonel.

Tears were running openly down Emerson's face as he reached out and put his hand on TJ's shoulder. Looking deeply into TJ's eyes, he saw the reflection of his own pain. Both men realized that no one was responsible for the deaths yet both men realized that everyone was responsible. The utter horror of war jumped forth in crystal clarity and both men knew that they had just visited hell, witnessing all of its agonizing brutality.

Their unspoken communication was clear and both men made a silent pact. TJ knew he had to blame the NCNWC for the attack. Emerson, grateful that TJ knew that this was the only acceptable answer, knew that he would have to live forever with the bitter truth of what really happened.

They embraced for a moment and then separated. Emerson returned to his HUMMER, while TJ attended to the grisly task of presiding over another nine, unwelcomed internments.

Glen Ellyn, IL (NCNWC bivouac area)
1101 hours
November 12

Pierce turned the page to the entry for October 30.

October 30 - Day Thirty-Nine

During the early morning hours, A NCNWC artillery shell hit the Tudor house that we were using as communal barracks. The nine people listed below were killed in the attack:

Bill Jenkins - 47
Jason Furgeson - 22
Joe Olive Jr. - 18
Frank Farmer - 70
Julia Farmer - 69
Nancy Sawyer - 30
Billy Sawyer - 5
Janice Pedopoulos - 42
Kathleen Granger - 30

Six people were injured pretty badly, but with Central DuPage Hospital being closed a few days ago after also being hit by NCNWC artillery, we were forced to make due here at the Country Club. Doc's not sure if all will survive. Most of the injuries were broken bones caused by the collapse of the roof. If no one has any internal injuries, everyone should make it. If any internal injuries do exist, well, only time will tell.

October 31 - Day Forty

Today is Halloween, but no one is dressing up. Actually, everyone is dressing up. Everyone one here looks like either a soldier, or a refugee.

We have just about lost track of time. The journal keeps me current with the date, but who gives a flying fuck.

Food and water are getting dangerously low. The deaths and injuries will allow us to stretch the rations a little further, but something's got to give pretty soon.

Medical supplies almost exhausted. Mostly bandages and cough syrup left.

The only thing we seem to have enough of is guns and ammunition.

We keep hearing more and more on the radio that the peace talks have started, stalled, started, stopped. No one wants to end this conflict. Can't figure out why not. Seems like everyone would benefit if we could just come to terms and like the song says, give peace a chance.

The women are taking this whole situation the toughest. Most of the kids are too young, or will at least have school and such after all this is over. The men will in all likelihood go back to work and rebuild the neighborhood. The women have it the toughest.

Now I'm not sexist, but most of the gals in the subdivision were moms, moms who didn't have jobs outside of the house, moms who stayed home, took care of the house, sent the kids off to school and were there when they returned. The problem now is that some of the moms don't have kids anymore. All they will have is the time to relive the pain and agony of losing their children.

You can see a couple of them walking around, trying to keep a stiff upper lip but failing miserably because of the misery they're feeling. We tried to collectively band together, but the moms who lost kids have turned into their own little group. Other kids, husbands and friends are excluded. No one can blame them and we do try to help. Hopefully the end of the conflict will give everyone the opportunity to recover. If not right away, maybe over time.

November 1 - Day Forty-One

Tried hunting again today and we had a little better luck. Didn't have much artillery fire over the last few days and the geese started to return to the ponds. By the end of the hunt we had bagged six geese and two ducks. Fresh meat will be well received.

Lieutenant Colonel Ralph Emerson, Illinois National Guard, stopped by today with a brief update on the local battle lines.

Seems the NCNWC have dug in and are trying to continue to disrupt the supplies lines with artillery interdiction fire. Very few troop versus troop encounters. The lines have stabilized and except for some patrol activities, Emerson believes the cannons will fight the battle for the next little while. He says both sides are trying to give the politicians time to sort out their differences and settle this bullshit.

Emerson thanked me for handling the situation regarding the artillery fire we sustained the other day. He appreciated the way in which we handled ourselves during that trying time and continues to marvel at our fortitude.

Other than that, not much else going on. Getting a little despondent. Waiting is worse than anything else. Also getting tired of trying to keep the journal up to date.

I just can't believe we've lost so many friends and neighbors. It just ain't fair.

November 2 - Day Forty-Two

Thank God we moved out of the old subdivision. In another 'friendly fire' accident, a squadron of F-15's dropped their entire load of bombs on our old area. Damn near wiped the place off the map. Somehow, the only area left undamaged was our little cemetery and the houses immediately surrounding it. Everything else was either wiped out or damaged heavily.

November 3 - Day Forty-Three

I hate talking about this, since its become a personal cross which I have to bear and I really wanted this record to be objective, but, I've been having this dream. It comes about once every two or three days. It's scaring the shit out of me and even the Doc has been unable to help me understand what I have to do to stop it from reoccurring.

I'm at home. The house is on fire and my family's trapped upstairs. I try like hell to help them but I'm always forced back by the heat and smoke. And I always wake up, never knowing if I'm able to help them or not.

The fucking thing is so real I swear I can smell the smoke on me when I do finally wake up. Joyce says it all in my head, which I guess is a true statement. But it's just driving me crazy.

Doc and I spoke about it for a long time and he said it's a result of the stress of trying to lead our group. He says the pressures of command are staggering and that I should expect some level of anxiety in dealing with the tremendous responsibilities.

Good words, possibly true, but not very comforting.

What I didn't tell Doc, but will share with you, is that these dreams started <u>before</u> CWII started. They actually started years ago. Clearly there are some buried subconscious reasons why I'm having these dreams, this one dream, but damned if I know why.

Another reoccurring nightmare I used to have during my teens and early twentys involved a train. I grew up pretty close to a large train yard on the west side of Chicago, about four miles

David A. Bragen

east of Midway airport. The yard was a switching point where two tracks fed in from both the north and the south. The yard had about thirty tracks branching off the in-feed lines. They broke down and reassembled trains there. There were also a few large building used for engine maintenance.

Anyways, in this particular dream, I was walking across the tracks where they crossed 55th Street, always stopping and looking both ways before I started to cross. At this point, twelve individual pairs of rails crossed the road. There were never any trains coming from either the right or left, but every time I got in the middle of those twelve sets of tracks, I heard a train whistle. I always looked left and seeing nothing, turned my head to the right. There was always a train coming towards me on track number ten. I would immediately turn around and start running for my starting point by track number one, not wanting to take a chance in running in front of the train. And every fucking time, I would hear this tremendous noise and looking over my shoulder, see that somehow, for some inexplicable reason, that the train had jumped the track and was headed right for me.

Now just like you would run either right or left of a tornado's path in an effort to get away from it, I would dodge right and left. But that goddamn train would weave like a snake and follow me. And just as a safe haven appeared to be reachable, I would always fall down, sometimes tripping over a track, sometimes just stumbling. But always going down, the train still headed right for me. And I always woke up, never knowing if the train hit me, never knowing if I survived, never knowing what caused the dream.

It stopped when I was twenty-three. I got married when I was twenty-four. The burning house dream started when I was thirty-one, two days after the birth of our second child.

I really wish it would stop.

November 4 - Day Forty-Four

We continue to hear reports of 'negotiations' that are underway between representatives of the NCNWC and the U.S. Government. The radio reports are sketchy at best and don't give us anything meaningful except for the hope that it creates in all of us. Admittedly, there is less gunfire than a week or so ago. Some sporadic cannon fire and maybe an occasional sniper. No more pitched battles, at least not near our little corner of the war.

The reports indicate that the only serious military actions are occurring in southern Texas. There are reports that forces of the Mexican Army have staged raids across the Rio Grande in an effort to expand their territorial claim. Doesn't make sense to me. There isn't very much in southern Texas, at least not at the sites of the alleged raids. My guess is that it's just muscle flexing on the part of the Mexican Government. The way I see it, they are hearing the same reports that we are about a potential settlement and are posturing for a slice of the pie. Can't tell if they want to actually annex part of Texas or are just puffing out their chest feathers in an attempt to gain respect.

Anyways, that's another one for the politicians to sort out.

November 5 - Day Forty-Five

Had another fight with my oldest son, Joe, today. He's still intent on going back to the old homestead to get that box full of souvenirs. I told him "no" once before and repeated the same thing to him today. Not only is it dangerous, the goddamn house is destroyed. Who could find anything in that mess?

So he gets all hyper about being a man now and wanting to do what he wants to do and that I shouldn't keep treating him as a child. I suppose he's got a point, but the father instincts inside me results in me telling him to quit acting like a kid if he wants to stop being treated like a kid.

Well, this verbal circle jerk goes on for about half an hour and starts to get pretty heated. I told him I understand the value of these trinkets, but that I'm really tired right now and don't want to hike back to the old house. Maybe tomorrow, maybe the day after. We'll go back and see what we could find.

I think this will work for a couple of days. I'm sure he'll forget about the damn box of stuff. Nobody's going to take it and it sure isn't worth getting killed over.

Wheaton, IL
0745 hours
November 6

Tony Joe awoke with a start; the same nightmare over and over again. Fighting through the flames, TJ desperately searches for his family. He briefly sees them only to once again, lose them in the thick, black smoke.

Opening his eyes, he realized once again that he was literally out of the fire, but into the proverbial frying pan. Fire wasn't his only challenge: bullets, booby traps, poor food, and just plain, old-fashioned fear.

"Joyce. Joyce!" he yelled.

Joyce, came running in. "What's a matter, TJ?"

"Everything. And nothing. This goddamn nightmare again. I can't get any rest during the day, and I can't get any rest when I sleep. I never should have pushed for control. I'm just a goddamn salesman. I just don't know what the fuck to do anymore."

"Honestly TJ, you have more excuses than your kids do. You have helped a great deal. You did what no one else wanted to do, take responsibility. You know how people look at you? You know what they see? They see the future. A future they were willing to fight for and yes, a future that only you can lead us to. You can mope around here all you want and feel inadequate, or sorry for yourself, but the indisputable fact remains; you're our leader," Joyce lectured.

He hated when she did that. He knew what she said was true, however, he was unwilling to always accept it for he thought it obscene to realize that his calling in life, like Patton, was to lead a group of people in a desperate struggle.

Yeah, give me a helmet and a couple of pearl handled 45s and look out Hitler!

"Joyce, I'm just sick and tired of it. I've seen too many people killed and maimed. I've seen our friends disappear. I've seen kids crying for their never to return parents."

"Stop it, TJ! Crying over spilt milk won't help," she scolded.

Not wanting to continue the debate, especially since he sensed he was losing, he got up and started to get dressed.

Reaching over to find his pants, he pulled on the set of army fatigues that the National Guard people had given to the Committee. *God bless those guys*, he thought. Without their occasional support, he and the group would have been up shit's creek a number of times. The food, medical supplies, arms and ammunition had helped keep them going. Had helped his small band of survivors survive.

Fifty-three days ago the Civil War started. Fifty-three days ago he was responsible for seventy-nine souls. Fifty-three days later, there were only forty-seven of them left.

Thank you God for letting my family get by so far. Better someone else than one of mine. He was immediately embarrassed that the thought jumped out, but what the hell; *This is the way I feel, God forgive me. Better someone else.*

The war had been pretty difficult on the little ones. When he walked into the building that served as the kitchen/eating area, he was immediately pounced upon by several of the seven and eight year olds.

"Hi, TJ!"

"Good morning, TJ."

"We didn't get enough to eat, TJ."

" When is more food coming?" asked one little waif.

"How come we can't go to the stores anymore, TJ?" moaned another quiet whimper

" We promise we'll be good, TJ. Please?"

Same litany that he's heard since the last food shipment was intercepted by the NCNWC.

How do you tell a kid, who should rightly be in school learning about pilgrims and coloring those turkeys you make by tracing your hand that there's a war on? That the grown-ups are too stupid to just live their lives? That there ain't going to be a Thanksgivings, or Christmas this year and that if we ever have them again, they'll never be like they used to be?

He answered like he did every day for the last seven days, "Sorry kids, not today. Maybe we can go to town tomorrow. But remember, ya got'a be good."

Seeing Joyce in the corner, fixing what little food was available for breakfast, gave him the excuse he needed to leave the little ones behind.

"Joyce, I'm not real hungry today. Just coffee."

"Come on, TJ. It's real admirable that you starve yourself and all that John Wayne macho bullshit, but you've got to eat something. You haven't had a decent meal in the last three days and you got'a have something," she said as a mother would talk to the bunch of seven and eight year olds he just left.

It pissed him off no end when she said stuff like that. Especially when she hit the nail on the head; the second time that morning. He simply grunted and picked up a couple slices of bread and walked away.

TJ wandered over to the main observation post that they had established near the big, old oak tree by the seventh green.

"How goes it, Ed?" TJ said to Ed Flanders, who was the Committeeman on duty during the 8:00 a.m. to noon shift.

"Hi, TJ. Nothing much doing. Jamison reported that not much happened during his watch. Some flashes on the horizon. He thinks it was artillery around Glen Ellyn, where it borders with Wheaton. Small stuff, didn't last too long, but getting a lot closer that it's been before," Flanders replied.

"You're a fountain of good news this fine morning," TJ said with a sly smile on his face. Flanders joined in when he realized that TJ was just kidding. Yet he knew that TJ was right. More shit happened on the midnight to 8:00 a.m. guard shifts than at any other time. In almost every case, by the time TJ got out on rounds, Flanders was the one to have to tell him the score for the night. TJ swore he would never kill the messenger, but sometimes, Flanders wasn't sure he'd keep that promise.

"Say, Ed. Have you seen Joe this morning? We were going to go back over to the cul-de-sac and see if we can recover the rest of the ammunition we cached just before we relocated up here to the Country Club."

Flanders flinched noticeably, sensing that this time, TJ might very well slay the messenger.

"Ah, well, ya see, TJ, ah, Joe said he wanted to give you a few extra hours of sack time this morning and that he didn't want to disturb you and all," Flanders stammered.

"Jesus H. Christ! Don't tell me you let Joe go out by himself, Ed? Don't tell me you're that fuckin stupid!" TJ yelled so loudly he started to spray spittle at Flanders like a machine gun. "How could you?" He's only a boy for God's sake!"

"TJ, I'm sorry. It's just around the block a little. Why he's probably on his way back right now, all proud that he helped in his own little way," Flanders said, hoping to calm down TJ's outrage, but realizing that his comments only threw fuel on the already blazing fire.

TJ looked at Flanders one last time, started to look through him, took a deep breath and walked away. He knew that if he didn't, he could very easily kill this man, his friend, his neighbor, for letting Joe go outside the perimeter alone. For letting his oldest son expose himself in such a foolish manner just so he could let his dad sleep a few extra hours. As soon as he saw Joe, he was going to give him such a talking to that he would never forget. He wasn't sure yet if he'd ever bother talking to Flanders again.

As he walked over to his tent, TJ saw Joyce and called over to her "Joe went over the wall this morning. Help me get my stuff together. I have to go find him."

TJ saw the look of panic flood across Joyce's face. She knew the seriousness of this statement. She immediately saw the danger surrounding her first-born and very nearly gave in to the hysteria; the peace found in panic when you realize that nothing worse can happened.

Together they ran to the storage shed to get TJ's backpack and rifle. Immediately upon entering the shed, TJ saw that the backpack was gone. Memories sprung upon him as his mind recreated the image of the ragged old backpack.

Joyce has started to go to college, junior college actually, immediately after high school. She didn't have a plan or the money and simply took a couple of courses each semester. She had completed about seven or eight courses when they had met, fell in love and got married. College was put on the back burner for a couple of years while they got settled into being married, searching for a house, starting a family and all that couple stuff. A course here and a course there, a move out of state and Joyce finally earned her Associates degree. Back to Illinois and Joyce told TJ in no small way that 'goddamn it, she was going to earn a real four-year degree and furthermore, TJ was going to pay for it'.

Well, Joyce received her Baccalaureate degree and TJ did pay for it. As a reverse graduation gift, Joyce had presented TJ with her Elmhurst

College backpack, the very one she had carried to and fro every day while she completed the last two years worth of credits towards her degree, the very backpack that TJ had calculated cost him just over $17,500, which she considered a good deal since they threw in the tuition for free.

Though the memory of their little joke brought a quick smile to TJ's face, he quickly realized that the absence of the backpack told him that Joe had 'borrowed it' so he could use the binoculars that TJ carried inside. He also noticed that Joe also 'borrowed' his Remington .303-caliber hunting rifle with the five power telescopic sight. Waves of fear coursed through his body. Joe wasn't simply going on a scouting mission, or a little jaunt to recover some buried ammunition. Joe was going hunting. Hunting for the enemy. Joe had ventured out as a solo sniper. Joe was looking to kill someone.

Grabbing a small bore .22-caliber lever action Winchester and a box of cartridges, TJ gave Joyce a perfunctory kiss on the cheek, smiled and ran towards the main observation post, his intended point of departure.

Reaching the big oak tree, TJ came upon Flanders, who was sitting dejectedly on a of pile of sandbags.

"God, TJ. I'm sorry. I shouldn't have let Joe go out alone. I, I guess I just wasn't thinking.

Feeling sorry for jumping on Flanders earlier, TJ was about to tell him to forget it, but it dawned on him that Flanders had fucked up, big time and not just because it was his son. He knew the rules; no one outside the perimeter alone. Not since Sara Hollis wandered off by herself on Day Twenty-Four. They had organized a search party about mid-day and looked all through the subdivision. No sign of Sara anywhere.

Later that night, they heard someone scream loudly off in the distance, several times. Then, one last, gut-wrenching, agonizing wail turned into a moan and finally slipped into complete silence. Prudence dictated that they wait until sunup to investigate.

They found her body early the next morning near the old barn across Geneva Road. It was obvious she had been violently raped. The area was disturbed so badly that it had obviously been by a large group of men. When they had finished taking turns, they had driven a sharpened stake into the ground leaving about twenty-five inches exposed. They had forced Sara's legs apart and impaled her on the stake, which penetrated her fourteen- year old vagina and probably stopped just below her heart. Doc figured it had taken her about five minutes to bleed to death, though she was probably unconscious from loss of blood after a minute or two. Susan Hollis, her mom and one of the committee members representing Food & Medical, collapsed when she saw Sara. She had committed suicide that same day.

"Flanders, don't say another word. If anything happens to Joe, you're a dead man. Now get the fuck out'a my face before I kill you," TJ said in a voice so calm and so soft that Flanders stood up and quickly walked away.

Jumping over the sandbag wall, TJ ran over to the tree line, a couple of hundred yards from the wall. Reaching the trees, he maneuvered down the slight decline until he was next to the creek. There he stopped and listened, and waited.

Artillery fire the night before in Glen Ellyn could only mean that NCNWC forces, either regular of irregular were in the vicinity. The National Guard Lieutenant Colonel has told them that they wouldn't use artillery unless they had to because of the damage that it caused to the community. You could repair a bullet hole in the siding, or put in a new window, but you sure as hell couldn't fix a house that got hit with an HE *(high explosive)* round fire by one of the Guards' 155 mm howitzers. Thinking back to the deaths at the Country Club caused by the 'friendly fire' of those same guns, TJ realized that he was the only member of the Country Club enclave who knew the real truth; that the National the Guard fired the fatal round.

Hearing nothing except for the chirping of birds, TJ dashed across the creek and up the slight incline on the other side, falling prone at the top of the rise. Before him lay the ruins of the subdivision.

It was hard to believe that a scant two months before, the subdivision had been a cacophony of typical suburbia noises; the hustle and bustle of life.

Now, the devastation was mind-boggling. Not one single house, other than the four residences surrounding their impromptu cemetery, remained unscathed. Between the artillery duel of mid-October, the air attack late last week and the continued probes of small bands of NCNWC irregulars, the homes simply fell into piles of so much brick and mortar.

Thank God we moved to the Country Club after that first exchange of artillery, TJ thought. *We never would have survived.*

He moved across Hagerty Street and worked his way across several backs yards, finally seeing MacArthur Lane. He was just about to stand up when he saw them coming around the corner. Three NCNWC soldiers dressed in white, gray, black urban camouflage. One working the point; the other two off to the flanks. Every twenty feet or so, they would stop and drop to one knee.

Looking for someone, boys? TJ thought with a grim grin spreading across his face.

He noticed that when they stopped, their camouflage blended in very well with the surrounding chaos and TJ made a mental note to warn the others that they will have to be extra caution in future excursions outside of the perimeter.

As the three NCNWC soldiers started to stand up again, TJ vowed to kill one. He moved back about a hundred feet and paralleled their westward movement on MacArthur. He knew when the Smyth house stood on the corner of MacArthur and Falcon. He moved quickly to get there first, before the patrol.

He hid behind the built up patio that Frank and Mary Smyth had added two summers before and waited.

Come in said the spider to the fly.

As the patrol rounded the corner, they moved forward about twenty feet and once again, performed their ritualistic genuflection. This motion resulted in the solider on the left completely exposing his back to TJ's view. Slowly raising his rifle, TJ clicked off the safety, took a deep breath while he lined up the open sights on the middle of the soldiers back, and let out half of that breath before gently squeezing the trigger.

The .22-caliber, long rifle, rim shot bullet spend to the target at about 1,200 feet per second. Though small, the bullet had a tendency to compact into a mushroomed shaped projectile upon impact, which also caused it to tumble during its continued flight through the body. The speed and entry point of the bullet, coupled with the slim build of the NCNWC representative insured that the small quarter ounce of lead shattered his spine, knocking him down instantly. A wound like that would at least cripple the sonofabitch, if he didn't bleed to death first.

No sooner had he pulled the trigger, TJ crawled back thirty feet, protected from view by the patio that he had visited so many times under more pleasant circumstances and once again found the creek. Working his way downstream, he essentially doubled back on his originally intended path in hopes of avoiding any reprisal from the two remaining NCNWC soldiers.

Where the creek finally crossed Pleasant Hill, TJ rambled up the culvert and dashed across the road. He stopped behind a clump of bushes and waited for quite a few minutes to make sure he wasn't being followed. Apparently the two remaining soldiers decided that chasing an idiot through the ruins of a subdivision, especially one with a gun, was a very foolish thing to do.

TJ followed the drainage ditch, which paralleled Pleasant Hill until he was directly across from his own backyard. About the only things left intact on his property was the tree line, which backed up to Pleasant Hill, and the massive three story fireplace that towered up out of the ruins like some gothic castle of old.

He sprinted across the street to the tree line and just as he had expected to, as he had hoped to, he caught a glimpse of Joe, looking through the ruins. He instantly knew what Joe was looking for and he was mad at himself for not having solved this problem in the first place.

TJ had told Joe not to take the money box with him when the evacuated the house to move to the country club. The box didn't contain any money of course, just the memorabilia that any eighteen-year old boy holds dear. First set of car keys, his own little black book with three girl's telephone numbers in it, a coin so old you couldn't even tell the date that his grandfather had given to him when he was four. That kind of stuff.

How could I have denied Joe. Why didn't I simply tell him it was okay to take the goddamn moneybox in the first place?

He was even more mad at himself for thinking that Joe had taken the Remington because he wanted to kill someone. Hell, Joe never even wanted to go hunting let alone play soldier with real bullets.

As Joe came into view again, not more that forty feet away, TJ raised his hands to his mouth to muffle his voice and drew a breath to call out his name when he heard the explosion. As the sharp report sounded, TJ watched as Joe was thrown into the air, his mouth open, half his young head puffing out into a million pieces.

He sank down to the ground in mute horror, not wanting to think about what he had just witnessed. He went down on all fours, his stomach revolting at the sight, his breakfast spewing out of his mouth.

He heard voices, strangely softened by the distance.

"Hey, Sarg! Take a look at this."

"Goddamn it, TY! Get under some cover before you get your ass blown away! How many times to I got'a tell ya we're still taking fire in this subdivision?"

"Whad'ya find, Ty?"

"Not sure, Sarge. It's pretty bad beat up. Look's like a diary or something. The damn thing is full of blood, and it's burned up on the one side."

"Looks like you're right on the money, TY. The first page has a title on it."

The voices faded as TJ finally gained control of his senses and moved backward across Pleasant Hill.

He sat for a long time in the drainage ditch. Thinking and getting more and more worked up.

Them fucking niggers just killed my boy. Now it's their turn. They even took my fuckin' journal and are reading it like some newspaper or magazine or something. Well fuck them to fuckin' hell! He screamed in his thoughts.

He move back across Pleasant Hill into the tree line behind the ruins of his house. He brought the Winchester up to his cheek and sighted down the barrel. Sure there were two of them, but if I can get lucky with my first shot, then it's one on one and he don't know where the hell I'm hiding.

He took a deep breath, put the sights on the larger of the two soldier's forehead and gently squeezed the trigger.

The Winchester Company has three locations in the United States where they manufactured .22-caliber, long rifle, rim fire cartridges. The particular bullet that leapt from TJ's rifle was actually made in a little town just outside of Rochester, NY.

Bullets are made by melting, then casting lead and other metals. Every once in a while though this process produces an anomaly. Some small particle of dirt or something, falls into the mold during the casting process. The molten lead is enough to essentially vaporize the dirt or particles of dust and nothing ever becomes of it. Every once in a while during those every once in a while occurrences, the particle that causes the anomaly is fairly large. Though the molten lead consumes the larger particle, it does so at a rate that results in a small hollow bubble forming within the supposedly solid, metal alloy head of the bullet.

The bullet that TJ had just chambered and fired had just such a small hollow bubble in its head. As the bullet sped on its path, the unevenly balanced weight at the tip caused a pronounced wobble, which altered the flight path of the projectile. The bullet moved slightly up and to the left and unbeknownst to TJ, because he was already crawling to a new position, struck the big soldier in the helmet, just over his left ear. And it was a good thing TJ moved because the other soldier was rapidly pumping five or six rounds into the very spot he had just vacated.

Every ten seconds or so, another five shots came flying out of the ruins, all wide of their intended target. And all obviously fired by one, scared, son of a bitch.

TJ crawled rapidly about fifty feet to his left. He looked up and saw no one. He was positive he got the big guy. Where was the second guy?

Just as he was about to move, he saw the small guy kneeling, offering his back as the perfect target. TJ couldn't resist this invitation. He threw caution to the wind and stood up, looking for revenge. He aimed square at the back of the soldier and was just about to take a deep breath when he saw a flash next to the soldier's ear, a dazzling earring of light, which struck him square in the chest.

TJ fell to the ground, just across the street from his own backyard. His last thoughts where of his family, struggling in the fire, thoughts that were quickly blurred as the thick, black clouds of nothingness hurdled at him like a freight train running out of control, knowing that he'd never awaken from this nightmare.

XXII

Philadelphia, PA (City Hall)
1300 hours
November 12

Paul Fitzpatrick, acting president of the United States of America, pushed back his chair, stood up and slowly walked around the table. He came face to face with Keshum Aguawada, leader of the NCNWC, extended his hand and as the men sealed the peace with the customary handshake, said "Mr. Aguawada, now that it is over, was it worth it?"

"Mr. President," replied Keshum Aguawada, "it is now our job, yours and mine, to make sure it was."

From across the crowded room, Reese Robertson led the congregation in a round of applause as the hands of the two leaders met. As he looked around the assemblage, he focused in on the gaze of one of the U.S. Army generals standing beside the President. Though the general's face held a smile, Reese could see the hatred burning deeply in the man's cold, steel blue eyes.

He wondered, *Has anything really changed?*

Manchester, MO (Pierce household)
1305 hours
November 12

"Mom. Mom!" yelled Shasa Pierce. "The man on the 'radio says it's over. Mom, come listen. Daddy's gon'na be coming home. Mom!"

Glen Ellyn, IL (NCNWC bivouac area)
1315 hours
November 12

"Corporal Brown. Go find Pierce. He and a couple of the guys are on patrol just south of the golf course. Tell'em to get their asses here pronto. Battalion just called. This here war's over. They called the fucker quits a couple of minutes ago!"

Wheaton, IL (Sandpiper Court subdivision)
1200 hours
November 12

He kept turning them, but the rest of the pages were blank. Pierce wondered what had happened to guy who wrote the journal. The kid that they took it from couldn't have been TJ. Clearly, he was too young.

"Come on, TY. Let's get back to camp. It's getting late."

"Sure thing, Sarge," said Jones. "Whad'ya think ever happened to that TJ guy?."

"Hard to tell. Probably still around here someplace."

As he started to walk away, Master Sergeant Franklin B. Pierce wondered if he would ever have the fortune to meet TJ someday. *He seems like one hell of a guy.*

"Hey, Sarge. Sarge!"

Pierce looked up and saw Corporal Brown running towards them.

"Sarge! Sarge!" Brown continued to yell as he ran across the cul-de-sac.

"What's up?" Pierce queried.

"LT told me to come looking for you guys. He saying there's a truce on. He's saying the war's over. Sweet Jesus, I hope this ain't no load of bullshit. The fuckin' war's over."

Pierce and Jones just stood there, with mouths open, staring at Brown.

God, could this be true? Could the war really be over?

The three of them, with Pierce in the lead, moved out in a hurry to get back to the encampment. They never noticed that they stepped over an old street sign, lying in the center of the cul-de-sac, the words SANDPIPER COURT almost obscured by the dust and filth of a modern battlefield.

ABOUT THE AUTHOR

David A. Bragen is the author of the **DAVEN Management Series** and founder of **DAVEN Consulting, Inc.**, a firm dedicated to helping publishers make the most cost effective vendor selections. In his career, David has held a number of senior management positions with **R.R. Donnelley, North American Directory Corporation, Quebecor Printing Inc., Quebecor World and John S. Swift Co., Inc.**

David holds both a BBA and MBA from **Loyola University** in Chicago, IL. He resides in Carol Stream, IL with his wife, two children and, a dog and cat. He enjoys hunting, golf, woodworking, and writing.